Also by Lisa Maxwell

Sweet Unrest

D1459951

For Helene, AdriAnne, Kate, and Kathryn:
Who helped to make this whole crazy ride a little more sane
and whose words inspire me every day.

GATHERING DEEP

LISA MAXWELL

Woodbury, Minnesota

Gathering Deep © 2015 by Lisa Maxwell. All rights reserved. No part of this book may be used or reproduced in any manner whatsoever, including Internet usage, without written permission from Flux, except in the case of brief quotations embodied in critical articles and reviews.

First Edition
First Printing, 2015

Book design by Bob Gaul
Cover design by Lisa Novak
Cover images by iStockphoto.com/11307378/©martinedoucet
        iStockphoto.com/14427275/©Kubrak78
        iStockphoto.com/32752266/©vectorarts

Flux, an imprint of Llewellyn Worldwide Ltd.

This is a work of fiction. Names, characters, places, and incidents are either the product of the author's imagination or are used fictitiously, and any resemblance to actual persons living or dead, business establishments, events, or locales is entirely coincidental.

Library of Congress Cataloging-in-Publication Data (Pending)
978-0-7387-4542-8

Flux
Llewellyn Worldwide Ltd.
2143 Wooddale Drive
Woodbury, MN 55125-2989
www.fluxnow.com

Printed in the United States of America

Once upon a time is for fairy tales, and besides, there ain't no once about it. There's only still is and ever was.

AFTER

Hair don't weigh no more than a soul, but taken all together, it's got the sort of gravity that anchors a person.

Shh. Shh. The scissors whispered their sharp commands, and pieces of who I was fell around me. I wanted to scream, to tell them I'd changed my mind. But I couldn't seem to make my mouth form the words.

Shh. Shh. Like each snip of those blades was telling me *Hush, hush. There ain't no use in arguing, so hush now.*

Two more coils slid into my lap, but my hands were clasped too tightly to bother with catching them. Even though I could almost feel the bite of my fingernails through the bone-deep numbness that had wrapped me up tight, I couldn't make my hands let go. It felt like I was trying to hold myself together.

Not that there was any reason to catch the pieces. As soon as they fell, the coils of hair were taken from my lap and tossed into the fire, where they crackled in fury.

But the scissors weren't done. *Shh. Shh.*

My momma always told me that I'd come into the world quiet, wide-eyed and ready, and with hair that was already locking on the crown of my head—a sign of who I would be. She told me to never let nobody cut it. Ever. She said cutting it would be a sin against who I was. But my momma was gone, and everything I'd ever been was balled up so tight, it didn't feel like anything worth preserving.

There was something else inside of me now, though—a scratching thing. Maybe that part had always been there, just waiting for its chance to break free, to claw and tear at the world until the pieces could never be put back. With each coil of hair that tumbled to the floor, that deep-down part of me became more and more unsettled. More and more sure.

Shh, the scissors whispered. *Don't tell them how much you want their world to feel like yours. Shh.*

I couldn't have argued with that whispered demand even if I wanted to. Because they were all still watching me with ready eyes, waiting for the shell of who I was to break.

Too late, I wanted to scream. But the words wouldn't come.

Shh, the scissors ordered, so I didn't tell no one that a part of me wanted to tear at their eyes and claw at their unbroken lives. *Shh.* I didn't warn nobody that a part of me felt so much bigger than what my skin should contain.

With each lock that tumbled into my lap, my head felt lighter, but my soul felt the weight of something more dangerous.

ONE

I don't care what anybody says, the house looked angry. Its shuttered windows were like narrowed eyes, and its once-welcoming porch reminded me of a broken smile. Like it was just waiting, and not for anything good.

Piers touched my elbow gently when I didn't get out of the car right away. "You don't have to do this, Chloe."

I shook my head, wanting like crazy to agree. It would've been so easy to turn around and go back to his apartment in the Quarter, but I'd been there two weeks already, and I was already starting to hate the way he was so careful around me. He handled me like I was spun from glass and hovered over me all the time, like he didn't trust me to be okay without him.

Or maybe it was that he didn't trust me.

Not that I blamed him for that, really. It had been barely more than two weeks since everything had happened, and I wasn't sure that he *should* trust me. I wasn't so sure I trusted myself.

I wiped the sweat that was already beading on my forehead. It was too damn hot to sit in the car anymore. The air conditioning hadn't worked right in my old Nova since it belonged to my momma, and the sticky heat of a Louisiana day in early August was maybe even worse than whatever I was going to find inside that house.

It was just a house. Just *my* house.

Giving the door handle a jerk, I forced myself out of the car. A moment later, Piers was by my side.

"Are you sure about this?" The dark curve of his head against the blue of the sky and the unexpected contrast between his country-club style and the black-as-night runes on his right arm were as familiar to me as my own face. But for the last two weeks, things had been different between us. Fragile and dangerous all at once.

"Sure as I'll ever be," I told him. Which, to be honest, wasn't very sure at all.

As though he could read my thoughts, he slid his broad palm into mine. Some of the anger and guilt I'd been feeling receded a bit as our fingers intertwined, but not all of it. The rest was still there, simmering below the surface. Some days, it took everything I had to keep all those hot feelings from bubbling over.

Piers waited a couple of seconds longer, giving me a chance to change my mind. He'd been arguing against me coming back to my house ever since I'd come up with the idea the day before. But I couldn't back down now. The more he'd argued against it, the more I knew that I needed to do this for myself. And for us, too, because love's a little like a fire—it won't grow if it can't get no air.

I gave him a tight nod, and then made myself start toward the house.

One step. Two. And then a few more, and we were standing at the foot of the steps that led up to the deep, shaded porch of my childhood.

How many times had I climbed those steps, skipping up into the coolness of that shade? How many times had I sat there, the only place I'd ever really felt safe and sure? Sometimes in the evenings my momma would sit me in front of her and rub my scalp with her strong fingers as she hummed some old song or another. Sometimes we'd sit in silence, letting the evening settle around us until the night buzzed with cicadas and the stars blinked themselves awake, one by one. Always just me and Momma. She was my whole world.

That was before I found out she was nothing but a lie.

I took a breath and tried to shake off the black thoughts that had flown up and taken roost in my head like a murder of crows that wouldn't be shooed. There wasn't anything to be scared of. It was still my house. Sure, I was going to feel lonely and left behind when I went inside, but I already felt that way and I was still breathing, wasn't I?

I lifted my foot to take a step toward the porch, but I couldn't seem to make myself keep going. Piers looked over, his hand tightening when he realized I'd stopped short.

"I can't," I told him, my throat tight with all the things I was feeling but couldn't say.

"You don't have to stay here. You don't have anything to prove." He brushed his thumb across my cheek and the tenderness of that one little touch about brought me to my knees. My Piers may look all tough and dangerous, but he has soft hands—a scholar's hands.

But he'd misunderstood. I hadn't changed my mind.

I had to force the words out past the tightening in my throat, past my own gnawing sense of dread. "No," I said, shaking my head. "I can't go up these steps. There's something stopping me."

I pulled my hand out of his and wrapped my arms around myself. It was ninety-something degrees outside, but my skin felt like ice—and that was before I looked up at the door and finally saw what was waiting there for me.

Piers's eyes followed mine. I could tell when he saw it too, because his body went all tense-like. He cursed softly under his breath.

"That's what I think it is, isn't it?" I asked him.

He didn't have to answer. There was no mistaking what we were seeing—a lifeless black rooster, hanging by its feet from the doorknob. Its blood had already gone dark and thick where it had dripped down from the missing head. Down to where it had pooled below, coating the threshold of the door.

It's not that I was scared of some rooster, dead and bleeding or not. No. It was that my feet felt like my shoes had taken on roots, and the air around me had gone thick and solid. I could barely breathe much less move. What kept my feet planted was something stronger than fear—it was something like magic. *Dark* magic.

"Thisbe," Piers said, using the name like a curse.

It was still strange to hear him call her that. Before everything happened, it had always been Mina or Amina or Miz Sabourin. Or Momma.

But that was before I lost whole days. Before Lucy Aimes and her family moved to Le Ciel Doux—the old plantation where I worked as a tour guide—and set everything in motion by unearthing the secret my momma had hidden for more than a century. Whatever had happened two weeks ago had killed any affection or respect my boyfriend once had for the woman who was my mother. Mina Sabourin was dead to him. There was only Thisbe now.

Piers and Lucy and Mama Legba told me it was my momma who'd killed my friend Emaline. They told me my momma tried to kill Lucy and her little brother, too. They told me she was evil, that she'd used the darkest sort of magic to keep herself alive for more than a hundred years past when any natural life should end. They told me that she'd possessed my body and used me, too.

I didn't want to believe any of it could be true, but I know I never would have stolen a photograph of Lucy's little brother so my momma could work a curse on him. And I don't think I'm even capable of threatening Lucy, much less trying to strangle the life out of her, which is what they told me I did. But as much as I wanted to deny all of it, I had whole days I couldn't remember. Whole days when those terrible things happened.

My whole life, Momma warned me about messing with the spirits, so it was hardly believable that their stories about what she did could be true. But my friends' proof sliced away at my doubts bit by bit, until the truth was bare and bleeding before me: A still-healing gunshot wound in Lucy's shoulder. The look of disgust and fear in Piers's eyes when he explained how my momma's voice had come out of my mouth. And the fact that my momma never did come back after the night

I woke up on the damp ground in a dark New Orleans cemetery without any notion of how I'd gotten there.

So when Piers told me that it was the red threads my momma had woven into the coils of my hair when I was just a girl that gave her the power to control me, I didn't have any fight left. I let them cut all my hair off, hoping it was enough to prove that I was on the right side of all this. I guess part of me had still been hoping against hope that my momma would come back and show everyone how it had all been some horrible misunderstanding.

But there was no way to misunderstand the vise-like pressure in my chest when I tried to take another step toward my own house. The porch wasn't even two feet away from me, and I couldn't set foot on the first step. It felt like claw-tipped fingers were gripping my heart, like they were trying to suffocate my love for her right along with my life.

I pulled my foot back and the pain around my heart eased enough so I could breathe again. "She don't want me in there," I told Piers, and I didn't even care how my voice broke. "She made sure to keep me out." *Out of my own home.*

He took my face in his hands. Even warm as it was that day, I could feel the heat of him against my cheeks as he made me look into his eyes. "This isn't about you, baby. This doesn't mean anything at all about you."

But I knew deep down he was all sorts of wrong.

At first, it had been a kind of numb shock that had kept my eyes dry after that night in the cemetery. Then, even with the constant ache building in my head, I'd refused to allow myself the luxury of grief. It would have felt too much like a weakness to give in to tears. So I'd held on to that ache as determinedly as I'd held on to the hope they were all wrong. Because allowing myself the freedom to cry would have meant an admission of my mother's guilt. Maybe even an admission of my own.

But something about that moment—the invisible wall that separated me from the only home I'd ever known, the ever-present pity and worry lurking in my boyfriend's eyes, and the absolute understanding that he was wrong about what all this meant—made me stop fighting that ache and give in to the truth.

The summer air was dead and still. No breeze dried the tears that traveled down my cheeks, so there wasn't any reason for the bottles to begin rustling in the trees like they did. *Clink clank clink*, glass clicking against glass. I'd helped Momma hang new bottles each spring—always with the rough, red thread she kept just for that task. To keep the bad spirits away, she'd told me, because red had a power all its own. Back then, I'd believed in her tales. I believed in her.

As my chest heaved with the angry sobs I'd held back for two weeks, the dull *clank* of the glass bottles grew louder.

Piers pulled away, sensing the danger, but I didn't pay him no mind. My body was shaking with all I'd been holding back for days and days. I couldn't have stopped the tears if I'd wanted to, and I wasn't sure I wanted to. Because the overwhelming relief I felt when the grief poured out of me seemed like the first thing that felt real in two weeks.

Then, all at once, the bottles went still.

I went still as well. A heaving sob caught in my throat at the unexpectedness of the silence around us. I waited with Piers for the unseen danger to reveal itself. I didn't bother to wipe the tears from my cheeks, just watched for what would come next.

As the first tear broke free from my cheek and tumbled to the ground, an invisible hand began cutting the strings on the bottle tree. *Pop. Pop. Pop.* One by one, the bottles fell in time with my tears, shattering the stillness when they hit the hard ground below. Shattering the last of my hope about my momma—and about who *I* might be—right along with them.

TWO

Once the last of the bottles crashed to the ground, Piers didn't waste any time in getting rid of the rooster. He took its stiff body by the feet and looked at the feathers dulled by blood for less than a second before he tossed the whole thing over the porch railing and out of my sight. Not that it made any difference—even once the blood was washed from the door, I still couldn't go any closer to the steps of my own front porch.

I didn't know whether Piers had noticed that the bottles seemed to have dropped at the same rate the tears had fallen from my cheeks, but I didn't think he had. He seemed more worried *for* me than afraid *of* me.

But *I'd* noticed, and the idea that I might somehow have been the cause of that invisible wind or of the bottles falling like suicides made my blood run cold. So when Piers insisted on driving back, I didn't argue like I usually would have. I was too shaken by what had happened, and for the first time in a long time, his watchfulness didn't chafe.

Mama Legba had been so certain Thisbe wouldn't have a hold on me once my hair was cut off and the red threads woven through it were burned up. They'd all assumed the red threads were the same ones she'd used in her darkest spells, and that those threads were what had let her have power over me. But there wasn't nothing natural about that wind or those bottles breaking—and my hair was gone.

Either they'd been wrong about all that, or there was something else going on. I wasn't sure which option worried me more, so I stayed on my own side of the car, thinking things through and trying to figure out what it could all mean as I watched my home get smaller in the side mirror and then disappear altogether.

Piers was on the phone, too busy talking with Lucy first and then Mama Legba to notice me worrying. He was making plans to meet them both back in the Quarter, and he was making those plans without even asking my opinion.

"We're going to meet at the shop," he told me when he finished the second call. It wasn't a question so much as a command.

"I don't see why we need to bother Mama Legba with this," I said, bristling at his tone, but also at the idea of having to rehash everything with the old Voodoo Queen before I'd had a chance to figure out anything for myself.

"You don't see why we would need to tell the one person who might be able to help us?" Piers glanced over at me, his face grim. "That rooster wasn't there when I stopped to get you some clothes a week ago, Chloe. You know as well as I do that means Thisbe's back."

Thisbe's back. The words sent a little jolt through me.

His words meant that my momma hadn't crawled off somewhere to die after they took away the source of her power that night. Until now, none of us had been sure how long she could last without the dark magic that had kept her alive for so long. An hour ago, I would have been relieved—maybe even excited—to hear that she wasn't gone forever. But now? I wasn't so sure.

It was painfully clear that whoever set the charm on my house didn't want me anywhere near it. A charm like that took powers my momma had never revealed to me. So maybe Piers was right. Maybe this Thisbe person was back and the mother I'd known my whole life really was gone for good.

"Besides," Piers added in a sour tone, "I thought you wanted to move back into your own house."

"I told you, it's not like that," I said, touching his arm. I felt the muscles twitch beneath my hand. Piers didn't pull away, but I could tell he was fighting not to, so I dropped my hand back into my own lap and let him off easy.

He kept his eyes level on the road. "I get it." But his voice told me he didn't.

"It isn't because I don't want to be with you," I told him, trying once again to figure out how to make him understand.

"You just don't want to stay with me anymore," he said.

I let out a frustrated breath. We'd been over this who-knows-how-many times. "I need to feel like I can make it on my own," I explained, searching for words to use that wouldn't bruise his ego any further. "I can't keep feeling like I'm a problem for you to solve."

"You're not a problem, Chloe. I *want* to help you get

through this," he said, glancing over at me. He took a hand off the wheel and laced our fingers together.

"I know you do," I said softly.

But sometimes wanting a thing wasn't enough. How was I supposed to explain to him that his hovering was driving me mad? I needed him to look at me like he used to—like we were partners, equals. Like he still wanted me.

"As much as that means to me—and it *does*," I assured him, "I have to know I don't *need* to rely on you to get through this."

He frowned, his brow creasing in irritation. "I don't see why you're afraid to let me help you."

"I'm not afraid." I pulled my hand away. It was almost the truth. "But you can't spend your life babysitting me. You're going to have to go back to Nashville soon, when the term starts. And then what? I need to be okay with myself and *by* myself before that happens, or your leaving is going to be that much harder."

"You think I would leave with Thisbe on the loose?"

"She's always been on the loose. We just didn't know it," I told him. "If anything happens, you'll come back, but you can't just sit around here waiting for her to make another move. You have work to do, work that's important to who you are."

"*You're* important to who I am, Chloe."

His words eased something inside of me. I'd been wondering how we'd weather this particular storm, if we'd ever get back to how it had been before. "You're important to me, too," I said softly. "Which is why I won't let you miss even one day of the term without a real reason—Thisbe or no. That's why I need to be okay on my own."

He took his eyes from the road long enough to glance over at me. The frown was still in place, but the tension had eased a bit.

"We have time to figure it all out," he said. Stubborn as always.

But I wasn't going to give in, because there was something else that worried me.

Lucy had told me a little of what happened that night in the cemetery. That night, she said, Piers had been forced to choose between me and Thisbe. For a moment, he'd thought he would have to kill me to stop Thisbe from taking my body over for good. After what had happened at the house—the invisible wind, the shattered bottles—I wasn't so sure she wouldn't, or couldn't, take me over again, and if I could keep from putting Piers in that position again, I would.

Still, I wasn't in any hurry to see Mama Legba. I'd had enough magic for one day. And one thing is for sure— Mama Legba has her finger on some powerful magic.

Piers had introduced me to the old Voodoo woman a while back, when he'd been doing some interviews of people who still practiced for one of his classes at Vanderbilt. Someone had told him Mama Legba was the best of the Voodoo Queens left in the city, and they'd been right. He'd enjoyed talking with her so much that he kept going back until they were friends. One day, he took me along, too.

From the first minute I glimpsed the pink-as-coral door standing out from the grime of the Quarter, I had a feeling about her shop. It's all Caribbean-bright colors and windows streaming in light—not at all what I thought a Voodoo lady's place would be like. But her shop had felt like a homecoming I hadn't even known I was looking for.

A year ago, I wanted to learn everything I could about the beliefs that structured Mama Legba's practice. I wanted her to teach me, because I thought I felt some connection to the things she was saying. I felt a pull toward her explanations of the spirits that move in this world, and I wanted to believe in the powers she talked about.

But with everything that had happened, and everything they told me my momma was, that pull had started to worry me. It was still there, and maybe even stronger than ever.

Piers and Lucy had been trying to get me back to her shop ever since that night, but Mama Legba reads auras, and I wasn't sure I wanted her to see mine. Even after cutting off all my hair, I still worried about what she might see in me.

There was a part of me, though, that *did* want to go back. A part of me that craved the afternoons I'd spent in the shop's sunny brightness, sorting herbs and learning everything I could about Voodoo and the way energy moves through the world. But I didn't trust that craving anymore, especially not after the brush with magic I'd had that afternoon.

Not that Piers was giving me much choice.

By the time we made it to the narrow alley behind the cathedral in Jackson Square, it was late afternoon. Once we stepped through the door of her shop, the dusty scent of sage and other herbs washed over me. I picked out the sharp bite of ginger root, the dry warmth of balmony, and a bit of citrusy lemon verbena to cut through the rest. There were so many I still couldn't name, but there were a lot that I could. I was learning.

Or I had been.

Lucy was already waiting for us. She was as disheveled as usual and looking every bit the artist I knew she was, with her always-present camera hanging from her neck. Girl never wears anything that doesn't slouch or slump, and somehow it fits her. Somehow it mutes that crazy red hair of hers just enough to make her look like someone you might want to know.

She looked so comfortable leaning against the counter where she'd propped herself to talk with Mama Legba, not at all like the skittish Yankee I'd met a few months before. Then, she'd been the one who was unsure about visiting the old Voodoo Queen's shop, but now I was the one looking in from the outside.

"Come on now, Chloe-girl," Mama Legba said gently, and I realized I'd stopped right in the middle of the doorway. There wasn't any kind of magic holding me back this time, though—just my own nervousness and fear.

But Mama Legba had a gentle smile curving at the corners of her mouth, and her eyes were steady and calm, not full of the dark worry and pity everyone else seemed to look at me with. If she saw anything in my aura to warn her off, she sure didn't show it. In the end, it was that small kindness that had my feet moving, one in front of the other, until I was all the way into the cool welcome of her shop.

Piers closed the door behind me and shut out the noise of the Quarter. It was just the four of us there—me and Piers, Lucy and Mama Legba. We were the only ones who knew what happened to me or what my mother had done, and still, not one of them seemed to be turning away.

Mama Legba held out her hand. "Come on, Chloe-girl. You come on over here and let me read your cards. You more than ready now." She glanced up at Piers. "Turn the sign? I think we need a bit of privacy for what needs doing."

"We need to talk about the spell Thisbe put on Chloe's house," Piers said as he flipped the sign and latched the door.

"Be time enough for that," Mama Legba said dismissively. "Evil never does go nowhere fast." Without another word, she turned with a little wave to indicate we should follow her back through the hall that led to the private area of the building where she lived.

The back rooms were washed in the same bright colors as the shop itself. To the left, a low couch and a couple of older, worn chairs were heavy with brightly colored pillows. On the other side, a white cast-iron sink and a range that looked to be as old as the Quarter itself anchored a small kitchen.

Mama Legba settled herself on one of the low, comfortable chairs and motioned for me to sit in the other. Lucy and Piers took their places on the couch without needing an invitation.

The deck of cards was already waiting on the low coffee table. Printed in the color of old blood, the backs of the oversized cards were covered with an angular design that reminded me of doors opening and closing. They looked so old with their yellowed and tattered edges, but I knew the cards' faces would reveal impossibly rich, iridescent colors as bright as the day they were made.

With deft hands, Mama Legba shuffled the deck and set it in front of me. "Go on, Chloe-girl. You know how this works."

I should have refused, but I *did* know how it worked, and I'd wanted Mama Legba to read my cards ever since I learned how good she was at it. So I pushed aside any reservations I might have had and cut the deck like I was supposed to.

With another deft flick of her wrist, she fanned the cards out on the table.

"How many?" I asked.

"I think three should do well enough for now—past, present, and future."

I took a breath and seriously thought about changing my mind. I wasn't sure I was ready to find out what any of those cards would tell me, because I knew that whatever she told me the cards said would sure enough be the truth.

But I've never yet been the kind of person who lets a little bit of fear stop me, so I took three cards and laid them facedown on the table. Then I balled my hands in my lap and hoped for the best.

Mama Legba tapped the back of each card before she found the first one she wanted to turn over. "This here card is your past," she said, flipping it to reveal the Two of Pentacles.

A woman with dark, waist-length hair swiveled seductively on the card as she held two orbs in her outstretched hands. Her long, flowing skirt hid her legs, but nothing except some heavy necklaces covered her breasts. When the light hit the surface of the card, the colors shimmered brilliantly and almost made the picture look like it was moving. The woman's hair flowed into the night around her like it was a part of it, and the orbs shifted as though about to reveal dark shapes that never quite came to the surface.

"This here card is all about duality," Mama Legba told me. "But you probably know that well enough. It speaks of living a life on the edge of chaos—that moment before everything is about to be changing. Clear enough, if you ask me, seeing what we know now."

She didn't seem to pay any attention to the way my cheeks flamed. *A life on the edge of chaos.* That didn't sound like my past, not as I'd lived it or experienced it. My life had always seemed so steady. Boring even. But Mama Legba wasn't wrong—I just hadn't understood what a lie the surface of my life had been.

"Let's see..." She flipped over the next card. "Your present."

My stomach went tight. "The Devil?" The card was painted in monotone shades of crimson and black. A monstrous horned beast stood over two naked lovers. Around their necks, each wore collars attached to chains held by the beast's claw-tipped hands.

Mama Legba made an impatient noise in her throat. "You know better than seeing the surface of these cards for the truth." She tapped the card. "These ain't meant to be taken as gospel, else anyone at all could do a reading. No, Chloe-girl, this here card ain't no more evil than you are."

That bit of information didn't exactly make me feel any better. Not after the bottles had shattered the last of my illusions about what my mother was. About what I might be.

"We all got some darkness inside us, child," Mama Legba said gently, "but we each gets to decide what to do with it. You try to deny that natural part of what's in you, it means you giving it too much power. Look here, these shackles ain't no real bindings," she said, pointing to the chains that the creature was holding in the card. "These two lovers could throw off they chains any old time. They don't because they is blind to the truth. This card is about freeing yourself—about making that choice to see past the things that most weigh you down and choosing otherwise. This card is about accepting the truth of our own selves. After all, ain't no shadow without the light, and ain't no devil but the one you create and let rule you."

I glanced at Piers, but his face was solemn and still, not giving away even a hint of what he was thinking. I hated that mask-like expression he'd taken to wearing in the last couple of weeks. I hated that I couldn't read him like I used to. He glanced up, meeting my eyes for a moment, but then he went back to studying the three cards.

Mama Legba turned the final card face up, and I couldn't stop the strangled gasp that escaped me. If the Devil wasn't bad enough, a man hanging from a tree like some sort of inverted lynching was the card I'd drawn for my future.

"Hmmm," Mama Legba murmured, her brows bunched as she considered the card. "You drew some mighty interesting cards, Chloe-girl." She tapped a finger against the man's body. "This here card is powerful enough on its own, but along with the Devil? Might could be something dangerous."

"Dangerous?" I whispered, thinking of the broken bottles. Because wasn't that exactly what I was afraid of—that *I* was something dangerous? That I was my mother's—Thisbe's—daughter in every sense of the word?

"Now don't be misunderstanding me, child." Mama Legba studied the card, frowning. "Look closer."

On the surface of the card, a man hung completely naked from a tree by one foot. A thorny vine anchored him to the branch above, and his arms were outspread at his sides. His face wasn't the face of a condemned man, though. Rather than agony or even the lifeless expression of the dead, the hanged man's eyes were clear and steady, his expression alert and almost hopeful. As I looked at the card, the vine seemed to twist farther down his leg and the sky seemed to undulate in blues and golds.

"This card is all about giving up your control to get something more, Chloe-girl. See here how this little man is? He ain't *been* hanged. He put his own self up on that there tree. His hanging there is a quest for knowledge." She frowned again. "But this here card is also about sacrifice. For what you seeking, you got to be ready to give something else up. We can't carry everything from our past into our future, child. That's what this card is telling you."

"You mean I need to give up on my momma," I said, not taking my eyes from the card in front of me.

"Maybe so," Mama Legba agreed. "But I don't know that life's ever so easy to understand as that. Might could be some other sacrifice you'll need to be making before you can move on into your future. But that sacrifice will bring you something better. Something greater than what you was."

I twisted my hands in my lap, afraid to meet Mama Legba's eyes. I could feel them all watching me. Waiting for something.

"Chloe-girl," Mama Legba said gently. When I didn't look up, she tipped my chin up so I had to meet her eyes. "Ain't nothing wrong with you. These cards sure enough look like trouble, but I promise they don't have to be. You got choices to be making, but what these cards tell me is that those choices is gonna be *yours*. That's a good thing. A *powerful* thing."

"I'll get to choose?" I asked, barely able to form the words.

"Ain't that what you been worrying about all along, child? You think that because your momma done took you over once that she could do it again. But we took care of that for you, didn't we? You already made one sacrifice. You already on your path." When she saw my look of confusion, she gave my chin a gentle nudge. "Most women would have needed to be tied down to have they hair taken from them like that, but you didn't so much as shed a tear. You did what needed to be done. You made a sacrifice, and in return you gained your freedom. Now you got to decide what to do with that freedom."

She took my hand and slid the card into it. "You need to start learning again, Chloe-girl. We've given you some space to grieve, but the rooster on your door should be telling you time is up. You need to be ready for what's coming."

I tried not to think about the way my heart had squeezed like it would stop when I went to my own house. "I think I've had enough of magic to last a lifetime," I said, pushing the card back toward her. "I'm surprised you'd even want me to get wrapped up with the spirits after everything that happened."

Mama Legba frowned down at the card. "None of that was your fault, Chloe-girl. And don't you be worrying that the cards on this here table mean a dark future for you. We gonna stand by you until this is done. But you is going to have to stand for yourself, as well." Mama Legba glanced up at Piers. "By the sounds of things, though, nothing sounds near to being done. Sounds to me like it's only getting started. Thisbe ain't gone after all, is she?"

Piers shook his head and begin filling in Mama Legba on the details of what happened at my house.

"Did *you* feel anything?" Lucy asked. "Or was it just Chloe that couldn't go in?"

"I didn't feel much but a general sense of unease, but Chloe couldn't even move. The color drained from her face, and she looked like she was about to fall over until she took a step back," Piers explained.

"Would take a mighty powerful bit of magic to do that," Mama Legba agreed. "Most warding charms I know of would only turn a body around. You might not even know why you decided to leave a place you meant to go, but you certainly wouldn't feel pain or harm. That's magic darker than any I know. But that don't necessarily mean it's Thisbe's doing."

"I can't imagine why anyone but Thisbe would want to keep Chloe out of her own house," Piers said.

"Is there anyone else around that even *could*?" Lucy asked.

Mama Legba considered the question. "Not many, and of those who could, I don't know why they would."

"Then we need to assume it is Thisbe's doing," Piers confirmed. "And if we assume that, we should be prepared. She's going to be getting more and more desperate, so we need to be ready for anything..."

They kept on talking while I stared at the cards laid out on the scarred table before me—the Two of Pentacles, the Devil, and the Hanged Man. Nothing about them looked safe or peaceful. They were cards filled with energy—mostly violent energy that spoke of changes I didn't feel ready for.

"It's a starting place," Piers was saying, when a loud thumping sounded from the front part of the building—out by the shop.

Mama Legba glanced up but didn't pay it no mind.

"Probably some tourists too drunk to read. They'll get the message soon enough."

But they didn't. After a moment, the thumps came again, louder this time, and Mama Legba made a disgusted sound and lifted herself from the chair. "Let me get rid of them."

"Are you okay?" Lucy asked me after Mama Legba disappeared down the hall that led back to the store. She was watching me with dark eyes that glinted with gold when the light hit them. Cat's eyes. Old-soul eyes.

There was still something different in them, though. Some new sort of knowledge. I'd been so consumed with my own losses that I hadn't noticed it until now, but I knew it must have been because of what had happened.

From what Piers had told me, Lucy had lost someone. To keep herself alive, Thisbe had been drawing energy and youth from the body and soul of a French boy named Alex, a boy Lucy had known and loved in another life. When Lucy's family had moved to the area earlier this summer, she'd found Alex again—or what was left of him. For more than a century, his soul had been stuck on the plantation where Lucy's daddy now worked as the museum director, and when she'd finally freed him, body and soul, from Thisbe's hold, she'd been forced to let him go.

Lucy's Alex wasn't coming back. Not in this lifetime at least.

I had to admit, skinny as she was, she had a sort of strength I hadn't noticed in her before. To lose a love like that? To know you have to set someone free to let them be whole? That's a hard thing, a brave thing. But Lucy had survived it, just like she'd survived everything else, and she'd survived it with a sort of grace I wouldn't necessarily have predicted.

She could have hated me or curled up away from the world, but she'd somehow managed to make herself go on. And for the last two weeks, she'd been right there, trying to bring me back to the world. She'd acted as though none of what happened had been my fault—not losing her Alex, not me almost killing her brother. Not even me threatening her life.

Even now, her face was open and expectant. Like maybe she still wanted to be friends after all. The thought made me feel a little better, even though my own guilt still pressed on me.

"I don't know that 'okay' is how I'd describe things," I told her honestly. "But I'm here."

"Yes, you are." Lucy gave me a small, almost relieved smile. "I'm glad. I've missed you."

In that moment, something shifted a bit between us, like some of my guilt lifted its heavy bottom and scooted itself over enough to give something else a little bit of room.

Mama Legba's footsteps sounded in the hallway, and when she appeared in the doorway, her face was pinched with worry and anger. She held up her hand before any of us could talk and shook her head, and then lowered her voice to a near whisper. "Stay here till I'm gone, then get yourselves home and stay there."

Piers stood up, ready to act on whatever threat had been pounding on Mama Legba's door. "What is it?"

She raised her fingers to her lips. "Police," she said. "They want me to come take a look at some crime scene—a body in one of the cemeteries. I don't need them finding you here and asking questions." Her dark eyes rested on me.

Because if they asked who I was, they might follow up and figure out that my mom was missing. And if that happened, there might be questions we wouldn't want to answer.

"We can wait," Piers said.

"Go on home before it's full-on dark. We'll talk tomorrow, when I know more."

Piers frowned, but he gave her a tense nod and didn't argue any further as Mama Legba grabbed a patchwork bag and her keys before hurrying back to the front of the shop and the waiting police.

None of us said anything until we heard the chimes on the front door go silent, but the quiet between us was filled with an unsettled energy. Like all the questions we wanted to ask and things we wanted to say were already there, waiting for us to call them to life by naming them.

Piers spoke first. "Well, if there was any doubt..." He looked at me. "There's no way you're going back to that house again," he finished.

"Excuse me?" It wasn't what I'd expected to come out of his mouth, and my hackles rose at the unexpected bluntness in his tone. I knew Piers meant well and all. I knew he was just worried, but the declaration of what I would or wouldn't be doing—on top of everything else that had happened that day—had my temper getting away from me.

"You heard what Mama Legba said, Chloe. Someone is found murdered in a cemetery after we find that spell on your house? This has Thisbe written all over it." He ran a broad hand over his smooth head, frustrated. "Even if we do figure out a way to break the charm on your house, I'm not going to let you stay out there by yourself if that witch is on the loose."

"You're not going to *let* me?" I asked, my voice rising right along with the fear. But fear felt too dangerous, and the anger was easier to hold on to.

"He has a point," Lucy admitted.

I turned on her. "It don't matter if he has a point. He doesn't get to say. Not without at least asking me."

"I don't get to say?" Piers snapped.

"No. You don't get to decide what happens to me. *I* do. You're not my mother," I snapped, the words lashing out before I could think better of them.

"Thank god for that," Piers said, his temper finally getting the better of him, too.

His tone silenced me, and we kind of glared at each other in the uneasy stillness. Lucy shuffled uncomfortably, like she didn't know whether to jump in or leave and give us some privacy.

I *knew* he had a point, but Mama Legba had been right too. Eventually, I was going to have to stand on my own. I couldn't keep letting people decide for me. Whatever happened, I needed to be the one to choose, or it wouldn't be any better than having my body taken over again.

"We just want you to be safe," Lucy said softly, twisting at one of the knobs on her camera.

"So do I, but I won't be told what to do. I don't need to be protected like that or kept like I'm some kind of child, Piers." I looked at him then, willing him to understand. "That ain't me, and you know it."

His mouth went tight. "You think that's how I'm treating you?"

He looked so downright miserable and guilty that I couldn't help but feel a bit of my anger fading. "I think you mean well, but you've been hovering over me for weeks now, acting like I might break at any moment. Or worse. You haven't done more than kiss me on the forehead since everything happened."

Piers glanced at Lucy, and I swear his ears went red at the tips. "I've been worried..."

"And I 'preciate that. But I need you to feel something more for me than worry. I can't keep living at your place and feeling like you don't see *me* anymore."

"I see you fine," he muttered.

I shook my head. "You see the broken pieces that you took out of that cemetery. I need you to believe I'm putting myself back together, that I *can* put myself back." I hesitated. "As long as I'm living under your roof, I'm not sure that you can see me any other way but broken."

"Where else do you think you're going to go?" Piers asked, and I could tell his frustration was mounting. "You can't go back to your home. Thisbe made sure of that."

The barb stung, but I kept myself from flinching. He was right again. I couldn't go home. And no way was any hotel going to let me rent a room on my own.

"She could stay at our place," Lucy volunteered.

Piers snapped his head around to look at her.

Lucy shrunk back in her seat a little. "I mean, if you want," she added weakly, chancing a glance in my direction.

"You don't think your parents would care?" I asked, ignoring the way Piers huffed his irritation. "After everything that happened..."

"They don't know what happened," Lucy said with a shrug. "As far as they're concerned, T.J. had some kind of mysterious illness that the doctors couldn't figure out and is totally fine now. They don't know your mom had anything to do with shooting at me, and I think it's probably better for everyone's peace of mind if they never find out about any of the rest. They already think your mom's helping a sick relative in Mobile, so it's not like we need a new story to cover for you."

I looked at Piers, really looked at him. He wasn't saying anything, but I had the feeling that whatever happened at this point would matter to him—to *us*. I could go back to his apartment and stay like I'd been staying. I didn't doubt that Piers would do anything he could to keep me safe. But I also knew that all his protection might smother whatever was left between us.

Or I could go stay out at Le Ciel Doux, at Lucy's place. Her parents were nice enough people, but I didn't know how I was supposed to live under their roof knowing what I'd done— or helped to do—to their family. Even if they didn't know a thing about it.

If I went to live with Lucy's family, the distance might make Piers look at me less like some fragile doll and more like the person he once loved.

"Well?" he said, his face settling into the mask I'd come to hate. There was a part of me—an uncomfortably large part of me—that wanted nothing more than to smash it from his face.

I shook myself at the abrupt violence of that thought. It

had to be the stress and pressure I'd been under. Or maybe it was the frustration and fear that had been haunting my every footstep these past two weeks. I thought about the shattered bottles and I prayed it wasn't anything more.

I took a breath and looked at Lucy. "I think I'd like to come stay with you for a bit, if you really think your parents wouldn't mind."

I didn't even need to look to know Piers wasn't happy.

THREE

After stopping by Piers's apartment to get my things, the two of us made our way from the Quarter out toward the River Road, where Lucy's family lived in the shadow of the antebellum mansion named Le Ciel Doux. Piers still wasn't really talking to me, but I figured that was better than arguing for the time being. As we drove, the land we passed was quiet and unaware of the frustrated energy thrumming between us in the car. The sun was settling into the lower part of the sky, creeping its way steadily toward evening, and the whole world seemed to be going on its way like nothing was amiss.

Once, sugar plantations around New Orleans held a large part of the entire country's wealth, but not anymore. Now the River Road is just a stretch of half-dead towns and the refineries that kept those towns breathing. Most of the fields that once grew sugar stood unplanted, and the only things that grow out there anymore are the throats of smokestacks retching their bile out into the world. On a good day, you can barely smell the stink of them. But the beginning of August is always too hot for it to be a good day, and that day, the stink was already coming in through the open windows and filling the car with its thick, chemical smell.

As we drove, patches of green interrupted the fields of concrete and piles of coal every here and there. Some of those patches had trailer parks planted on them, but others held stately homes—pretty little pictures of the past, all brought back to life by one committee or another. All of them were a testament to the glory that had been the South, once upon a time. Busloads of tourists liked to follow the winding roads, like ants drawn to the sugar that once made the area rich.

Le Ciel Doux is maybe the biggest and prettiest piece of green. It sits back from Route 18, popping up like a surprise. My momma had worked at Le Ciel since I was little, so I basically grew up on the grounds. But it didn't matter how many times I drove through the ornate wrought-iron gates that separated the plantation from the rest of the region—seeing that big house sitting at the end of the row of ancient oaks, all shadows and bone-white stone, always gave me a creeping feeling right up the back of my neck.

I don't think anyone was more surprised than me when I applied to work as a tour guide there, but I decided I'd rather wear a hoop skirt than work the night shift at one of the refineries like a lot of folks do. And if I wanted any pocket money, I had to work for it—one of Momma's many rules.

Or, it had been.

I turned up the gravel road toward the big house and that creeping feeling came back, like cold fingers tickling at the short hairs on the nape of my neck. Like someone warning me to stay away. I was so used to it that I didn't even shudder anymore. Guiding the car left at the fork in the drive, I brought it up next to an old Volvo wagon parked in front of a pretty-as-a-postcard cottage.

"You're sure about this?" Piers asked, and I knew he meant more than what he was saying. I wasn't sure, but I had a feeling that giving us some space was the only way our relationship would survive.

I didn't even have my bags out of the trunk when the front door of the cottage opened and Lucy came out. Piers took the bag from me and took my hand as she came down the front porch steps to greet us, a tentative smile on her face.

She glanced at Piers as though to read his mood before she said anything. "Everybody's excited you're here," she told me. "Come on in, and I'll show you your room."

I wasn't even to the porch when Lucy's little brother T.J. popped his dark head out the door. Even my forgot-how-to-smile mouth couldn't help but turn up a bit at the sight of his impish face.

This was a bad idea, I realized. I'd put T.J. in danger once before. My staying at Lucy's could put her whole family in danger again.

Piers squeezed my hand, and I realized that I'd stopped moving. I knew Lucy was watching me, too.

"It's okay," she said softly. Like she knew exactly where my thoughts had gone. "Mama Legba did some protective wards on my house after everything happened. You'll be safe here."

I didn't know how she could sound so sure, because I sure wasn't.

"She doesn't have a hold on you anymore," Lucy added gently.

"You could still come back to my place," Piers suggested. I could tell by the tone of his voice that he was still frustrated he hadn't been able to change my mind about staying with Lucy's family.

"Why don't you stay for tonight and see how you feel?" Lucy offered. "If you decide to go back to Piers's place in the morning, you can. No hard feelings. But you're here now and they're already expecting you. If you leave, we're going to need an excuse for why you changed your mind. We don't need anyone trying to call your mom."

I glanced over at Piers. He still didn't look happy, probably because he knew that Lucy was right.

"Okay," I said with a sigh. "I'll stay for tonight." But I wasn't going back to Piers's place. I'd figure something else out, if it came to that.

When we got inside, both of Lucy's parents were there to greet me. Dr. and Mrs. Aimes look exactly like parents should—late forties with bodies that have started to go soft, clothes that have long since gone square, and lines etching themselves into their faces. You can tell they're good people, though, because their lines are a map of all the smiling they've done through the years. A lot of people's lines map out a different kind of story.

I wondered for a moment about the lines my face might show someday. Then I thought about the lines my momma's face had never shown, and I felt that much worse.

"I'll show you to the guest room," Lucy said, rescuing me from their fussing.

By the time I'd finished settling my stuff, Lucy, her dad, Piers, and T.J. had gathered in the front parlor to look at some old crate that Byron, the preservation manager at the plantation, had brought over to show Dr. Aimes.

Byron was in his mid-forties, and he had that kind of nondescript, doughy look to him that some men start to get at that age when they sit too long and eat too much. Lucy had hated working for him earlier that summer. Her dad had promised that working at Le Ciel would mean an opportunity for her to take pictures for a new book the university was putting together, but Byron never let her do anything but fetch coffee or hold his equipment. I hadn't had much experience with him myself, but every time I'd seen him around the property, he always seemed to be sweating.

As I walked in, Byron was wiping his brow with a rumpled blue handkerchief. "Thought you'd want to see it, so I brought it right over," he was saying to Dr. Aimes.

"You say you found this in the attic?" Lucy's dad asked, peering at the crate through the thick lenses of his glasses. "I thought we cleaned that out back in June?"

Byron tucked the handkerchief into his back pocket. "We did. But when the electrical crew went in to redo some of the wiring, they ran into this tucked away in the back of one of the eaves."

Piers motioned for me to come over to the table. I stood near him, and he wrapped an arm around my waist as we watched Byron and Dr. Aimes carefully pry open the lid. We all leaned forward a little to see what the crate contained, but at first I couldn't make out anything but some old fabric gone black with age and mold.

It took them a little longer to make sense of the box's contents. That whole big crate, and all that was inside was a couple of old books wrapped in yards and yards of the moldering old material.

"That's it?" T.J. asked, clearly unimpressed.

"Amazing, isn't it?" Dr. Aimes answered, completely missing his youngest child's disappointment.

T.J. shook his head, like he couldn't believe he'd waited around for nothing, and then took off into another room.

When they opened the first of the books, Lucy let out a small, strangled gasp.

"Would you look at that," Dr. Aimes said with a kind of satisfied triumph that made it clear he hadn't noticed his daughter's distress either. He turned the book to show us that the object wasn't a book at all. Beneath the cover, a startlingly crisp image of a couple peered out from behind thick glass.

I recognized who they were immediately—in the big house there were matching portraits of Roman Dutilette and his *much* younger French wife, Josephine. But seeing them like this, I understood Lucy's reaction. The images were so clear, so lifelike that it seemed like the pair had been shrunken and trapped under the glass.

"Did you have any record of Roman commissioning a daguerreotype?" Dr. Aimes asked Byron, but he didn't wait for an answer. He was already moving on to the other book, which turned out to actually be a book this time.

"It appears to be a journal," he said, holding the slim volume in his gloved hands and opening it carefully. It was covered in dark, cracked leather that looked near to disintegrating, but the edges of the pages were tipped in gold. Even I could see that at one time, it had been a rich man's book.

As Dr. Aimes turned the pages of the book carefully, his whole expression was rapt and almost possessive. He was looking at the book like it was some kind of buried treasure for him alone. "From my very meager French, it looks like a journal that belonged to Roman Dutilette. But much of it is written in some kind of code."

"Why would he write in code?" Lucy asked doubtfully.

"Probably to keep his thoughts private. It's not like he would've been the first," Piers explained. "William Byrd's is probably the most famous example of a slave owner keeping a coded diary, but I doubt he was the only one." Piers leaned forward, his brows drawn together as he looked at the book. "Can I see it?" he asked.

Dr. Aimes frowned, like he wasn't quite ready to give up the volume, but Piers was already pulling on a pair of the white gloves they use for handling the old stuff. Reluctantly, Dr. Aimes handed it over.

"It's not a code," Piers said after a few moments of studying the pages.

"What do you mean?" Dr. Aimes looked completely baffled.

"It's a language," Piers explained, pointing out something on the small volume's yellowed pages. "See here, this marking is the Nsibidi symbol for woman."

"En-sigh-what?" Byron asked, narrowing his eyes at Piers.

"Nsibidi. It's a language that's used in Western Africa by the Igbo people," Piers said. "I did a paper on some of the ceremonial uses of it a few years back for Professor Lamont's grad seminar. It's still used, but there are hundreds of secret symbols that are only passed between family members or between teachers and their students."

"Why would Dutilette be writing in some African language?" Byron asked, scowling at Piers.

"Oh, there could be any number of reasons," Dr. Aimes said. "It's possible that he didn't write it, or it's possible that one of his slaves taught him."

Byron snorted.

Dr. Aimes didn't acknowledge Byron's derision. "Can you read any more of it?" he asked Piers.

Piers shook his head. "Languages aren't really my thing," he said. "But if I'm right about what it is, it shouldn't be all that hard to translate."

"Leonard, you're going to have to put that away now." Lucy's mom peeked her head through the door. "Dinner is almost ready, and we have a guest." Mrs. Aimes gave me a smile that was a welcome and apology all at once. It was a motherly smile, and it felt like a punch to the gut. "You're staying too, Piers?"

"Yes, ma'am," he said, flashing her a smile. Then his eyes met mine, and the smile dimmed.

"Byron?"

"No, ma'am, but thank you. I'll just be getting these artifacts back," he said, reaching for the book.

"Oh, I can bring them later," Dr. Aimes said, still studying the book with a resolute intensity.

Byron scowled. "I think it's best if I take them to the office, where I can secure them," he said, determined.

Dr. Aimes looked up, clearly irritated. "Byron, I understand that you worked for the last owner, but *I'm* the director of the project now. The house and its contents are *my* responsibility. Not yours."

"You might be director, but I'm in charge of the artifacts," Byron shot back darkly. "Anything happens to them, and it's my ass on the line."

"I'll walk them over later tonight," Dr. Aimes said. His tone was so stark that it was clear the decision was final.

"I really think we need to follow protocol on this..."

"Are you implying that I don't know how to handle artifacts?" Dr. Aimes asked. I'd never heard his voice go steely like that.

See, Lucy's dad is all gangly limbs and tufts of hair sticking out at odd angles, and he has a way about him that makes you think of a snug corner in an old library when he speaks. Like there's book dust in his voice. He'd brought his whole family to Louisiana because restoring Le Ciel was his dream, and his family loved him enough not to hate him for it. But glaring at Byron like he was, I saw a side of him I hadn't noticed before.

For a moment, Byron looked like he wanted to argue, but he didn't. He glared at Dr. Aimes before he sullenly took his leave, looking back more than once before he finally left the parlor.

Dr. Aimes took a moment longer to look over the book before he set the two artifacts back into the crate reluctantly.

"Oh, Piers," Dr. Aimes said, his voice back to its usual softness and his expression relaxed. "Hold on. There's one other thing I wanted to talk to you about... Let me just grab it." He stood abruptly and disappeared into another room.

"Are you okay?" Piers asked Lucy. "For a second there, you looked like you were about to fall over."

Lucy's cheeked flushed in embarrassment. "The picture took me off guard."

"They seem to have a tendency to do that with you," Piers said with a smirk. "Strange for a photographer…" he teased.

Lucy slapped his arm. "Shut up. You know why I fainted the last time."

Earlier in the summer, Lucy and Piers had been with Dr. Aimes when he'd found a daguerreotype of Armantine Lyon, the girl Lucy had dreamed she was in a past lifetime. The unexpected sight of seeing Armantine's face in her waking hours had made her faint dead away. I hadn't realized back then what was happening to Lucy—or to me—so I'd teased her about it mercilessly.

"I remember what Josephine Dutilette was like to Armantine," Lucy went on. "When I saw Josephine's eyes staring up at me…" She shuddered. "Let's just say, that woman was a piece of work. I don't have any desire to ever run into her again, not in any lifetime."

Lucy's father returned a moment later with a foam cube. He set it on the coffee table between us and opened it. Inside was a small, dark piece of wood that at first looked like a misshapen star. Then I realized it was a carved doll of some sort that had a bit of ancient-looking, rust-colored thread wound about its body.

"You still have that thing?" Lucy sounded horrified.

"Of course," Dr. Aimes replied. "After we recovered it from Thisbe's cabin, we cataloged it, same as the other artifacts."

The University of New Orleans, which owned the plantation and ran its living history museum, had also managed to buy an adjoining plot of land containing a cabin that once belonged to Thisbe. The historians all knew that Thisbe was an ex-slave and influential in the life of the area, but none of the university staff—Dr. Aimes included—had any idea of how powerful she'd really been. And they certainly didn't know she was still around.

"Mama Legba told you to get rid of that, Dad. She told you how dangerous it was," Lucy said.

Piers shifted next to me, and when I glanced over at him, he was looking at the small doll with the same wariness as Lucy. He'd been there the day they discovered the charm, and I knew he was as upset as Lucy to see that Dr. Aimes still had it.

"It's *history*, Luce. This is probably more than a hundred and fifty years old," Dr. Aimes said, his voice gruff with more than a little irritation. "You can't get rid of something like that because of some superstition. And besides, while I'm sure Ms. Legba meant well enough, since when do you put any stock in stories about spirits and curses?"

Lucy's mouth shut abruptly, and she glanced at me like she didn't know what to do. It's not exactly like she could explain to her father why she thought the charm was dangerous, not without explaining everything else. Not that he would have believed her anyway.

After all, the charm didn't look like much—just a gnarled little piece of dark wood—so I understood why Dr. Aimes wouldn't have paid much attention to Mama Legba's warnings about it, but the unease that filtered through the room once the foam crate had been opened was so thick and obvious that

I couldn't understand why he wasn't sensing it. I couldn't imagine why he'd even want to have that thing near him much less keep it in his own house.

"I was talking to Professor Lamont about this," Dr. Aimes told Piers. "He said his lab up at Vanderbilt could run some tests on it before we put it in the museum. I thought maybe you'd like to take it for me? I could get a courier, but if you go, you might get some extra lab time under your belt," he finished with a smile.

"Oh," Piers said, shifting again in his chair. "I don't know…Things have been pretty busy around here with the preservation crew," he hedged. "I'm not sure if I can get the time off."

"I can talk to Byron," Dr. Aimes told him, waving away his excuse. "It shouldn't be a problem to give you a few days off from your usual shifts. Besides, now that we've found the journal, I'd like Lamont to take a look at it as well."

"Thanks, but—"

"It sounds like a great opportunity," I interrupted. I knew Piers was about to turn it down so he could stay close to me. Which was exactly what I'd been afraid of him doing—giving up pieces of his life to protect mine. It was exactly what I didn't want him to do, because I knew in the long run, he'd end up hating me for it.

"I don't know," Piers said, clearly frustrated with me.

"I'll be fine," I told him, pasting on a smile that I hoped looked genuine. "Besides, it'll only take a couple of days, right?" I asked, glancing at Dr. Aimes, who gave me a nod in answer. "You'll be back in no time. No big deal," I said, trying to send him the not-so-subtle message that he should agree.

Piers didn't respond. He frowned at me with an undecipherable look in his eyes. But he must have known he was stuck. Between me and Dr. Aimes, he didn't have any other excuse that wouldn't have raised suspicions. "I don't know…"

"Well, give some thought to it," Dr. Aimes said.

"Lovely," Mrs. Aimes drawled from the doorway to the kitchen. "Now if you would be so kind as to put that away so we can eat?"

Dinner was pleasant enough, but I could tell Piers was pissed about me insisting he go to Nashville. It hadn't done anything to help the tension that was already between us, and I was more than a little nervous about what he would say when he pulled me aside after dinner.

Alone in Dr. Aimes's cluttered office, Piers again went through all the reasons he shouldn't go to Nashville or leave me to myself.

"We haven't even talked to Mama Legba like we planned," he said. "We need to meet up with her tomorrow, because you know that if the police came to her, they think the killing had something to do with the occult. Thisbe has to be involved."

"So we'll talk to her first. But you know as well as I do that if you don't go, you're going to have to come up with a better reason. Usually, you'd jump at a chance like this. I thought we were supposed keep acting like everything's normal so we don't have to involve anyone else. Wasn't that the whole purpose of my story about Momma visiting a sick relative?"

"You're right," Piers said, running a hand over his head. "But I don't like the idea of leaving you alone right now. Not with bodies turning up in the Quarter."

"It's just for a couple of days," I told him again. "Until

then, I'll be staying with Lucy in a well-warded house that's been covered twice over by Mama Legba's protective charms. I'll be fine."

He still didn't look convinced. "I still can't help but feel like you're trying to push me away, Chloe."

I pretended like I didn't hear the question in his tone as I walked over to the table where Dr. Aimes had left the foam container and lifted the lid. Again, that uneasy energy whispered through the room. "This was Thisbe's, right?"

Piers nodded.

"Did you ever consider that it might be able to tell us something about her, or about what she might do next? If you're in the lab, we wouldn't have to wait to find out what they learn about it."

He frowned, and I could tell he didn't like where I was going.

"Think about it," I pushed. "If you're the one who delivers the charm to Professor Lamont, and if you get to help out in the lab, you'll have first-hand knowledge about anything they learn. That would be a lot more help to figuring out what Thisbe might do than all of us sitting here waiting for something else to happen."

The way he scowled at me told me that he knew I was right. "I still don't like it," he said.

"Me neither. Look, like Dr. Aimes said, you don't have to decide right this second. Let's see what Mama Legba has to say, but at least consider it?" Without thinking, I reached out and ran a single finger across the rough thread of the little doll.

A shuddering unease ran through me, and then all at once, the room around me was gone.

The smell of woodsmoke burned my nostrils and the light from the fire in the brick hearth cast a strange, pulsing glow over the meager furnishings in the room. My skin felt the fingers of the cold night beyond reaching for me through the sparse warmth of the fire, but I shrugged it off.

What did a little cold matter when I had power settled over me like a heavy cloak?

A bone-deep sense of absolute rightness and conviction flooded through me as I looked at the body of the man lying on the narrow bed. He was beautifully built, with strong features that even in sleep looked formidable and sure. Simply looking at him, knowing he was mine, had a warmth curling low in my belly. I had an overwhelming urge to press my lips against his broad and generous mouth.

But I didn't. There would be time enough for that later—a lifetime of days. But tonight, there was work still to be done.

I pulled a low three-legged stool close to the bed where he lay and rested his palm in the skirts that covered my lap. I already had everything I needed, but still I hesitated.

"No," I thought wildly.

No more hesitation. No more second thoughts. I knew what needed done, and I would do it. I would keep him safe.

I took the knife I'd prepared and carefully shaved a bit of his hair from his temple and added it to the lock of my own hair that I'd already cut, binding them together with a few drops of red candle wax. Always red for power.

Then I took a bit of sewing thread and pierced the clump of wax as I murmured the words that would bind him to me. The man shifted in his sleep as I finished the incantation, but I ignored him. Working more quickly now, I fastened the clump of wax to the small figure I'd carved from one of the great oaks on the neighboring property. I'd selected the largest of the trees for its constancy and power.

When I was finished, I looked at my handiwork for a moment, sensing the warmth that built in my palm where the charm rested. Magic like this should have been more than enough to bind most, but he wasn't like most. He had a strength and a power to him that everyone could sense—the others, who made way when he passed by. The slave driver, who'd never raised the whip to mar his back. Even his master, who refused to sell him, no matter the price offered.

I knew well enough it would take something stronger than a simple binding to hold him safe when he was so determined to die for the sake of living. Not that he'd told me any specifics of what he was planning. But he didn't have to, because I could smell it in the air, cutting through the smoke from the fires that boiled the cane. Disquiet and recklessness has its own particular perfume—sweet and thick smelling, with a little rot underneath. For weeks now, that scent had been thick in the fields, wafting through the cabins filled with uneasy bodies, and following Augustine everywhere he went.

Before she'd walked off into the swamps and left me behind, my mother had whispered to me secrets that her mother had taught her. Secrets of blood and life, of power and magic so thick it could smother a person. My whole life I'd hidden away those secrets from the hateful eyes that looked at my skin like it was my fault. From those who saw her in my blood, like I had any choice.

But I'd use those secrets now. I'd save him.

Taking the bright blade of the knife, I made the smallest of incisions in his palm. He didn't so much as stir this time, so I pressed the knife deeper, carving through the skin of his hand, following the strong, steady curve of his lifeline. As the blood welled, dark and shining in the flickering light, my mouth formed words that my tongue had never tasted. Words I hadn't even realized I knew.

When his palm was filled with the inky darkness of his own blood, I took the small figure and I placed it in the pooling blood. Dark rivulets ran over the edges of his cupped palm, staining the material of my skirt, but I didn't waver. Ignoring my ruined dress, I twisted the little carved man until it was coated with Augustine's lifeblood.

My mouth kept on chanting those strange words until my throat went hoarse and the blood began to slow. Gently, I bound up the wound and placed his bandaged hand back on the bed. Only then did I allow myself to relax any, satisfied at the work I'd done.

Only then did I allow myself the pleasure of pressing my lips to his.

As I pulled back, the sleeping man's eyelids flew open. But all I could see was the whites of his eyes.

I jerked away from the carved doll and gasped as I came back to myself. I wasn't wearing a long, roughly spun skirt but the same shorts I'd had on earlier. We weren't in a fire-lit room but still in Dr. Aimes's cluttered office.

"Did you hear anything I just said?" Piers asked, his tone dripping with irritation.

"What?" My voice came out breathy and unsure.

He let out a sigh. "See, this is exactly what I was telling you. You're not ready for me to go anywhere yet."

I tried to focus on what Piers was saying and not on

the fact that I might be losing my mind. "I'm fine," I said, failing miserably to keep my voice steady. "I just got a little lightheaded or something." I couldn't quite meet his eyes. "It's stuffy in here," I added, which wasn't exactly a lie.

Piers took me gently by the arms and brought his face down to mine. The irritation in his expression had been replaced by concern. "You still feel lightheaded? Do you need to sit down?"

I could still practically feel the man's lips against mine, and I felt unaccountably guilty. I had to force myself not to pull away from Piers. "I just need some air. I'll be fine," I said, hardly able to breathe with him so close, watching me like he was waiting for me to prove him right.

"Okay. Let's get you some air." Piers finally released my arms to put the lid back on the box. I wasn't sure if it was him giving me some space or that the box was closed that made it seem like air in the room around me sighed with relief.

I didn't think Piers had any idea what had happened to me. Whatever that vision had been, it was clear he hadn't seen or experienced it.

I took a breath, forcing myself to hold it together. There had to be some sort of magic clinging to that dark charm that caused the vision, and I was more certain than ever Piers needed to be the one to take it to Nashville.

Even the sultry warmth of the evening air didn't make me feel any better. I knew I needed to tell him about what happened when I touched the charm, but he was acting so protective and nervous about me being a little lightheaded that I couldn't seem to find the words. I told myself that I only needed a few minutes of peace to let my thoughts settle and to figure out what I wanted to say, but Piers kept hovering so close.

The farther we got from the charm, the more unreal it all felt, and I told myself that maybe I'd only imagined it. But no matter what I did, I couldn't shake the image of my skirt stained with blood and the whites of the man's sightless eyes.

FOUR

Outside, we found Lucy waiting for us on the deep-set front porch, but then T.J. bounded up to us and wouldn't be shooed. We couldn't get rid of him without being mean, and we couldn't talk about curses and dark magic in front of him, so Piers ended up leaving before I found a way to tell him what had happened when I touched the charm.

I didn't feel like hiding anything else that night, so I made up an excuse about being tired and turned in early. After I washed up, I ran my fingers along my scalp, scratching it a bit as I studied myself. I might look just fine with my hair so short, but I didn't think I'd ever get used to feeling so naked and exposed. For as long as I could remember, I'd looked out at the world through the dark frame of my curtain of hair, but now, everything seemed a little off. The whole world seemed a little too close.

Studying my profile in the mirror, I searched my face for I don't know what. Some hint of my mother's features?

Or maybe I was looking for some hint of my mother's evil? But the only face that looked back at me was my own.

I didn't have any more doubts that my mother was powerful, and I knew enough about what had happened to understand she was most likely evil. But I couldn't shake the idea that evil doesn't sing you to sleep when you're up with worry or keep you alive when you're burning with fever. I'd always believed that evil doesn't know how to love.

But when I thought about the vision—the way I'd felt drawn to the sleeping man on the bed, the warmth that had flooded through me when my lips touched his—I wasn't sure I understood what evil was at all anymore.

I raised my hands to my own mouth and tried to rub the feeling of that man's lips from my skin, but it didn't work. The memory of the soft warmth of his mouth against my own clung to me like a spiderweb.

Even after I'd climbed under the covers and tried to fall sleep, I couldn't shake the memory of the vision. The vivid *reality* of it. I knew almost instinctively that what I'd seen had something to do with Thisbe. She'd been working some sort of spell to bind the sleeping man to her, but I couldn't quite let go of the idea that I hadn't sensed any malice when she sliced through the man's lifeline, only calm certainty and affection. I didn't know what to make of that either.

She'd thought of her mother, too. The hurt and anger that had throbbed through her heart when she thought of being left behind still made my throat feel tight and my eyes ache. Or maybe that was my own hurt, my own understanding.

Finally, I found sleep, but it wasn't restful. All night, I dozed on and off, plagued by strange dreams of a lonely grove of pines. The cool night air was filled with the sharp bite of resin, and the world was still and completely silent. No insects buzzed in the trees. No breeze could be heard rustling the branches. And no matter how far I walked, I never found the end of the grove.

Above, the endless pines towered into the sky like the roof of a cathedral. They were so thick, so dense I could barely make out the stars above. Moonlight found its way down to the ground below in narrow shafts, like dim spotlights revealing a path through the forest. But the path never led anywhere.

After wandering for days or weeks or lifetimes, I stopped, settling myself against the base of a pine, and waited. And as I waited, something stirred in the trees beyond. I couldn't hear it, but I sensed it and I knew that something was out there. Pacing. Hunting.

I stood, bracing myself against the rough bark of the tree behind me. Waiting. I didn't even breathe.

You really think I would ever leave you behind?

The voice came out of the darkness, soft and low, and it echoed through my mind. *Flesh and blood. Heart and soul, baby girl.* Then softer, like a promise or a prayer. *Soon, baby girl. Very soon. You're meant for great things.*

I knew that voice as well as I knew my own. "*Momma*," I screamed, looking around the dark grove for the source of the sound, wanting an answer. But not even my own words came back to me. The pines were silent, and I was alone.

Or maybe I wasn't, because right before I woke up, I felt something in the darkness smile.

———————

Sometime after dawn, I pulled on some clothes and eased myself out of the house into the hazy morning air. At first, I sat on the front steps trying to shake the unsettled feeling my dreams had given me, but I was too restless and needed to move. Before I'd really consciously decided where to go, I found myself walking down the path that led out, away from the big house, to the fields beyond.

Even once I realized where my feet were headed, I didn't turn back. Resolute, I made my way through the tall grass on the far side of the plantation's property, through the wooded area surrounding the pond, and out toward the abandoned cabin they all said my momma used to call home so many years ago, when she still called herself Thisbe.

The cabin was small and low to the ground. Spindly pines partially hid the ancient-looking structure from view. Some of the trees still had the remnants of faded, rust-colored string hanging from their branches. Someone had cut the bottles down that had hung there, and now the wisps of thread, like forgotten webs, were all that remained.

I hesitated as I studied a burned-out spot a few yards away from the cabin, but I'd come this far. I wasn't going to turn back now.

As I stepped a little closer, into the copse of trees, I kept expecting something to stop me, like it had at my own house. I waited, holding myself steady against the crushing defeat of being pushed away and held back from understanding once again. But as I took tentative steps toward the cabin, nothing seemed to be blocking my way.

Near about everyone in the area had heard tell of the lonely cabin just beyond Le Ciel Doux. Most people heard stories about the ghosts that supposedly haunted the woods and swamps around it and stayed away. I'd never been out to the cabin myself, not even after the university managed to buy the property. At least, I didn't remember going out there, which in my case doesn't really amount to the same thing.

But standing a few steps from the front door, I wasn't in no hurry to face whatever it was I'd come to face. So I waited in the lacey shade and tried to imagine what the place must have looked like way back when an ex-slave named Thisbe lived there. I tried to see the ramshackle structure through her eyes—what had that rusted-out roof been made of back then? What would that wide front porch have meant to a woman in her position? And why had she decided to stay once her owner—and father—had freed her, when she could have left that life behind?

I stepped toward the house and ran my finger along the uneven boards of the porch, closing my eyes as an image of the past rose up softly in my mind, the colors burned-out and faded like an old photograph. *The cabin with its walls washed white in the heat of a summer day with its doors open and welcoming.*

She must have been powerful even then to rise so far for someone in her position. I could almost see her, a little older than I remembered my mother ever being, but not quite old, sitting in the shade of that porch and never alone. Always surrounded by people who believed in her power and feared her because of it, but who knew she'd care for their needs just the same. As I imagined it, a warmth that felt like fingers began stroking down the tense cords of my neck. Easing out the knots that stress and sleepless nights had put there.

When I opened my eyes, the fingers disappeared. The cabin was gray and worn, the doors shuttered now instead of open.

Stupid. I was imagining what I wanted to feel. After the rooster and the curse on my house, I shouldn't have had any illusions that my momma wanted anything to do with me, or at least nothing good. Giving myself a mental shake, I mounted the steps before I could change my mind. It took a bit of time to wrench open one of the French doors at the front of the house, but once I did, it was easy enough to step into the closed-up warmth of the interior.

Inside was dim and smelled strongly of new plaster and something damp and old beneath it. I detected another scent, too—something earthy and heavy—an almost oily smell that reminded me of the jars sitting on Mama Legba's shelves. Maybe some herb I wasn't familiar with? But I couldn't tell if it was the ghost of a scent from years past or something more recent.

The interior of the cabin was mostly empty. The floors were worn in certain places where furniture might have once stood, and everything was covered with a layer of dust from the restoration the university was doing. But small as it was, it was a comfortable space, and the way the rooms flowed one into the next reminded me of my own house.

I took my time walking around, wondering what it would have been like to live there a hundred years ago. Imagining the furniture that must have stood against the walls.

The walls would have been washed white, I knew, to protect against the diseases that ran so rampant in the slave quarters. Like a little whitewash could stop cholera. And there would have been some furniture, maybe even a picture or two on the walls.

I ran my fingers along one of the jointed boards of the wall.

A finely wrought chest stood there, its wood gleaming darkly. Opposite, a velvet-covered settee…

I shook my head, disrupting the image. No way would an ex-slave woman in Thisbe's position have had anything so fine as what I was imagining. And yet, if I closed my eyes… I reached out and pressed my hand against the wall again. All at once, I could see it. All at once, an image rose up stronger than before, wiping away my present and pulling me back, back into a distant past…

Strangers filled the rooms—and friends, too. But all of them wanting something. All of them needing something. All they had to give me in return was a couple of limp chickens or a few handfuls of meal.

And they would give it.

They'd give the fish they stole from their master's stream, and the scuppernong they pilfered from the wild vines in the forest. They'd give near anything for one of my charms. Anything for the hope of something more than the narrow lives they clung to. Some would trade their very own soul for some protection against the dangers of this world.

Always filling up my rooms and wanting and needing. And not one of them ever bringing what I really needed. What I'd been waiting for so long.

I pulled my hand away, startled at the thoughts that had tumbled through my mind. The image had been so vivid that I could have reached right out and run my hand across the velvet. Still, I could almost smell the bodies with three days of labor clinging to their skin and feel the pressure of the crowd pushing down on me with their need, when all I wanted to do was breathe free. When all I craved was the cool night air and something else that I'd been missing.

But it wasn't *me* that was missing and craving something. Like yesterday, I was seeing through another pair of eyes, feeling another person's thoughts.

Yesterday, I'd thought that the vision happened because the charm still contained some of Thisbe's magic, and I wondered if that explained this vision, too—maybe the cabin itself still held a bit of her power. But I didn't sense any power here, not like I'd sensed the almost spiteful energy that radiated off that charm. I wasn't sure what to make of that.

I followed the rooms until I reached the back of the house. The university had recently rebuilt the fireplace there, and the new brick stood out strikingly red against the blackened remains of the hearth. The furniture in that room had been pushed up against the wall—a low bed, a worn cabinet with an amazing number of doors and drawers.

That room felt strangely peaceful. The whole cabin was silent as a grave, but the back room was somehow even more so. It felt like a private place, but nothing there looked like the mother I knew. Nothing felt like her.

I sat carefully on the low, platform-like bed, and the moment my hands touched the worn slats, the room around me shifted, changed...

A fire was burning low in the hearth, the room dark except for its subtle glow. On the low-slung bed was the body of a younger man with sharp features and hair like spun gold. His face was slack with something stronger than sleep.

I bent over him, my mouth curving into a smile. "You're going to give me more time," my mouth said, moving on its own. "You're gonna give me everything."

I gasped, standing up and releasing my hold on the low bed, and when I did, the room came back to me as it truly was. But my heart was thundering in my chest, and my breathing was fast and anxious. It had seemed *so* real.

Forcing myself to take a slow, steady breath, I considered what had just happened. Slowly, because I wasn't sure that I was making the right decision, I reached out and touched one of the small drawers in the cabinet next to the bed.

I pulled out the tiny man I'd made for that particular purpose, excitement coursing through my blood. Last time, it hadn't worked. Augustine had left and he'd never come back. But this boy wouldn't be going anywhere.

My other hand held a bloody knife, and I turned to the man lying still and barely breathing and I raised that blade …

When I pulled my hand back, the knife was gone. I was me again.

If I had any doubts about what was happening, that last vision erased them. The blond boy on the bed, the knife and the voodoo charm—Lucy had told me enough about her dreams for me to know that I was seeing what had happened in this place long ago. I was seeing *Thisbe*, but I wasn't dreaming the way Lucy did when she learned about her own past life.

I looked at my hands in horror, not understanding what was happening or why. I'd never been able to see anything like that before, and I shouldn't have been able to see anything like that at all, not when they'd taken my hair. That sacrifice was supposed to have stopped Thisbe from having any connection to me. I couldn't let myself believe it had been for nothing.

But again, I felt the sensation of warm fingers stroking my neck.

My skin prickled, and the room felt suddenly too warm, like a fire was burning in the empty hearth. Every cell in my body said run, but I couldn't.

Didn't *want* to.

Because the truth was, part of me still wanted to find my mother before anyone else did. Even though I knew what she was, I wanted the chance to ask her, face-to-face, the one question that had been running through my mind for two weeks now—*why*?

A familiar chuckle rumbled through my brain, so deep and dark I felt like I was drowning in it. But familiar as that dark laugh was, as much as it sounded like the musical tones of my momma's voice, I didn't trust it.

"Momma?" I whispered, my voice barely breaking the uneasy silence that surrounded me.

You miss me, sweet girl? The voice that sounded so much like my mother's echoed in my head. The fingers were still there, their ghostly rhythm soothing me. Rubbing away my doubts.

Of course, I wanted to say. Because I did miss the momma I had known once. But I didn't say anything.

I might have wanted to believe the gentle hands stroking my neck belonged to her, but I was raised on enough tales of spirits and tricksters to know that not everything is what it appears to be.

"Give me a sign," I whispered. "I miss my momma, sure enough, but you gotta show me that you are her before I'll believe a thing you say."

The warm fingers were gone and a grip like ice stole my breath.

Do I now? The dark chuckle echoed through my head again. *You say you miss your momma, but you're still running around with those who would end her. You don't trust the very person who gave life to you.*

I struggled to take a breath, but it was impossible. My throat ached from the strength of the invisible grip squeezing it, and my lungs had seized up.

You listen, baby girl. You think about which side you want to be on. You think about who you owe your loyalty to. And when you're ready to be the dutiful child I raised you to be, you come on back to me and we'll be together. We'll be together always.

The icy fingers released me, and I gasped for air, but the lungful I got tasted heavy and dark.

Shaken, with my clothes stuck to me with sweat, I stood on unsteady legs. I loved my mother. I would always love the mother I had known, but I knew in that moment, my throat still aching from the pain of those invisible fingers, that I wouldn't take the side of a monster. No matter how much part of me might want to if it meant having my mother back.

My vision swam a bit as I made my way back to the front of the cabin, and I wasn't exactly sure on my feet as I walked toward the front door. I stumbled a bit and used the frame of the door to catch myself.

The man from that first vision—Augustine—looked up at me. He wouldn't come in and he wouldn't come any closer.

I'd give this all up, I told him. We could leave all this behind. I'd give it up now if you'd walk away with me.

But his eyes were dark with frustration and he wouldn't answer me. He only turned away...

I pulled my hands back, like the door was on fire. I needed to get out of there. Needed to be away from the closeness in the air and the voice that echoed through my mind with its dark laughter.

I stepped onto the porch and then kept walking until I was down the steps and safe on the ground. I drew a deep breath into my lungs, trying to erase the memory of the cabin and the unsettled feeling I had. Trying to make myself breathe steady and easy.

That's when I realized how late it was.

I'd come to the cabin right about the time the sun was barely warming up the horizon. By the time I came out, it had already climbed high into the sky. It had to be well on into late morning, which wasn't possible. I hadn't been inside the cabin for more than ten or fifteen minutes at most.

My hands shook as I took out my phone and checked the time. I'd lost *hours*. Whole hours that had felt like minutes.

Just like before, I thought with a sinking sense of dread. A whole morning gone, and I had no real memory of where all that time went. Or what I'd been doing during it.

The screen of the phone lit suddenly, and a list of texts greeted me, all from Lucy and Piers. As I scrolled through them, I saw that the messages had become more panicked with every one I hadn't answered. I tried to text Lucy back, but the reception wasn't strong enough for the message to get through.

As I walked, I shivered in the heat, wrapping my arms

around myself to ward off the icy dread that had settled over me. Last time I lost time, Thisbe—my momma—had taken over my body and used it to hurt innocent people. I examined my hands, my legs, but found no sign that I'd been anywhere but the cabin. Which didn't make me feel much better. It's not like I knew how to tell if Thisbe had possessed me again.

As I ran a hand over the close-cropped cap of what was left of my hair, tears burned in my eyes. Thisbe was still out there, and she maybe still had the ability to get hold of me.

"What do you want from me?" I said to the wide, lonely world around me. "I need the truth."

Silence was the only answer I got.

Giving up, I made my way across the unplanted field, but as I reached the line of trees that would take me back to Le Ciel, I heard the dark chuckling again, right up close to my ear.

You make it sound like the truth is an easy thing, the voice that sounded so much like my momma told me. *Like it's a fruit you can pluck off a tree, whole and sweet for you and you alone.*

I stopped, waited with my heart in my throat.

A wind rushed through the trees, brushing against my legs and arms, turning my sweat-damp clothes almost icy in its wake.

Truth is something that lies buried. Like a body in a grave. You want the truth, baby girl? You're gonna have to dig.

FIVE

As I made my way up the gravel path to the Aimes' house, Lucy's slim figure appeared as a silhouette in the wood-framed screen door. By the time I'd made it to the steps of the porch, she'd stepped outside, and a second, taller and broader figure had joined her. *Piers.*

At first I was startled to see him, but then I thought of the frantic texts. Of course Piers would be waiting.

He sure didn't look happy to see me, though. Actually, neither of them did. Their faces were matching masks of frustration and concern, and they didn't make any move to greet me. At first they both just stood there, side by side, at the top of the steps, dual sentries blocking my way.

Piers moved to meet me first. "Where have you been?" he asked, his arms still crossed against me, his face not registering any emotion but frustration.

"I had a hard time sleeping, so I took a walk," I told him, ready to explain everything. I needed to talk through what had happened out at Thisbe's cabin, because I still didn't know what to make of it all, but before I could say anything he was talking.

"You took a *walk*?" he said, his brows rising in mocking disbelief.

I'd known he was upset, but the anger in his tone had me taking a step back. "I lost track of time," I told him, knowing exactly how weak that excuse sounded. But with Piers looking at me like that—with more irritation than worry—I suddenly wasn't sure how to even begin explaining everything else. He was already looking at me like he didn't trust me.

"Why didn't you answer our texts or calls?" Lucy asked from her vantage point a few steps above us. Her voice didn't have the demand in it that Piers's did, but I could tell she was upset.

"I must have lost service," I told her, holding up my phone and waving it a little. "My phone never even buzzed until a couple of minutes ago, and I got all your messages at once. By then I was already on my way back."

Piers looked doubtful, like he'd already decided not to hear me out, but Lucy studied me with those ageless eyes of hers. I couldn't quite tell what she was thinking.

"You disappeared, Chloe," Lucy said, an unspoken question in her tone. "You didn't leave a note or tell anyone where you went. And you've been gone for *hours*."

"I . . ." It was harder than I thought it would be to start. My throat was still tender from the grip of the icy fingers, and the weight of everything that had happened out there in that cabin pressed down on me so I felt like I couldn't even breathe.

Something out there had spoken to me. Something had

offered me a choice—or maybe it had issued a threat. Either way, I didn't know what that meant about the danger any of us might still be in. Or the danger I might be to them.

"We were worried about you," Lucy told me, and I knew from the way she spoke, she wasn't really mad. Scared, maybe, but not mad.

Piers didn't say anything, though. Just kept taking me in with wary, watchful eyes.

"I'm sorry," I said, finally forcing out the words I knew he wanted from me.

Piers relaxed his shoulders a little, but he still didn't uncross his arms. It was like he was waiting for me to explain completely before he'd open himself back up.

But conditional love ain't no kind of love at all, and his closed-up expression made me feel all kinds of empty inside. It also made me hesitate, because I didn't know how to explain where I'd been or what had happened without that frustrated look changing to something else.

We stood there in uneasy silence, Piers waiting for me to explain myself and me not knowing how. Lucy's eyes darted between us as she retreated back up the steps. "I'm going to go in and grab my things. Let me know when you're ready to go," she said before she slipped through the door. I could tell she was trying to give us some privacy to sort things out.

When she was gone and we were finally alone, Piers let out an impatient sigh. "Come on, baby. Just tell me where you went so we can get on with things."

The way he asked, without any warmth at all and like he had a right to demand, made something inside me want to lash out. "I told you. I went for a walk," I said. But I still hadn't calmed all the way down, and there was more attitude than I meant in my tone.

"Chloe, it's almost noon. Lucy said she's been up since around nine, and you were already gone by then."

I glanced away, pushing down the panic that inched along my spine as I thought about the hours I'd lost out at that cabin.

"You didn't try to go back home, did you?" he asked, his brow furrowed like he was watching for a lie.

"Home?" It hadn't even occurred to me to walk back to my own house. True, it was only a couple miles west of Le Ciel and an easy enough stroll if you had the time, but after the rooster, it certainly didn't feel like no kind of home anymore. "I wouldn't try to go back there. Especially not on my own."

"Then where were you?" he pressed, not giving an inch.

When Piers meets any kind of a problem, he attacks it with a kind of single-minded attention. I'd seen him do it a hundred times before when he was reading over some study or trying to make headway on a project for school, but right at that moment, he was looking at *me* like that. I didn't like that feeling one bit, but I knew he wasn't going to let go of this. And I didn't really have anything to hide.

"I went out to Thisbe's cabin," I told him.

"You *what*?" Disbelief and fury flashed in his eyes. "Why the hell would you go there?"

I winced at his tone. "I don't think I meant to go at first," I said, trying to explain. "But when I started walking, that's where I ended up."

The scowl on his deepened at what I'd admitted. "You didn't go inside, did you?"

"Of course I went inside."

He stared at me, incredulous, shaking his head at me like I was some kind of misbehaving child. "Why would you think it was safe for you to go in there?"

"It didn't seem like that big of a deal at the time," I said weakly. "You and Lucy both have been in there and nothing happened."

"Lucy and I don't have an evil witch for a mother," he snapped. As soon as the words were out, his eyes widened, like he realized what he'd said. "I'm sorry, baby. I—"

"Forget it," I said, cutting off his apology. I didn't want to hear it, and I certainly didn't want to think about the implications of what he'd said—that he saw something wrong with me because of the blood in my veins. My throat was as painfully tight as it had been when those icy fingers had squeezed it.

"I'm trying to keep you alive," Piers told me, a pained expression dimming his eyes. He took a step toward me, but I pulled back. I didn't want his pity or apology.

"I don't need a keeper, Piers."

But he didn't respond to that, so maybe he thought I did need one.

"You're going to have to step back some and trust me again," I told him. "I can't keep living with you breathing down my neck and questioning every choice I make."

The stiffness in his shoulders broadcast all his frustration, all his worry without saying a word. "You don't have any idea what it was like that night, Chloe. You don't know what you put me through all those weeks leading up to it—you were so cold and distant."

"That wasn't me," I reminded him.

"I didn't know it wasn't you at the time," he said, his eyes shadowed with the memory of those days.

"But you know now."

"Yeah." Piers's jaw was tight. "I know a lot of things now," he said, but there was something in his tone I didn't like.

"What's that supposed to mean?" I asked warily.

He looked me dead in the eye before he spoke again, like he wanted me to know that what he was about to say was important. "It means that I know what it's like to stare into the face of evil and realize it's a face I've known and laughed with and actually *liked*. And I know what it's like to aim a gun steady at your chest and know that I could pull the trigger," he said, his voice so rough it broke at the end.

My shoulders sagged a little at the emotion in his words. "Is that what this is about?" I asked. "You still feel guilty?"

"It's more than guilt," he said softly, before he finally glanced away.

I took an uneasy breath as I thought about all the other things that might be causing the way he'd been treating me lately, but none of them were good. "You would have saved me," I told him.

"By killing you," he said darkly. His eyes met mine and I saw the pain in them, the horror of that night still haunting him.

"But you didn't kill me," I reminded him.

"Chloe, there was a moment in that cemetery when I knew I would—that I *could*—pull the trigger if I had to." He let out a ragged breath and shook his head. "Every time I look at you, I keep seeing that moment over again. There was a split second where I knew what it was going to be like to lose you, and I was going to do it anyway."

I took a step closer, my heart aching even as I couldn't quite shake off all the anger. "You can't save me from any of this, Piers. You can't keep standing in front of me, either." I laced my fingers through his. "You're going to have to let what happened that night go, or eventually there'll just be you and me and nothing between but what used to be. Is that what you want?"

He squeezed my hand and for the length of a heartbeat, I thought he understood. I thought he would tell me all the things I needed to hear.

"Why were you gone so long, Chloe?" he asked instead.

For a moment, I was too disappointed to speak. He hadn't heard or understood a thing I'd just said to him, and I wasn't sure what to do with that.

But that bit of hesitation on my part was apparently all he needed to pull his hand away and take a step back from me. "We should get going," he said, changing the subject. "Lucy and I have been waiting all morning for you to get back so we can go see Mama Legba."

"Piers—" I started, but my voice sounded so damned pathetic that I stopped myself. Not that he heard me. Not that he even looked back. He was already up the three steps and through front door before I could stop him.

SIX

The drive back into the oldest part of New Orleans wasn't a pleasant one. None of us really said much—Lucy seemed to be giving us some space, but Piers seemed perfectly happy to let that space grow in the uneasy silence of the car. By the time we found a place to park a few blocks down from Mama Legba's, I was on edge, and I think Lucy and Piers were, too.

The atmosphere in the Quarter didn't help much. The streets were already swarming with tourists out seeing the sights or weaving drunkenly on the sidewalks. To get to the alley that led to Mama Legba's shop, we had to push our way through a group of people who had gathered to listen to a mournful brass band moaning out some life-done-me-wrong blues. But even those lonesome notes sounded too cheerful for the dark mood I was carrying with me.

Mama Legba had a couple of customers when we walked into the shop, so we pretended we were browsing the selection of Gris-Gris and amulets until she finished up with them. But as soon as they had paid and she'd bid them a blessed day, the smile slid from her face. She flipped her sign and locked the front door behind them.

"I was expecting you earlier," she said, the question clear in her voice.

"That was my fault," I volunteered before Piers could speak up. "Sorry."

Mama Legba pinned me with an inquisitive look, but then gave me a nod. "Well, come on back then. We got things to talk over."

She already had a kettle of water on the stove that she set to boiling. She didn't say much as she poured the steaming liquid over the herbs already waiting in the four mugs on the table. She handed us each one before she had us sit around the table. The tea smelled like flowers and tasted sweeter than I would've expected from something so green, but when I sipped it, I finally felt the ghostly memory of those icy fingers around my throat melting away.

Once we were all settled, Mama Legba took a breath as though to center herself before she spoke. Her usually smiling face was serious, and I knew that whatever was going to come out of her mouth wasn't going to be good.

"If I'd been having any doubts about Thisbe being back, I don't have any no more," she told us bluntly. "Even the police could tell plain as day that poor soul was killed the same way as that girl back in June."

"Emaline," I corrected, my voice breaking as I said the name. It hurt even to think about her, but I needed to remind everyone *that girl back in June* had a name. "Her name was Emaline."

Everyone at the table went still. I didn't look up to meet any of their eyes, but from the way they shifted in their seats, I could sense them having a silent conversation about me while I was sitting right there.

Finally Mama Legba reached out and rested her soft hand over mine. "You weren't to blame for what Thisbe did to her, Chloe-girl," Mama Legba said. "You know that, right? The death of that poor girl ain't on your head."

She could say what she wanted, but that didn't change the truth. "I let her come with us, didn't I? Emaline might never have even been at the St. John's Eve ritual if not for me. She would have been safe, maybe even still alive."

"Even so," Mama Legba said. "You had no way of knowing what would be. You came out to the Bayou to celebrate a new season—to ask the spirits for blessings, not to harm. You didn't have no way of stopping what happened to her."

I pulled my hand away from Mama Legba's. Whatever she might say, I couldn't shake the feeling that she was wrong. Everything had changed that night—that was the night my momma discovered I'd been learning from Mama Legba behind her back. It was the point when everything seemed to start spinning out of control for me.

Or maybe I should say it was the point when Thisbe starting taking control, because after that night I started having hours and days disappear.

"Now when that girl was killed—*Emaline*," Mama Legba corrected herself, "everyone knew well enough that her throat had been slit. Couldn't keep something like that out of the news when there were so many people around that night. But the police didn't officially release none of the other information."

"You mean about the other cuts on her body," Lucy said.

Mama Legba nodded. "'Course there been rumors about the way her killer carved symbols into her arms and legs, but the police were careful to keep the specifics quiet. They showed me the pictures, though," she said with a little shudder. "Over the years there've been plenty of wannabes 'round these parts, but something about those markings didn't look like the work of no amateur."

Mama Legba looked around the table, meeting each of our eyes. "Just like Emaline, the pictures they showed me yesterday had a body with his throat slit clear across. The poor soul was wearing the exact same sort of markings on his arms and legs that Emaline had been wearing on hers. Ain't no doubt in my mind that the same person killed him."

"You think it's another ritual killing," Piers confirmed.

"Sure enough," Mama Legba said. "But more than that— the ground weren't near as soaked as you'd expect from wounds like that. Whoever killed the boy did it careful-like. They wanted his blood," she said.

"Which means that Thisbe's making more of the thread again." Lucy's voice was strangely hollow when she spoke. "That's what happened in my dreams—a girl turned up dead and a little while after that, Thisbe bound up Alex with the string she'd made from the girl's blood. She's going to find someone to replace Alex, isn't she?"

"That'd be my guess," Mama Legba murmured, staring solemnly into her cup of tea. "But I don't think she'd be able to do nothing right away. It'll take her some time to make the thread, and more time to find an old enough and powerful enough soul to do her any good." She glanced up at Lucy.

"You mean a soul like me?" Lucy said softly as she raised her chin.

Mama Legba's mouth went tight. "We don't know for sure that she knows what you is, Lucy-girl."

"Thisbe knows I could see Alex. I'm sure by now she has some suspicions about how I figured out who he was and where she was keeping him," Lucy said. "And if it's anyone's fault that she's desperate, it's mine. It would make sense for her to come after me." Lucy's voice was steady enough, but I didn't miss how her hands shook as she held her quickly cooling mug.

"That's true enough. We'd be mighty foolish not to expect her to try something." Mama Legba frowned. "But there's no telling about the where or the when."

"We can't just wait for her to kill someone else," Piers said, his voice tinged with frustration.

But what if we didn't have to sit around and wait?

I still wasn't sure what to make of the visions I'd had, and I certainly wasn't sure how they'd react to hearing that I was possibly seeing past events through Thisbe's eyes, but I couldn't shake the feeling that maybe, dangerous as those visions might be, they could help us.

"What if there was a way to figure out what her next step will be?" I asked carefully.

Mama Legba quirked a brow in my direction. "How you propose we go about doing that?" she asked.

"Maybe something she's done in the past might give some clue?" I asked, measuring their reactions and response to my words.

Mama Legba made a surprised murmur. "That might work," she said, but before I could tell them anything more, Mama Legba looked at Lucy. "How do you feel about taking a little nap and seeing what you can see?"

Lucy looked startled for less than a second. Then, understanding dawning, she said, "You want me to dreamwalk?"

"Last time, you was able to break from your past actions and follow that boy. Seems like you might could follow Thisbe just as well. Maybe there's something we been missing from way back."

"But—" I started, confused at the turn the conversation had taken. That wasn't what I'd meant at all.

"Don't worry yourself about it, Chloe-girl," Mama Legba told me, misunderstanding the reason for my protest. "Lucy be safe enough trying this. Ain't nothing can hurt a ghost in a dream."

I wanted to correct her, but Piers was watching me with a pinched expression on his face. Like he was waiting for me to prove him right about me needing a keeper. So I didn't say anything else as Mama Legba got everything ready.

I hadn't exactly been myself when Lucy dreamwalked before, but from what I understood, it was an easy enough process. Lucy was an old soul, which apparently made her powerful, and she was able to access her past lives through her dreams about them. A few weeks before, though, she'd discovered that she could break free in the dreams and walk separate from her memories, making the dreams serve as a kind of portal to the past.

She couldn't change anything, because she wasn't anything more than a memory in the dream, but she could see things and learn things. It was how she'd figured out what Thisbe had done to Alex back in the 1840s, and it was how they'd discovered how to free him and find Thisbe.

Mama Legba lit a stick of sage and juniper and smudged the smoldering herbs around the room, clearing out any negative energy. Speaking in a soft, low voice she asked the spirits for protection and guidance before she let Lucy lay back on the couch. I settled back in one of the comfortable arm chairs, curling myself around a pillow, and watched as Mama Legba placed the smoldering herbs on the table and lit three white candles at Lucy's head and three more at her feet.

Little by little, Lucy slowed her breath and softened her features. After a few minutes, she drifted off into a deep sleep. Mama Legba and Piers watched her carefully for any sign of a problem, but it looked to me like she was resting peaceful. Occasionally, her forehead would wrinkle, like she was struggling with some sort of puzzle, but mostly she laid there, quiet and still as a sleeping princess.

From the way Piers and Mama Legba were all focus and concentration, I knew something important was happening, but it wasn't like we could see into her mind and know what it was.

Since I'd had such a hard time sleeping the night before, I was tired enough that I almost started drifting off myself. Maybe that's why I didn't notice the way my neck was growing warmer and softer at first, like firm fingers were rubbing gently down my nape. Little by little, I relaxed into the cushions of the chair, almost humming at how soft and boneless I was starting to feel.

They really think that's gonna work? The voice came soft and low. Familiar.

I blinked my eyes open. Mama Legba and Piers were still watching Lucy.

"What?" I started to ask, but when I opened my mouth, I found I couldn't speak. My words came out as a gasping breath as the soft, finger-like warmth at the back of my neck changed. I struggled to draw a breath as something took hold of my throat.

The noise I made must have been loud enough to catch their attention, because both Mama Legba and Piers looked over at me, confusion on their faces.

"What is it, baby?" Piers whispered.

I opened my mouth to speak, but nothing would come out. My vision started to go dark around the edges as I tried to pull air into my lungs. As I struggled, I felt a breeze course through the room, swirling around and turning my skin to ice.

"Chloe?" Piers was there suddenly, kneeling beside me. I could see his mouth move, but I couldn't hear the sound that came out.

Soon, baby girl. Soon. The echoing voice hummed along the inside of my skull. Reminding me, as the icy breeze lashed at my skin.

But then Mama Legba was there, her soft hand warm on my arm, grasping my wrist like she meant to hold me there to the earth. The wind died and the icy fingers released their hold on my throat.

"You okay?" Mama Legba started to ask, but across the room, Lucy's unconscious form jerked.

I took a gasping breath, trying to tell them. "Lucy," I

rasped through my still-tender throat, but the sound didn't come out anything like her name.

But Mama Legba understood at once. She turned and, seeing that Lucy had gone white as death, went to her side. "Come on, Lucy-girl," she said, shaking her to wake her. "Come on," she said over and over, but Lucy was deep, deep in sleep.

Little by little, my lungs started working again.

Piers had his arms around me, but I could barely feel the warmth of him and the only thing I could hear was the sound of my own breathing. I tried to push away from him, but before I could untangle myself, the icy wind was back.

"What *is* that?" Piers asked, searching anxiously for some indication of where the breeze was coming from.

One of the candles at Lucy's feet sputtered, and we both turned to look at it just in time to see it go out.

Mama Legba went still for a moment, and Piers tightened his grip on me.

"What—?" he started to say, but before he could, a second candle snuffed itself out.

Something inside me leapt at the sight, but I pushed it down and ignored it as I watched, one-by-one, the rest of the candles snuff themselves out. *Ssst.* Like wet fingers were pinching out the flames, so not even a curl of smoke was left behind.

As the last candle died, Lucy's eyes flew open and she lurched up, gasping and panicked like she didn't remember where she was.

Piers wouldn't ease his grip on me, but for the moment, I didn't mind. "She okay?" I rasped as Mama Legba rubbed

Lucy's back, whispering soft words in her ear until her breathing was almost normal.

"She'll do well enough," Mama Legba said as she helped Lucy to sit upright.

"What the hell was that?" Piers asked.

"I don't rightly know," Mama Legba said, glancing at me from the corner of her eye.

My stomach turned. It hadn't been me. It *couldn't* have been me... could it?

"It all went dark." Lucy had her arms wrapped around her middle, like she was trying to hold herself together. "It was the time I went out to Le Ciel with Alex. I was going to try to break away and walk to Thisbe's place. I thought maybe I could find something there, but before I could even start, everything went black and the dream faded into nothing. I couldn't move and I couldn't find my way back..." Her voice trailed off. "That's never happened before. Alex was there and then he was gone... *everything* was gone." Lucy's voice rose in a panic as she looked at Mama Legba. "She can't hurt him, can she?"

Mama Legba gave her head a shake and cupped Lucy's chin with her broad hand. "No, child. You made sure he was safe already. What's done is done, and not even a witch as strong as Thisbe can change the past."

Lucy gave a tight nod, like she wanted to believe Mama Legba but didn't. "I need to try again," she said, determined.

"I think you've done enough for one day," Mama Legba told her in a worried tone.

"But I didn't get anything," Lucy said, frustrated. "There has to be something there we can use. We can't let Thisbe do what she did to Alex to anyone else." Her voice went a little quiet. "I can't have lost him for nothing."

"Oh, child," Mama Legba said, patting her on her knee. "You didn't lose him forever. You know that, right?"

Lucy's mouth went tight, but she didn't answer. "At least let me make sure he's okay."

Without another word, Mama Legba gathered the stick of herbs that had long since stopped burning and the candles that had gone dead. She dumped the whole bunch of them into the trash. "Not today. I won't have nobody putting themself in any more danger till we knows what happened here."

"Mama Legba's right, Lucy." Piers glanced back down at me, but not long enough to really *see* me. Just long enough to check on me. "It's not worth the risk."

"But my dreams are the only lead we have right now," Lucy pushed.

"What if they're not?" I said softly.

Everyone turned to look at me, but I ignored the unease I saw in their eyes and forced myself to say what I knew I needed to say.

"I didn't only lose track of time this morning. Something happened out there at the cabin."

In a rush of words, I told them everything about the visions I'd had before I could change my mind again. " … It's like the present world sort of fell away, and I was back there—back in her world. It was almost like I was in her skin. I don't think what I saw was random," I said. "I think I'm seeing what Thisbe saw way back when, and I feel like I'm dreaming about pieces of her past."

"That sounds a lot like what I experienced when I

dreamed about Armantine in the past with Alex," Lucy told me, her forehead wrinkling in confusion.

"I don't see how that could be." Mama Legba was considering me with an uncomfortable intensity. "We took care of the link between you and your mother when we took the charms in your hair."

"But what if you didn't?" I pressed, voicing the worry that had been plaguing me ever since those bottles at my house fell from their strings.

Mama Legba grimaced like she didn't enjoy being contradicted. "You have any other markings on you, Chloe-girl?"

I shook my head. "Not that I know of, but maybe you were wrong about what the threaded charms in my hair did. Maybe they weren't meant to let her control me. Or maybe they weren't *only* meant for that," I amended when Mama Legba frowned at me. "Maybe they also kept me out."

"Kept you out of what?" Lucy asked.

"Out of her head. Out of her past, maybe?" I asked, voicing the fear that had been plaguing me. "I never experienced anything like this until my hair was gone."

"That only makes sense if Thisbe knows we cut your hair," Mama Legba said.

I thought of the fingers rubbing my throat, the icy grip that tried to strangle me. "Maybe she does know," I said, unable to keep the unease out of my voice.

"You think she's watching you?" Lucy sounded horrified.

"If that's the case, maybe it's nothing you're doing to get these visions," Mama Legba said darkly. "Maybe it's still Thisbe pulling the strings, making you see what she wants you to believe."

"But even if Thisbe's the one doing this," I said, "it doesn't mean we can't still use the visions I'm having. It happened so fast the first time, it took me off guard, but if I could touch that charm again, maybe we could figure out what's happening. Maybe even figure out what I'm seeing. If Thisbe's still manipulating things, maybe she'll give something away, and if she's not, if it's really just a vision of the past, maybe we could learn something more about what she's trying to do, or why she's trying to do it."

"Does it matter why?" Piers asked.

"It might," I said, not at all liking the way he was looking at me.

He thought about it for a moment, not even blinking as he stared at me. And then, finally, he spoke. "Absolutely not," he said stiffly, shaking his head.

The abrupt finality of his words had me on my feet. "Why not?" I challenged. "You were willing to let Lucy try looking into the past."

"Yeah, and look what happened."

Without thinking, I rubbed at the sore spot at the base of my throat. "I'm willing to take the risk if it could help us find her—"

But I couldn't finish before Piers cut me off. "Did you stop to think that if you opened a connection between you, you might let Thisbe in again?"

My stomach twisted. Of course I'd thought of that. All I'd been thinking about was how I'd lost hours at the cabin that morning. Hearing him say it out loud, though, made it all that much more real. But it also made something else painfully clear.

"You really don't think I can fight her. Even with my hair gone, you think she's going to win, don't you?"

"It's not about that, Chloe," he said, but the way he was holding himself off from me told me it was exactly that.

"Piers is right to be careful," Mama Legba said gently. "But you also got a point. That charm might indeed be one place to start."

"So you'll let me try?"

"Not until I know for sure it's safe, child." Mama Legba gave me a doleful look before turning to Piers and Lucy. "Do you think I can get a look at that charm?"

Lucy shook her head. "There's no way my dad's going to let you anywhere near it after you told him to burn it." Her expression brightened. "But Piers could get it, maybe. My dad's already asked him to deliver it to a professor's lab up in Nashville."

Understanding dawned on Piers's face. "You want me to steal it?" He didn't look happy about the idea at all.

"Not steal it," Mama Legba said, "but maybe we could borrow it long enough for me to take a good hard look at it. If it's safe, maybe—just *maybe*—we can let Chloe take another look."

"To do that, I'd actually have to take it to Nashville."

"So take it," Lucy said. "Maybe the tests will tell us something."

Piers shook his head. "I don't want to leave New Orleans right now, especially not with this latest murder."

"But if I could get a good look at the charm, we might could tell something about the magic it holds and understand where these visions Chloe's been having come from."

82

Mama Legba took a thoughtful sip of her tea. "Wouldn't take but a few hours, and then you could take it on to that professor of yours and let him do whatever tests they want. I can keep Chloe safe until you get back."

Piers frowned, and I could practically see the thoughts spinning around that brain of his. He knew the plan could work, and he didn't like it one bit. His expression was strung so tight I thought for sure he would say no, so I was surprised when he finally spoke.

"I'll do it on one condition," he said, his voice as firm and determined as I'd ever heard it. "I won't have Chloe anywhere near that thing again until and unless Mama Legba can tell it's one hundred percent safe."

"Excuse me?" I said.

"You heard me." Piers met my eyes and didn't look away. "I saw how you looked at it yesterday. I don't even know if you realized how focused you were, but you didn't hear a thing I said to you. If I do this, I don't want you around while Mama Legba looks at the charm."

I crossed my arms. "Last I checked, I don't take orders from you."

Piers sighed and rubbed a hand over his smooth head. "That's not what I meant, baby. It's not an order."

"No, it's a condition, and maybe that's even worse."

"You have to understand—"

"I do understand," I snapped, interrupting whatever bit of nonsense was about to come out of his mouth. "You make it sound like I'm some kind of idiot who doesn't know how dangerous Thisbe can be."

"Chloe…"

I shook my head, refusing to hear anything more. "You want to push me out of this, but you don't seem to realize I'm already wrapped up in it, Piers. If we're going to look at that charm, I want to be here. I *deserve* to be a part of this."

Piers's jaw went tight, and I knew he didn't like what I was saying. But he didn't even bother arguing with me. Without another word, he turned to Mama Legba. "That's my only condition. Take it or leave it. You want to study the charm to see if it's safe, fine. I'll bring it to you, but I won't have Chloe here while you do it. Until we know there's no way the visions are coming directly from Thisbe, she stays away from it."

Mama Legba looked to me, her mouth turned down like she was considering her options.

"You saw what happened here just now with Lucy," Piers pressed. "That's never happened before."

I understood what he was implying—that maybe it happened because I was there. I wasn't sure how I felt about that, but I had a bad feeling that he was right. The wind, the snuffed-out candles...all of it felt linked to me somehow.

"You don't really think Chloe had anything to do with what happened?" Lucy demanded, and I felt a spark of hope for how she stood up for me.

"I don't know what I think about it, but I'm not going to put her at risk by underestimating Thisbe's power again," he said to Lucy. "If y'all want the charm, fine, but it'll only be me and Mama Legba until she can guarantee it's safe."

Mama Legba was still watching me as she considered Piers's offer.

"Don't..." I pleaded.

"I'm sorry, Chloe-girl," Mama Legba said, and I knew that her mind was made up. "I don't agree with keeping you out of this, 'cause you do have a right to it. But Piers'll be taking something of a risk by doing this, and he got a right, too."

SEVEN

When we finally got back out to the plantation, Lucy sent me a tight, pitying sort of smile before she excused herself, leaving me alone with Piers. Not that the privacy she gave us did any good. Neither one of us seemed to know how to step across the space that was growing between us. I wasn't even sure I wanted to anymore.

"I need to talk with Dr. Aimes about delivering the charm," Piers said after a couple of awkward moments of silence. "If I'm going to do this, I'd like to get it over with. Are you coming in with me?"

I stared at him, waiting for him to say something more. "That's all you have to say to me?" I asked when it was clear he wasn't going to offer me anything more.

Piers let out a frustrated breath and shook his head. "What do you want me to say?"

"If I have to tell you, I don't want it," I said.

"Chloe…" He stopped, and then let out an irritated huff

of breath. "I get that you're mad at me, but I'm doing the right thing here." Piers was still frowning at me, but now there was even less tenderness in his expression. Instead, a guarded distrustfulness filled his eyes. "You told us that Thisbe might have bound another man in the past, but when you were talking, it sounded to me like you might think she isn't all evil. Did you ever stop to wonder if you just imagined what you wanted to see in her actions?"

I had plenty to say about that, but I knew he wasn't going to hear it, so I kept quiet.

He let out a ragged, frustrated breath. "Fine. Stay out here and be mad at me then." Without another word, he mounted the steps up to the house, leaving me and my angry thoughts behind.

Like I was going to follow any more of his orders.

My limbs were practically vibrating with all the frustration and fretfulness I'd been carrying around all day, so I let my feet take me out toward the big house. I followed the path that led up over a small rise and cut through one of the big gardens to come up on the back side of the mansion, the side facing the river.

On the upper balcony, a group from one of the last tours of the day was taking pictures of the alley of oaks that led toward the Mississippi. Those ancient trees had been there long before Roman Dutilette built the house, even long before his father, Jean-Pierre, bought the property in the 1790s, though no one quite knows where they came from or who planted them. Anyone's best guess is they were put there long before any of the French or Spanish settlers moved in and took over.

Centuries have passed with those big, graceful limbs watching over the river. The planters and their descendants came and went years ago, but the trees are still there. I've always felt like there was something about those oaks that spoke of a different sort of power—one that couldn't be bought or stolen. I knew then that if my visions could be trusted, Thisbe would have taken wood from one of those trees to make her charm, for that very reason.

But thinking of the vision made me remember the way the unnatural wind had spun through Mama Legba's rooms and how the invisible fingers had snuffed out the light of the candles. I thought of the bottles in the tree outside my own home crashing to the hard earth below, and something inside me shifted uncomfortably.

I wanted to believe Thisbe had been the cause of all those strange happenings, but there was a part of me that wasn't so sure. I felt like there was some part of me getting stronger and more unsettled ever since they'd cut the last of my hair and tossed it into the fire. It was like that particular part had been balled up tight so long, and now it had time to stretch itself out.

When I'd felt the wind whip across my skin in Mama Legba's shop, that unsettled feeling had eased a bit, like a cat ruffling up its spine and flexing its claws. I didn't trust the spark of excitement I'd felt thinking that maybe I'd caused that wind, and I certainly didn't want to feel so drawn to it.

After a while, Piers found me there, under the canopy of one of those old oaks. I sensed him before I heard his approach, but even once he was standing a few feet away, I refused to turn and greet him. I was still too hurt and too angry that he could push me aside and try to fit me in some box. And I was still uneasy about that part of me that sometimes felt too big for my own skin.

"I'm taking off," he told me. "Sooner I go, the sooner I can get back."

"Have a safe trip," I said, picking at a piece of grass that had been tickling at my leg.

He was silent for a long moment, like he was waiting for something else. But I wasn't about to give it to him. Not until he realized that what he'd done to push me out of this was wrong.

"Are you really going to let me to leave with things like this between us?" he asked, his voice soft and low.

I glanced up at him then. "You're the one that made them that way."

His mouth went tight and he let out a tired-sounding sigh.

I picked at another piece of grass. I wasn't going to go through all this with him again. I knew what he was going to say—that he was trying to protect me, that I didn't understand—and I didn't want to hear any of it.

"Chloe?" he asked, and then waited, like it was my turn to speak.

"What do you want me to say, Piers? You want me to thank you for treating me like I can't take care of myself? I'm not going to." My voice came out more tired than angry. "I understand you're worried, but I feel like you aren't even *trying* to hear what I'm saying. I get that you want to keep me safe from Thisbe, but you can't protect me from my own life."

"Thisbe isn't your life, Chloe."

I looked up with him then. "She's my momma. You said

so yourself, and I can't just set that fact down and walk away from it." I glanced away. "Like it or not, she made me. I'm her flesh and blood, and I need to be part of what happens to her."

"You're not your mother, Chloe," he said, and his voice was so kind and gentle it made my teeth hurt.

"I know that," I told him. "But sometimes I wonder if *you* know that, Piers. Sometimes when you look at me, I get the sense that you're seeing her."

A muscle in his jaw clenched. "That's not true," he said, but the words sounded hollow, like he didn't believe them himself.

"Isn't it? I see how you look at me sometimes, like you're waiting for her voice to come out my mouth again. But trying to protect me from all this ain't gonna stop the fact that I'm still her daughter. What happened might not have been my fault, but that don't mean I don't bear some of the guilt just the same. Whatever happens next, I need to be part of making it right."

Piers only shook his head, like he didn't want to listen to what I was telling him, much less really hear it.

I took a breath and got myself ready for what I needed to tell him. "You've been trying to keep me away from anything and everything involved with Thisbe, but you don't seem to want to even consider that my connection to her might be able to help us stop all this if we use it. I need to be there, Piers. I need to touch that charm again so I can know for sure."

His jaw was tight. "I can't," he said finally.

I shook my head. "More like you won't," I told him, and I started past him.

He snagged my arm gently to stop me from going. "Don't be like that, Chloe."

I let out a hollow laugh as I jerked away. "You lost any right to tell me how I should be when you stopped believing in who I am."

The frustration vibrating between us felt like some kind of runaway train, and I didn't know how to stop it without getting broken up myself.

He studied me with those dark, soulful eyes of his, and then let out a great, frustrated sigh. "Okay then." He stepped forward, finally breaching the spaced we'd kept between us. "Maybe you're right. Maybe we need a little distance and me leaving for a few days will be a good thing, so we can *both* get our heads back on straight."

I didn't like the way he said that—like he was talking more about me than himself—but I didn't argue. I'd had enough of fighting with him for one day.

When I didn't disagree, he took my head gentle-like, cupping the sides of my face in his hands, and placed a kiss, warm and soft, square in the middle of my forehead. Then he stepped back, and the distance was there between us again.

"I'll call you when I get to Nashville. We'll figure everything out when I get back."

My throat had gotten so tight-feeling by that point, I couldn't hardly swallow. So I couldn't have said anything to stop him from walking away even if I'd wanted to. All I could think was *no,* but I wasn't sure if I meant *no* to him calling me later or *no* to him leaving. And before I figured it out, he was already gone.

EIGHT

That night, I avoided everything and everyone. I went straight back to that sterile little guest room and sat with myself until I couldn't stand my own thoughts anymore. Eventually, I sent Piers a text telling him that I was sorry for how we'd left things and asking him if he got in okay, but I didn't get a reply before I finally drifted off to sleep.

I woke in the thick grove of pines again. The night was as cool and dark as it had been before, and through the thick canopy of trees, the sky was clear and the stars looked like salt spilled on a dark table.

The world felt like an empty place, and that emptiness crept along my skin, up my spine, and made the nape of my neck go tight. I could feel that emptiness more than any-thing else—more than the air around me, more than the rhythm of my own breath, more even than the cold that had my muscles shivering for warmth.

I needed to be free of that silence and that cold and

the stars that were looking down like they were laughing at my foolishness, so I started walking. But like before, the grove of pines never ended. No matter how far or long I walked, I never reached the end of them. Still, I felt boxed in. Trapped, like there was no way out.

Exhausted and still cold despite the good sweat I'd worked up, I stopped and waited. I didn't know what I was waiting for, exactly, but the longer I waited, the more I felt like I was there in that endless place for a reason.

Then, just as I couldn't stand it no more, right about the time I felt like I would scream from the frustration and the fear, a figure appeared in the darkness a ways off. He was cloaked in the shadows and moving slowly and carefully through the trees, creeping his way closer to me with every step he took.

My every instinct screamed for me to run, but I'd done that already and hadn't gotten anywhere. So I forced myself to be still and wait until the figure got close enough that I could see it was only a man.

He was tall and broad, and he had a way of walking that marked him as a man who knew what he was, who knew what he *always* would be. When he stepped into a shaft of moonlight, my heart leaped straight up into my throat, because for a moment, I thought it was Piers.

Before I could stop myself, I stepped forward, too. Because even with all we'd said to each other, I missed him and regretted the distance that had grown between us. Because relief shot through me to know he'd come back, even with everything that was keeping us apart. Now that he was there, we had a chance to make everything right between us again.

But when the figure turned to me, the glow of the moonlight lit up the planes of his face and I realized my mistake.

Not Piers. Not Piers at all.

It was the man I'd seen in the vision—the sleeping man that Thisbe had kissed after she'd sliced open his hand. Just like in that vision, I felt a sense of rightness, or possessiveness, when I looked him. Even knowing it wasn't Piers, something about him pulled at me, made me want to move closer. But I forced myself to ignore that pull, and I held my ground.

After what felt like an endless moment, the man took a step toward me. His face was so steady and determined that I could barely think much less move. I was stuck, paralyzed with something that felt like a cross between fear and want.

He smiled then, a flash of straight, white teeth that had my heart thundering in my chest. His eyes glinted like obsidian as he took another slow, steady step. And then another. He was only two steps away by the time I could finally make myself move, and I stumbled back on the uneven ground as he reached for me.

But he didn't grab me.

He didn't even touch me.

One second he was in front of me, reaching with his broad, callused hands, and the next second, he was through me.

Through me.

Like I wasn't even there.

Like I didn't even exist.

I felt the warmth of him as every cell in my body vibrated from the violation of being passed through, like I was nothing more than a ghost. I turned, and he was still there—still walking, but I saw then that it hadn't been me he'd been reaching for after all.

A girl stood in the clearing behind me with sharp cheekbones and hair that pillowed out around her face, settling about her shoulders like a dark cloud. Her broad mouth was curved up in a smile as welcoming as the warmth in her eyes as she lifted her arms to the man, and there was something in the curve of that smile that reminded me of my mother.

Augustine, I heard a voice say in my head.

The world flashed warm, like the heat of the summer was washing over me when his lips settled onto hers, and I had to look away. But even looking away, I could still *feel* their kiss—the want, the need, the desperation and love all mixed up together.

I woke up, my skin cold to the touch and my body shaking from the fear and adrenaline. Flushed and uncomfortable from the intensity of the dream.

He hadn't been all that much more than a boy, I realized then. Tall, yes. Broad, most definitely, but now that I thought back on it, there had been something about him that seemed young and untouched despite his strength. He must have been a few years younger than he was in that other vision— he couldn't have been older than nineteen or twenty.

"It was just a dream," I said out loud, needing to hear a human voice after the deafening silence of the pines. But hearing it didn't make it feel like the truth, and even though I could feel the warmth of the covers over me, I couldn't stop shaking.

NINE

Most of Lucy's family was still sleeping in their beds when I went into the kitchen to get something to eat and found Dr. Aimes already sitting at the table with a cup of coffee and the newspaper open wide in front of him.

"Morning, Chloe. Did you sleep well?" he asked, barely looking up over his paper.

"Well enough," I said, skirting the truth.

I poured myself a glass of juice and made some toast before I sat down at the table with him. Wordlessly, he offered me a section of the paper, but I waved him off. I still couldn't shake the memory of the dream—I couldn't stop thinking about that cold place or the voice that called to the man named Augustine.

"Dr. Aimes?"

He looked up over the paper and raised his brows. "Yes?"

"You don't know if anyone who lived on the plantation was named Augustine, do you?"

Folding the paper, he frowned as he considered my question. "I don't know off the top of my head that I've heard that name before. It definitely didn't belong to any of Roman or Josephine's children. They only had two girls, and neither made it to adulthood."

"What about a slave, maybe?"

"That I couldn't tell you offhand. Byron would know better." He leveled a serious gaze at me. "Why do you ask?"

"Uh…"

"Hey, Chloe." We both turned to find Lucy coming through the door of the kitchen. "Morning, Dad," she said, giving him a kiss on the top of his head.

"You're up early," he said, smiling at her. Then he turned back to his paper, apparently forgetting all about the last question he'd asked me.

"Hey," I said to Lucy, relieved that her appearance had provided a welcome distraction.

Her mess of hair was a fiery nest on top her head, and she looked barely awake as she walked over to the coffee pot and poured what was left into a mug. She started doctoring it up with cream and sugar, and then turned to me like she'd thought of something. "You already got some, right?"

"I'm fine," I said, lifting my glass of juice in a small salute.

"Did you ever hear whether Piers got in okay last night?" she asked after she took a sip. Her voice was casual enough, but I knew she was really asking if I'd heard anything about Mama Legba and the charm.

I frowned, realizing suddenly that Piers hadn't called me. "Actually, I didn't hear from him," I said. I pulled out my phone to check my messages and felt a little better when

I saw a short text that had come in sometime early in the morning. "He must have gotten in pretty late."

"He didn't say anything about the trip?" she asked, giving me a pointed expression over the top of her dad's head.

I shook my head, glancing at Dr. Aimes. I didn't think he was paying any attention to the silent conversation we were having, but it wasn't worth the chance. "Just that he got in and he'd talk to me later." I shot him a quick *good morning* text, but I didn't get an immediate reply. "If he was driving late, he's probably still asleep. I'm sure he'll call later." If he wasn't still mad about how we'd left things.

Lucy frowned as she sat down with her coffee. She gave her dad an impatient look as he took his good time reading his paper.

"I was thinking that I'd take a drive into town and see Mama Legba this morning," she said in a too-casual voice. "I thought you might like to come. Especially if you didn't hear from Piers?"

"Sure," I said. We needed to find out what they might have learned about the charm—and why no one had contacted us about it. "I want to stop by and talk to Byron first, if you don't mind?"

Lucy's brows shot up. I knew she didn't have much love for the guy, but I sent her a silent look, hoping that she'd understand that I would explain later.

The meeting with Byron was a total bust. He was in a doubly foul and less than helpful mood because he had to deal with all of the museum interns on his own for the next couple of days. Piers had been handling most of that for him, but Piers was in Nashville.

Byron had less than no interest in digging out the old plantation registers for us. He said we didn't have the right training in archival preservation to handle them without supervision and sent us away without even telling us where they were.

"So you really think this Augustine person could be linked to Le Ciel?" Lucy asked as we drove into the city.

"I don't know," I told her. "But you see the past in your dreams, so maybe." I shrugged.

"But I see my *own* past."

I shrugged. "I guess I hoped there might be something in them that could help us."

Lucy frowned, but she didn't say anything more.

It was early enough that it didn't take us long to find a parking spot near Mama Legba's shop. But when we got to the door, it was clear something was wrong—the sign hadn't been turned to *open* yet and the lights were all off.

"She's usually open by now," I said as I peered through the windows at the empty shop.

Lucy turned the knob of the door, and I think we were both surprised when it clicked open. We glanced apprehensively at one another. "Do you think we should go in?" Lucy asked.

"I doubt she'd leave the door open if she wasn't in there," I said, but I had an uneasy feeling about it.

We walked into the dark shop and waited as the bell fell silent behind us, but Mama Legba didn't come out to greet us like she usually did.

"What do you think's up?" Lucy whispered.

"I don't know. Something." Then I called out, "Mama Legba? You here?"

There was a shuffling from the rooms beyond the hallway that had us exchanging nervous looks, but then we heard Mama Legba's voice call out for us to come on back.

When we got to her private rooms, Mama Legba was sitting on the low couch, her face in her hands. She looked to me like one of those ancient statues that lasts through wars and earthquakes and everything going wrong, but somehow survives.

All around her, the room was in chaos. Chairs were overturned, their stuffing spilling out of knife-slashed slits. Cupboards were torn open, their contents shattered on the floor like jagged-edged puzzles that wouldn't ever go back together. The back door's frame was splintered and busted, and it stood wide open, spilling light into room.

"Oh my god," Lucy whispered.

"Mama Legba," I said, taking a step toward her. "Are you hurt?"

Mama Legba raised her head then, like someone had just shaken her awake. I was relieved to see that the look in her eyes was as much anger as it was fear and uncertainty. "I ain't been harmed," she said.

"Have you called the police?" Lucy asked, pulling out her phone.

"No, and don't you be calling the police into this now, neither. I've had about enough of them for today." She stood and made her way through the mess toward the kitchen-side of the room. "That's where I was when all this happened."

"You were with the police again?" I asked, still trying to take in the mess that someone had made of her home.

"Was it another body?" Lucy asked in a strangled-sounding whisper.

Mama Legba shook her head. "No, just more questions about the markings on that poor soul they found the other day. I told them before that I didn't have no clue about what those were. Those marks ain't nothing to do with Voodoo, but they didn't want to be hearing that then, and they wanted to hear it even less this morning. Somehow they got the idea in their heads now that I might have had something to do with the killings. Thank the spirits for customers giving me an alibi, or I doubt they'd have let me go at all. And then I come home to this mess?"

She crouched down to look under the sink. The piece of fabric that usually served as an apron beneath the basin had been torn away, exposing the ancient plumbing beneath. After rustling around for a moment, Mama Legba let out a muffled curse as she righted herself.

"I really think we should call the cops," Lucy said again.

"Put your phone away," Mama Legba told her with a voice that meant business. "Ain't nothing they can do about *this*. What are you girls doing here anyway?"

"We came to see if you found out anything from looking at the charm last night," Lucy said.

"I didn't look at no charm last night."

"Didn't Piers bring it over?"

Mama Legba frowned. "Was he supposed to?"

"I thought that's what he was going to do," I told her. But I'd been so angry, I hadn't really asked him. Maybe I'd assumed wrong. "Maybe he meant to bring it by on his way back from Nashville instead." I pulled out my phone and sent him a quick message to confirm.

"I don't know," said Mama Legba. "But we got other things to worry about now." She gestured to the room, and then she grabbed her large, patchwork bag and was out the door in a matter of seconds.

"Should we follow her?" Lucy asked, looking more than a little shell-shocked.

I frowned. "I don't think we should let her go off alone right now. Not with all this," I said, gesturing to the mess all around us.

So we took off after Mama Legba, through the back alley that led to a larger street and then east through the Quarter. She didn't bother to pause at any intersections or pay any mind to the cars that almost ran her down. Marching on with her shoulders set and her arms swinging like a determined soldier, she crossed each street and let the traffic stop for her. Amazingly, it did.

Lucy and I were a little more careful as we tromped along, following the determined path Mama Legba cut through the heart of the Quarter.

The farther we got from Jackson Square, the quieter the streets became. Even with the humidity of the day pressing in on us, even with the worry clinging to my back, walking those lonely streets wasn't all bad. Walking through the Quarter never is.

Some places in this world might be well loved *despite* the grit and grime and age, but people come to the French Quarter because of it. Like a worn-out madam who still has enough sparkle to keep the fellows knocking on her door, there's something beautiful about the way this part of the city has stood, steadfast and sure, over the centuries. Even with the usual smell of the puke and piss from the night before's carousing, it's a place people can't help but want to be.

But Mama Legba didn't stop, and the farther east you go, the more the neighborhoods change. On the other side of Elysian Fields Avenue, things get a little more hit or miss—there might be a cute little shotgun house next to a building covered in graffiti. Or there might only be a row of run-down shacks. Once you pass the quaint homes in the wedge of streets that make up Marigny, you're in Bywater, and then just beyond Bywater is the Lower Ninth Ward, which still hasn't come back all the way from Katrina.

They don't bother marking those parts of town on any of the fancy tourist maps, but those places are home for a lot of people, even if the streets there have their problems. Still, I was starting to worry that Mama Legba might not ever stop walking.

"Are you going to tell us where we're going?" I asked when we made it as far as Bywater.

She didn't bother to answer, just shot me an impatient look and kept on walking. But after a few more turns, she slowed to a stop in front of a cream-colored house on Desire Street.

It seemed like a nice enough place, but nothing fancy. It had an air conditioning unit drooping out the front window, the motor clicking away and dripping condensation on the ground, and one of the shutters was tilted off its top hinge, hanging like it was trying to decide if it wanted to fall down or to climb back up. In the window was a hand-lettered sign that said *READINGS* with a picture of something that might have been a cat beneath it and a phone number.

Mama Legba didn't hesitate. She marched straight up the steps and rapped a rapid-fire cadence on the door as she called, "Odeana! I need to talk with you!"

"Who's Odeana?" Lucy whispered.

"Hell if I know," I told her.

Even though it sometimes felt like I'd known Mama Legba forever, I realized then that none of us had really known her long enough to have any idea who the other people in her life might be. She'd always seemed like this solitary figure to me, and I guess I'd sort of felt like Piers and I were adopting her rather than the other way around. But maybe I'd been wrong about that.

After a couple of seconds, the curtains rustled and then, a moment after that, the door opened.

"That you, Auntie Odette?" A boy who was a year or two older than me stepped out with a confused and then an almost pleased look on his face.

"Odette?" Lucy whispered, her voice kind of high and strangled. She was still staring at the guy.

I shrugged. I didn't know what was going on, but I couldn't blame Lucy for sounding the way she did—the boy was something to see. He knew it, too, if the swagger in his shoulders was any indication.

He stood at the top of the steps with his hands on his hips and grinned at Mama Legba before he noticed Lucy and me waiting on the sidewalk below. His smile barely faltered as he took his time looking us over. When he caught me looking right back, he winked. That wink was so unexpected that

I had to remind myself to scowl at him. Which, of course, made the teasing glint in his eye all the worse.

I hated that he knew I'd been looking, but to be honest, it was kind of hard not to. The guy wasn't wearing much besides some low-slung basketball shorts and a necklace around the base of his throat made from smooth wooden beads and bits of sharp shell. A blind woman would've agreed that his chest looked it was designed by someone who knew what a man's chest should look like.

"Don't Auntie Odette me," Mama Legba told the boy, poking at his bare chest to punctuate her words. "Where's your mama?"

The guy gave a lazy shrug, the kind that's all attitude without saying a word. His eyes lighted on Lucy and me again, and his full mouth kicked up into a grin.

"Don't even, boy," Mama Legba said.

The grin turned into a full-on smile, and I knew he was only playing. "Aw, Auntie. Don't be like that."

"I'm not in the mood for your sass today," Mama Legba said, but she looked like she was holding back a smile of her own. "Now, is you gonna let me in to talk to your mama, or do I have to make you?" She narrowed her eyes, but her mouth was definitely twitching with something like amusement by then.

He laughed at that, a rich, rolling laugh filled with the same teasing humor that sparked in his dark eyes when he looked at me. I made myself meet his gaze without flinching and did my best to scowl some more.

"I'd like to see you go on and try, but you best come on

in," he told her, stepping aside. "I don't need you hurting yourself, Auntie."

Mama Legba smacked his bare chest as she brushed past. "Go put on some clothes. Like your mama didn't teach you nothing at all, answering the door without a stitch on."

"I got more than a stitch on," he said, running his thumb along the elastic waistband of his shorts, causing them to dip enough that I could make out the dark band of his boxer briefs. When I looked up, his teasing eyes were on me again.

It took everything I had not to look away and let him know exactly how much that laughter in his eyes felt like a tickling in my gut. I gave him another purposeful scowl that seemed to make him smile even more, his eyes lighting with a challenge.

"Y'all coming, too?" he asked.

We weren't going to stand there on the sidewalk all day, so we followed Mama Legba into the house. It had a welcoming, lived-in feeling, and it smelled like someone had been cooking something heavy with spices the day before. The air conditioner was whirring and rattling in the window, but it wasn't doing much for the closeness in the air.

"Where's your mama, boy?" Mama Legba asked again as she looked around the house and seemed to realize it was empty. She ignored the boy's indication that she should have a seat.

"Don't know," he told her, slouching into a well-worn easy chair and ignoring her order to put on some clothes. "I got back from the rig late last night, and I haven't seen her yet today. But I'd 'preciate it if you would stop calling me *boy*, Auntie. In case you haven't noticed, I outgrew that some years back," he said, waggling his eyebrows playfully.

Mama Legba glared at him. "You sure do seem to want everyone to know," she said, gesturing to his still-bare chest. "You worried somebody's gonna miss you, strutting around like that?"

The guy laughed and ignored the question. "How you doing, Auntie O? It's been too long since I seen you."

"That's only 'cause you never come visit. Out there living in the middle of that water. You think you some sort of fish? A body's meant for the dry land." Mama Legba's eyes softened a little then, and despite her blustering, the affection she felt for him was clear as day on her face.

"Working on the rig is a good enough job," he said. "Had to do something with myself."

"You could've taken yourself off to school, like your mama wanted."

The boy shook his head, his carefree expression faltering. "That wasn't for me, Auntie, and you know it. I can't stand being cooped up in a classroom just to someday be cooped up in an office. The rig suits me fine for now."

Mama Legba seemed to be examining him. "That's true enough, I guess. You too wild for four walls to hold you in." She smiled softly. "But what about for someday? You been practicing any?"

"Some," he said, but he made the word sound like "not at all."

Mama Legba nodded. "That's what I thought. Well, as you said, you ain't a boy now, so soon enough the question gonna be what you want to do about what you've been given."

The boy frowned. "I got time."

"Maybe you do and maybe you don't…" She paused for a moment, and something passed between the two of them that made the room buzz with tension. Then, all at once, Mama Legba seemed to let it go. " You really don't know where your mother got off to, Odane?"

"No," he said. "I really don't. What do you need her for anyway?"

Mama Legba frowned. "I need to talk something over with her."

The boy's brows went up. "It sure must be something if you came all this way just to talk," he said. "But I don't know when she'll be back."

Mama Legba finally took a seat on the edge of the couch, her arms crossed over her ample bosom. "I can wait."

The guy—Odane—scooted to the edge of his chair, his forearms resting on his knees and his brows drawn together. "What's this all about, Auntie?"

"I bought up some aloe from Laveau's this week, but somebody done come into my home and tore it up so they could steal it," she said with a frown. "My dishes is broke all over the floor, my furniture is all torn to bits, and my back door's been busted in. But nothing else is missing but that aloe."

The expression of doubt on Odane's face didn't change. "You came all the way over here because somebody stole some plants?"

Mama Legba's brows drew together. "They wasn't just plants. They'd been curing already in black cat oil, and you know that ain't easy to find neither."

Odane considered that information with a thoughtful

frown. "What do you think my mom can do about it? She ain't no police. Besides, you tear up a person's house, you're doing something personal. You're trying to take a piece out of the person's security and peace of mind. That's nothing to brush aside."

Mama Legba shook her head as Lucy gave a told-you-so huff and elbowed me.

"No," Mama Legba told him. "I need to think this all through . . ."

"What is there to think through?" Odane asked. "Someone broke into your *home*."

"They sure enough did, but you don't understand." She ran her hand up over her cheek, like she was comforting herself and trying to think all at once. "I had all the protections set," she told him.

"Somebody got through *your* protections?" Odane's shock was clear.

Mama Legba nodded, her expression grave.

"Who around here is strong enough to do something like that?" he asked.

"Only one person I know of that would," Mama Legba said, her dark eyes finding mine. "Question is, what she wants with that aloe."

TEN

"I think you best come on back to the kitchen," Odane said with a long-suffering kind of sigh. "I'm gonna need something to eat before I hear what you're about to say. Something tells me I'm not going to like a word of it."

He got up without another word and headed back into the kitchen that opened onto the parlor we were sitting in. Instead of stopping there, he went on back through and disappeared through another door.

A second later, the front door opened. "Odette?" the small woman said as she stepped through the door and saw Mama Legba sitting in the parlor. "What are *you* doing here?" The woman didn't sound at all pleased to see Mama Legba, and then her eyes drifted to us and she seemed even less pleased.

If I hadn't already known we were in Mama Legba's sister's house, I might not have guessed the two women were even related. Where Mama Legba was broad and ample, this woman was small and slight, almost frail looking. Her hair was loose around her face in a short bob and didn't have any of the gray that shot through Mama Legba's. But there was something in the similar tilt of their eyes that marked them as family.

The woman came in, but her steps were labored and uneven because of the crutch she clasped in one hand and the way her right foot didn't exactly go straight.

"Odeana, honey," Mama Legba said with a nervous sort of smile. She stood to greet her sister.

"Don't honey me," the woman told her without an ounce of warmth. "What are you doing in my house?"

But before Mama Legba could reply, Odane came back through the kitchen, this time fully clothed. "Mom?"

The scowl on the small woman's face slid away and her entire expression brightened, like her argument with Mama Legba had never happened. She dismissed us completely and went to wrap her son—who towered above her—in a hug that made my throat go tight.

My momma used to hug me like that. The thought was as sudden as it was awful. And I had the sudden realization that whatever happened next, I was never going to have that again. Even with everything that had happened, there was a small part of me that still craved my momma's arms around me.

Odeana made some more noises of delight over her son—how much she'd missed him, how good he looked, and how that sea air must have made him grow another three inches. He glanced up at us once, over his mother's head, clearly embarrassed, but then he turned back to her preening approval.

"You done yet?" he said, when it was clear he couldn't take any more.

"I'll let you know," his mother said. But then she glanced over at Mama Legba. "Just as soon as I find out what *she's* doing here."

"Someone smashed up her house," Odane said, taking the opportunity to get himself free of her arms.

Odeana turned to Mama Legba, her face slack with shock. "They did what?" All at once, the anger and suspicion she'd worn like armor was gone.

"Broke up my place," Mama Legba said, still clearly uncomfortable. "Ripped up the furniture, smashed up my pottery, made a mess of every blessed thing. Not my shop. My *home.*"

"Why didn't you tell me that straight off?"

"You never gave me no chance," Mama Legba said wryly.

"But smashing up your home?" Odeana's hand came up to her mouth. "Oh, that's—well, that's lowdown, ain't it?"

"It sure is," Odane said, all sincerity.

"What did the police say 'bout it?" Odeana asked.

"I didn't call no police," Mama Legba said.

"Why not?" Odeana's eyes were wide with confusion.

Odane frowned. "That's what she was about to explain."

Odeana looked at her expectantly.

"Because there ain't nothing the police can do about it," Mama Legba said. "Besides, calling them probably would cause more trouble than I already have…"

She gave Odane and his mother a very brief rundown of everything that happened earlier in the summer, only leaving out some of the details about how my own mother had possessed me.

Watching them talk—finishing each other's sentences,

arguing over the finer points of Voodoo here and local history there—it was hard not to smile. They bickered pretty much constantly through the whole telling, but even I, a total stranger and outsider, could see that they were a family. Despite their differences, whatever they were, they seemed tightly knit, and I had the sense that each would have the other's back when it counted.

I'd only ever had my momma. We didn't have any big extended clan like a lot of folks do. It had always been just her and me, through thick and thin. Or so I thought. Now, I wasn't sure I'd ever had even that much.

"You 'member when that little white girl up and got herself killed at St. John's Eve?" Mama Legba was saying. "They called me in—to consult, you see."

Odeana's mouth pulled down. "Does this story have a point, or did you come all the way over to my side of town to brag on yourself?" she drawled.

"I'm getting there." Mama Legba shot her a look. "See, the body they found yesterday had some particular similarities to the girl who was killed on St. John's Eve. It wasn't no copycat. Those cuts was in the same sort of pattern."

"So it's the witch?" Odeana asked.

"That's what I'm thinking," Mama Legba confirmed. "But for some reason, the police started looking at me. That's why I haven't called them about my house. Last thing I need is them getting up in my business while we're trying to stop Thisbe before she does any more evil."

"You think they'll be more victims," Odane said.

I glanced up at the anger I heard in his words, and found him watching me like this was all my fault.

"I don't know for sure," Mama Legba said. "But I would expect it."

"And you're sure you trust *her*, Auntie?" Odane asked, gesturing in my direction.

"I want to stop Thisbe as much as anyone does," I said, finally speaking up for myself.

Odane's expression was clouded with suspicion. "She's your mother," he challenged. "You'd give up your own family? You'd really turn her in and let us put a stop to all this?"

"There ain't no us," Mama Legba snapped. "I just need some information. I didn't come here to drag you all into this." She looked pointedly at Odeana and Odane.

Odeana snorted, a sound of disdain that sounded so much like Mama Legba it startled me. "You always did think you could boss me around—always have, still trying to. Lot of good that's done you over the years." Odeana leaned forward. "You already dragged me into this when you brought it right up to my front door."

Mama Legba didn't seem to have a response to that. The two women stared each other down, but it was Odeana who broke the silence by speaking again. "You know as well as I do that you might be good at telling what is, but what *will* be hasn't never been your strength."

Mama Legba didn't seem all that pleased to hear this appraisal.

"You came to see me because the aloe is gone." It wasn't a question the way Odeana said it, but more a way of reminding everyone of the point.

Mama Legba shared a look with her sister, and I couldn't tell what that look meant.

"What's the deal with the aloe?" I asked.

"If everything she told us here is the truth, there's not much chance that witch stole it for a beauty treatment," Odeana said.

"What are you thinking she wanted it for?" Mama Legba asked.

"Oh, well … you can use aloe for all sorts of reasons and things, of course, but if this Thisbe stole it, another use for aloe, 'specially aloe curing like it was, is to summon a demon."

ELEVEN

Panic raced through me. "What do you mean, 'a demon'?" I looked at Mama Legba. "You were trying to summon a demon?"

"Of course not." Mama Legba frowned. "I was making the ointment for a ceremony, because it can help channel the energy to help figure out what might be coming next."

"That's one use, all right. It works to channel energy because of the power it has to summon," Odeana explained. "But if it cures for the right amount of time, and someone who knew what they were doing had enough power, that person might could call forth a demon."

"That's what I was afraid of," Mama Legba murmured, leaning back in her chair.

"What kind of demon?" Lucy asked.

Mama Legba looked at me, her face registering her worry before she glanced back at Lucy. "She don't exactly be meaning the horned, pits-of-hell type of demon."

"Is there really more than one kind?" I asked.

Odeana lifted one eyebrow. "You can be calling a demon any old thing that don't come from the light," she explained. "We're all just energy, but some of us channel it for and through the darkness."

"That doesn't really tell us anything," I said, hating the way she was talking around it.

"You add the right things and know the right words," Odeana explained, "and you could use an ointment like that to summon Cimitière."

"Cimitière?" I asked. Something about the word felt familiar, but I couldn't place it.

"Oh, he goes by other names—La Croix, Samedi—"

"Samedi." Now *that* was a name I knew. "You mean, like Baron Samedi?" He was the Loa, or spirit, who had power over death and life and served as guardian of the cemetery. Trickster and cheat, he wasn't a spirit to trust or make deals with.

The memory of my momma's voice sifted through my head: *Truth is something that lies buried. Like a body in a grave. You want the truth, baby girl? You're gonna have to dig.* I tried not to shudder at the memory of the cold certainty in that voice.

Is this what she'd been hinting at? When I'd heard that voice before, I didn't think to take the words literally. But if my momma was messing with Baron Samedi, maybe I'd been wrong.

"Samedi, sure enough. Different names, all the same energy," Mama Legba replied, her voice dark as the mood that had settled over the room.

"*Dark* energy," Odeana added.

"Who is this Samedi?" Lucy asked.

Mama Legba turned to her. "He's the spirit who stands guard at the gate to the world of the dead. He accepts those who pass over and keeps the living out."

"But there have been plenty enough people foolish enough to believe they could make a deal with him to get back the person they lost," Odeana finished.

"Could he really bring a person back?" Lucy said, and I didn't like the curiosity in her voice, not one little bit.

Neither did Mama Legba. "Don't you even think on it, Lucy-girl. A soul ain't meant to go backward in their journey. Souls is only meant to move on. You bring someone back, you doing him a serious harm. You making them something unnatural and breaking the journey they supposed to be on."

Lucy shifted a bit in her seat, her face a little red from what might have been embarrassment.

"Usually, when someone summons Cimitière, they want to raise a soul," Odeana added. She glanced at me. "The question is, which soul does she want to bring back, and why?"

"I don't remember my momma even talking about anyone she knew who had died."

"That don't mean she doesn't have someone she misses," Odeana said. "Cain't never tell what a person has stored up in her heart. Sometimes the most painful, most important things are the ones we never speak a word of. Parents certainly don't speak every truth to their children."

Odane's eyes flew to his mother, but she kept her gaze steady on me. Like she didn't want to look at her son in that moment, and I couldn't help but wonder what truths she hadn't yet spoken to him.

And then I thought of the girl in the dream, and of the

longing in the voice that called out for Augustine. I thought of my vision, and the desperation she'd felt to keep the sleeping man safe, and I wasn't sure what other truths my momma had kept from me.

"You need more than just the aloe to summon, though, and even then, if you leave it to cure less days or more, the ointment could be used for something else. For healing a wound or giving a blessing. But if this is your mother's doing, I doubt she's wanting it for any sort of kindness," Odeana said. "From what you told me of this Thisbe, I don't think she's got no blessings in mind." She paused a moment, considering. "You know who might could help you with this? Ikenna."

Mama Legba's eyes narrowed. "Oh, no. No, no, no. Ain't no way we're bringing that good for nothing—"

"I won't have you speaking ill of my son's father," Odeana warned, cutting Mama Legba off before she could really get started.

"My mom's right, Auntie," Odane said. "I hate to admit it, but if we're talking about someone summoning Cimitière, you know as well as I that he's one of the only people who might be able to help you."

"No." Mama Legba stood up in a motion so swift and sure there was no mistaking it for anything but a final pronunciation.

"Do you even know the other ingredients you'd need for the summoning?" Odeana asked.

Mama Legba frowned. "I don't play with no darkness," she told her sister carefully. "You know that."

"You sure remind me often enough. But you don't need to play with no darkness to understand the game," Odeana said.

Mama Legba shook her head. "I understand enough to know that evil's a sticky sort of thing."

"Is that why you still pushing me away and trying to protect me?" Odeana asked, amusement tingeing her voice.

"Do you get the sense that they're talking about something else?" Lucy whispered to me.

I nodded, though I didn't know what. But the intensity in the sisters' words made it clear that there was something else between them that none of us understood.

"Auntie..." Odane started, but Mama Legba waved him off.

"I'm not making no deals with that devil," Mama Legba added before Odane could interject anything. "Y'all know his price would be too high for any of us to pay."

An uncomfortable silence descended around us. No one seemed ready to argue with Mama Legba's assessment of the situation, and no one seemed interested in explaining anything more than that. Lucy looked at me, uncertain.

"Then let *me* help," Odeana said.

Mama Legba shook her head, her expression grim. "I can't risk wrapping you up in any more of this."

"I can take care of myself well enough," Odeana said.

"You think I don't know that?" Mama Legba smiled softly then. "You probably could take care of us all well enough, but y'all mean too much to me."

"Now, Odette..."

But all I heard was a roaring in my ears. I couldn't help but feel tainted somehow, like my blood was a stain that I couldn't be rid of. The idea that I was part of the darkness that Mama Legba didn't want rubbing off on her family had something lurching inside me in fury—and agreement.

The lights in the room flickered, not enough to snap off, but enough that Odeana went still, stopping mid-thought. "What the . . . ?" she murmured, her eyes warily considering the lamp.

I took a breath and ignored the something deep inside me that practically purred at the sight of the wavering lights.

"My mind's made up," Mama Legba cut in, as though she hadn't noticed what had just happened

I forced myself to unclench my hands, and as I did, the lights burned brighter and the air conditioner hummed steadily again. It took everything I had to force myself to breathe even and slow so that no one else noticed. But when I glanced up, Odane was watching me thoughtfully.

"Seems like you already let it touch us, Auntie," Odane said. "Another person's dead, there's something powerful out there killing them, and you brought that something's flesh and blood up into our home."

"Hey—" I said, the anger and the hurt spiking all at once.

The lights flickered again.

"Chloe's okay," Mama Legba told him before I could say anything else. "Just because you have someone's blood, don't mean you have to become them. You of all people should know that, Odane." She sent the boy a chastising look.

Odane frowned as though her words had hit a nerve, and he didn't say anything else.

"Y'all ready?" Mama Legba asked us. "It's past time we go."

"Don't be going off mad," her sister said.

"Come on, girls," Mama Legba announced, ignoring Odeana. This time she didn't sound like she was asking.

"At least let me drive you back," Odane offered.

Mama Legba looked like she wanted to refuse, but it had been a long walk and already the day was hot and sticky. "Okay, then," she said. "But that's all. Just take us back."

So he did. We wedged ourselves into the too-small cab of his rusted pickup truck, Lucy perched almost on my lap and my side pressed up against the warmth of Odane.

Odane managed the traffic, and I tried to manage my thoughts.

"How many days?" I asked.

"What?" Lucy said.

"Your sister said that if the aloe cured for a certain number of days, it could be used to summon Cimitière," I told Mama Legba. "How many?"

"Five days," she said, her expression grim. "Sundown on day one to sunup on the fifth day."

"So if we're right and Thisbe is the one who took it, we have a little less than a week to stop her?"

"Less than that, Chloe-girl. That aloe has been in the black cat oil for a day already."

I wasn't sure what to say to that. None of us were, it seemed, because as Odane drove us the rest of the way through the narrow streets of the Quarter, the interior of the truck's cab was silent, like none of us wanted to say a word.

TWELVE

By the time we got back to Mama Legba's shop, it was nearly evening.

"Your parents know where you are, Lucy-girl?" Mama Legba asked once we'd climbed out of the Odane's truck. "It's getting late, and I don't want them to be worried."

"I texted my mom back at your sister's, so they know it might be a while," Lucy told her. "We can help you straighten things up before we head out."

Mama Legba studied her for a second, like she was considering it. Finally, she shook her head. "No. I don't like the idea of you two running around here once night comes. Not with everything that's happened and might happen still. Y'all had best get on back."

"But your door—" I couldn't imagine it was a good idea for Mama Legba to stay in a place that didn't even have a door you could secure against the night and all its wildness.

"I'll take care of it for her," Odane said. His words

were friendly enough on the surface, but underneath, they sounded like a challenge. Like he was stepping forward to claim his family.

Fine enough. I'd do the same if I had a family of my own to worry about.

"Y'all need a ride over to where your car is?" he asked in an easy drawl that covered the tension I could feel radiating from him.

"No. We're only a block over," I told him, and I sensed he was glad to have us gone.

The ride back to Le Ciel was quiet, but uneasy. Seemed like Lucy didn't want to talk about anything that had happened any more than I did. At least not at first, but right about the time we hit the highway leading to Le Ciel, she spoke up. Of course, she'd start with the very thing I didn't want to think about much less talk about.

"So this Cimitière guy, he's bad?"

Funny thing—a few months ago, Lucy could barely conceal her disbelief of anything to do with Voodoo. It hadn't been all that long, but now she sounded like she really wanted to know.

"I wouldn't say that he's bad, but from what I know, he's not exactly good. I've always been told he's more of a guide and guard for the dead than Death himself. He's a trickster— a kind of spirit who doesn't exactly play by the rules. He likes smoking, and drinking, and making deals that benefit him and him alone. From what my momma told me..." Which was probably damning evidence right there.

"Go on," Lucy said after I hesitated.

"From what she told me, Baron Samedi's deals are all

tricks. He always works something into the deal to make sure that he wins."

"Like what?"

"I don't know exactly," I told her honestly. After all, my momma might have told me stories to warn me off, but I knew well enough that she'd left more out than she ever told me straight. "But I always got the sense that Baron Samedi would require something impossible from the person summoning him, and when the person can't or won't hold up their end, the deal goes south in a hurry."

Lucy seemed to consider what I'd said. "But if your mom was the one who told you this, she'd know she couldn't make a deal with him."

"I would have said that my momma should know that, but who knows what Thisbe knows or thinks. Maybe she's overconfident in her own power?"

"Maybe," Lucy agreed. "After what she pulled off with Alex to live for so long, I guess it's possible."

"In a way, she's already pulled one over on Samedi. She should have made his acquaintance some years back," I said. "Still, I don't know who she'd go to all this trouble to summon him for. She never talked about anyone …"

"What about Augustine?" Lucy said.

I'd thought of that, too. "Maybe," I told her. "But I don't know for sure that he was real. Piers could be right—I could be dreaming or imagining what I want to think about my momma."

"But you don't believe that," Lucy said. I could feel her watching me. "You think there's something to the visions and the dreams you've been having." I was relieved that it didn't sound like any kind of condemnation.

"I do, but I also want some sort of proof there even *was* an Augustine before I put too much into believing anything about the dreams."

"Well, we can go back and ask my dad to get us into those records. We don't need Byron to get them for us."

"Maybe," I said, and even though everything seemed like it was tumbling down around me, I felt a little better. Because I had at least one person who still believed in me. One person who still seemed to be on my side.

By the time we were almost to Le Ciel, the fields were ribbons of darkness spooling out, broken only by a single shaft of lamplight here and there. I blew through the wide gates at the entrance of the plantation land and guided the car into a spot next to Lucy's family's Volvo.

"Any word from Piers yet about why he went to Nashville without stopping at Mama Legba's?" Lucy asked as she opened her door.

"I don't think—" But when I clicked my phone on, a message was sure enough waiting for me. I couldn't help but smile. "Yeah." Relief washed over me like water. "He sent me a text."

Lucy smiled as she adjusted her bag so it didn't hit her camera. "And?"

I looked at the five words on the screen:

Change in plans. Talk later.

It wasn't much, considering how we'd parted. "He didn't say much."

"Really?" Her face bunched in confusion.

"We had a fight right before he left," I told her. "He must still be irritated." But it didn't seem like Piers to be so short with me.

Lucy frowned. "It seems weird that he would change plans like that, though."

I stared at the phone for a minute. The message was so damn short—I couldn't get anything from it. "I think I'm going to try to get ahold of him before I come in."

"It couldn't hurt," Lucy said as she went inside.

I dialed Piers's number. It rang for a while, and just as I thought it would click over to voicemail, he picked up.

"Piers?" I said after a second of awkward silence.

"Yeah?"

Even if his tone was gruff, the relief of hearing his voice on the other end of the line washed over me like water.

"Hey," I said. "How'd the drive go?"

"It was fine," he said stiffly.

"We went to Mama Legba's today. She said you never stopped by." I hoped he'd hear the question in my words.

"Had a change in plans," he said. "I told you that."

"I know, I was just wondering why … "

"Something else came up, and I couldn't stop before I left town."

"Something like … ?" I let my voice trail off as casually as I could, but he sounded so irritated that I was starting to think calling had been a bad idea.

"Is there something you wanted? I'm a little tied up right now."

"Oh," I said. "Right."

"What did you want?"

I cringed at the stiffness and impatience in his tone. "I thought you'd want to know someone broke into Mama Legba's and stole some things."

"Did she call the police?" he asked.

"No, not yet. We think it was Thisbe."

"It's good you didn't call the police then. They couldn't do anything about that."

"Right. That's what we thought. But I thought you might want to know and—"

"Great. Thanks for letting me know," he said, cutting me off. "Look, I have to go. Can we talk later?"

"Later? But—"

"I don't really have time to talk right now."

"Oh. I see," I said, hating how disappointed my voice sounded. "When will you be back?"

"Now that I'm here, I'm not sure how long this will take," he told me, and I could feel his impatience through the silence after his words.

"Okay, well...Be safe and let us know if you find anything?"

"I will," he said.

"Love y—" But the line had already gone dead.

When Lucy poked her head out of the door who-knows-how-long later, I was still staring at my phone, trying to tell myself it wasn't as bad as it sounded. Piers had been frustrated with me to start with, and he hadn't wanted to leave town in the first place. And I knew how he got when he was working.

But that didn't make me feel any better. I'd thought

hearing his voice would help, but all it did was make me feel farther away from him than ever.

That night I dreamed again of the pines, but I didn't dream of the man named Augustine. Instead, I dreamed of a man who was more skeleton than human. When the man appeared, he walked out of the night. Not out from a distance, but from the darkness around me—*poof*—an apparition fully formed. One second I was alone, and the next, he was there.

Snake-like dreads spilled from his skull and writhed around his face like they were alive. He had deep-set eyes, empty and dark, a wide nose, and a sharp chin. When he smiled, his teeth flashed white as the bones of his fingers, and one of his front teeth was a little crooked.

He was dressed all in black, and his feet were bare. He had the face of a man, but he was missing his skin everywhere else—long, white bones for fingers, long, white bones for toes peeking out beneath the tattered hem of his black pants. On his head, a velvet top hat of deep purple perched at a confident angle, and stuck into its crimson band were three black-as-night feathers that glinted iridescent in the pale moonlight.

We were in the pines again, but this wasn't like the other dreams. The grove didn't feel like an empty, cold place anymore. There was something in the air that hummed across my skin, like it was teasing at me. Threatening and daring me all at once.

The skeleton man looked right at me, and unlike in the other dream, I knew that this man was seeing *me*.

He took a couple of steady, not-in-no-kind-of-hurry steps toward where I was standing. Every bit of me—body and soul—wanted to run, because he looked so wicked and dangerous. He looked like the kind of death nobody wants. But I couldn't seem to make myself move.

When he was a little more than an arm's length from me he stopped and, cocking his head to the side, he looked me over. Up and down, his eyes moved over my body as he took his time about it. Like I was something he could bid on or buy. Like he had all the time in the world to decide whether he would.

Then, amusement sparking in those otherwise empty eyes, he took out a cigar, lit it, and inhaled. He closed his eyes as he sucked the smoke deep, deep into his chest, and then he blew it easily into a ring that floated toward me. The smoky ring wreathed my head, never breaking its shape. It smelled thick and earthy, the same heavy and almost oily scent I'd smelled in Thisbe's cabin.

The man took one look at my puzzled confusion and started laughing. He laughed and laughed, and the air bursting from his throat sounded like wind whistling through a cave. All around me the forest rustled as his laughter echoed off the trees and stirred the air, disrupting the quiet and calm.

At first I didn't hear the rustling noise, because I thought it was part of the laugh, but all at once I realized it wasn't. No, the rustling I heard was coming from something else, something alive, but I didn't understand that in time to avoid the thick swarm of flapping wings.

Dark-as-night crows barreled down on me, flapping around me so that the little bit of night was swallowed up by their inky, dark wings. Through it all, the wheezing, rustling evil of the skeleton man's laugh wrapped itself around me like a noose.

All at once, I was sitting up in my bed, panting from the struggle I'd been through and still smelling the thick, oily scent of Baron Samedi's cigar heavy in the air.

THIRTEEN

The early hours before dawn found me bleary-eyed and frustrated. I hadn't been able to get back to sleep after I woke from the dream I'd had of Baron Samedi in the pines. I didn't doubt that someone summoning him would be a very bad idea, and I'd spent the rest of the long, dark hours thinking about what I could do to stop it from happening. We had maybe two more days left before someone would be able to use the aloe. We needed to know what other ingredients Thisbe would need, and we needed to know what Thisbe might want from Samedi if we were going to stop her before it happened.

It wasn't quite light out when I decided I was tired of waiting. I knocked on Lucy's bedroom door. When I didn't hear anything I knocked a little louder and heard her mumbled reply, so I peeked my head on in.

"Lucy?" I whispered. "Are you awake?"

"No," she grumbled.

She didn't seem all that upset about me bothering her, so

I eased myself into the room. "Lucy," I hissed, a little louder now.

"What?" she groaned, turning over and regarding me with a half-open eye. Then, seeing who it was, she blinked herself awake, sitting up before she was really steady. "What is it?" she whispered, her eyes widening with something that looked like panic. "Did something happen?"

"No," I said, cringing inwardly. I hadn't meant to startle her like that. "I wanted to ask you for a favor."

"Now?" She slumped back into her pillows. "It's not even morning yet."

"Sure it is. It's past five," I told her.

"Chloe, that's still basically the middle of the night."

"The sun's almost up," I argued.

She glared at me and turned back over.

"I need your help," I said, and that seemed to get her attention again.

She rubbed at her eyes a bit and pushed that wild hair of hers back from her face. "With what?"

"I want you to come with me . . ."

"With you where?"

"I want to go have another look around the cabin," I told her, "and I don't want to go alone."

"The cabin?" Her brain must have been as sluggish as her voice sounded. "Wait. You mean *Thisbe's* cabin?"

I nodded.

"Are you crazy?"

"No. I mean, maybe, but I'm thinking there might be something there that everybody else missed. A clue or some-thing." Actually, what I thought was that I could try touching different parts of it again, maybe see if I would have any more visions. But I didn't want to be alone when I did it. And after Piers's reaction the first time, I wasn't ready to tell Lucy my plan.

She frowned as she stared at me. "You're serious."

I nodded. "I think maybe there might be something in her house that might help us figure out if Augustine was a real person or something Thisbe conjured up to play at my sympathies. Or now that we know she might be trying to summon Baron Samedi, maybe we'll see something that we missed before—some clue as to what else she might want with him."

Lucy thought about that for a second. She still probably thought I was nuts, but at least she was considering it.

"You're half right," she said, flopping the covers back and popping out of her bed all business and ready to go.

"So you'll go with me?" I asked, surprised. I really thought she'd say no.

"Not to the cabin, no way. There's nothing there, anyway," she said, waving her hand dismissively. "Dad's crew searched that place top to bottom after everything went down a few weeks ago. If there had been anything to find, they would have found it already."

Lucy was more alert by now as she pulled on her clothes and looked in the mirror to untangle her nest of hair.

I couldn't help but reach up and touch mine—or what was left of it.

"Anyway, there isn't any reason to go back there—and not just because that place creeps me out," she said with a shudder. "But the idea to go search Thisbe's home is actually a great one. We need to go to Thisbe's *other* home."

She looked at me with those old-soul eyes, and I could tell I wasn't going to like what came next. "To *your* home," she clarified, her voice going soft and low.

Sometimes I hate it when I'm right.

––––––––––

I wasn't as sure as Lucy seemed to be about going back to my house. To be honest, I didn't want to face that feeling of being held out and all alone again, but I couldn't argue with her, really, because she was right. We didn't have any other leads, and my momma—Thisbe—had lived and breathed under that roof for most of my life. It was the one place where there should be *something* of hers, and I had a feeling that we would find something there. Why else would Thisbe have worked so hard to keep me out?

Which was the problem—I couldn't set foot across the threshold. Not that a little thing like that was enough to talk Lucy out of it.

"So this spell on the house," she asked as I drove down the back roads that connected Le Ciel to my neighborhood. "Did it hurt when you tried to get in, or did it just make you feel uneasy, or ..."

"I couldn't move," I told her. It came out a little sharper than I meant it to, but even thinking about that morning had me feeling all kinds of wrong. "I got to a certain point, and I, literally, couldn't take another step. It felt like there was concrete drying around my feet and a vise squeezing my heart. I couldn't even breathe. All I could do was stand there, because it felt like moving might kill me."

I turned off the road and began to steer my old Nova up the long, unpaved driveway that led back to my house. When I was little, I'd ride my bike up that very same drive, knowing all the while that my momma would have something cool to drink and a smile just for me. When I got older, I'd drive home from school and the windows would be open, like my momma's arms had always been. And at night, coming home after a party, the windows would be aglow and waiting.

That morning, though, the windows were dark glass, reflecting the still-sleeping world back to me. But the house seemed to be waiting just the same. The closer we got, the more the pressure behind my eyes built.

I didn't pull all the way up to the porch.

"Ready?" Lucy asked after I put the car in park and killed the engine.

"Not even a little bit," I said, but I got out of the car when she did.

By then the sky had started to turn from a shade of lurid pink to the hazy blue of the day. It hadn't been a hopeful kind of sunrise. It had been the kind of sunrise that once might have made sailors lower their sails and secure their ships.

"I'll make it quick," she said. "In and out, and nothing's going to happen."

"Says you." I couldn't take my eyes off the glaring windows or shake off the unease I felt just looking at the place I'd once called home.

"Right." Lucy started toward the house, and I didn't have much choice but to follow.

When we got close to the porch, I could feel the beginnings of something. My feet felt heavy, sluggish. "I don't think this is going to work."

"Do you feel it?" she asked.

"Yeah. Don't you?"

She shook her head.

Still I tried to walk on toward the house, but there came a point where I couldn't go on. The same solid, invisible wall greeted me, and my feet felt like lead. When I tried to push through it, the same squeezing panic filled my chest to bursting until I stepped back to the relative safety of just feeling uneasy.

Reluctantly, I handed Lucy the key. "Be careful."

"Any idea about where I should look?"

"I don't know," I said, trying to think. "I'm not even sure what we're looking for."

"Something private," Lucy told me. "Something she wouldn't have wanted you to see, even before you knew what she was."

"Then you'll need to try her room," I said. "She never let me in there unless she was with me." She used to say that a woman had a right to her privacy, but now I wondered if she was keeping me out to keep her secret safe.

"Anywhere else?" Lucy asked. She was studying the house with an intense look of concentration, like she expected something to change or jump out and attack at any second.

I combed through the house in my mind, trying to imagine a place where my momma might have hidden that other part of herself. "The basement," I said at last. "She never wanted me down there when I was little."

"Right," Lucy said, but it didn't look to me like she was in any hurry to go into the house on her own. Especially not into any basement.

"We don't have to do this," I said. "We could wait until Piers gets back."

She shot me another sharp look. "You know we don't have that kind of time. I won't let her do to anyone else what she did to Alex."

"Okay, then. Be careful," I told her.

Lucy took a deep breath and then started up the stairs of the porch, her steps tentative like she was expecting the floor to drop out beneath her at any moment. When it didn't, her shoulders relaxed a little and she unlocked the door.

"If you're not out in ten minutes, I'm calling for help," I told her as she pushed open the door. She turned back to me and nodded her agreement before she stepped inside.

FOURTEEN

I held my breath as the door shut behind Lucy, and I kept it held until I saw a light come on inside the house. I couldn't go any farther, but I wasn't about to go back, either, so I stood and kept watch, taking in the angry-looking house and wondering how my whole life had gotten so far off course.

A moment later, a light came on upstairs—my momma's window—but the curtains stayed still. No movement gave away anything happening inside. I checked my phone for the time, but when I turned it on, Piers's last message was there, staring me in my face.

Talk later.

Except we hadn't talked, not really. The short, gruff conversation we'd had when I called him felt almost worse than silence would have. More real and more hopeless somehow.

But if I was honest with myself, I'd known for a while this day had been coming. Ever since Piers had gone off to

Vanderbilt instead of staying at one of the colleges around New Orleans, I'd been worried that he was really moving away from me. Maybe him being a couple of years older hadn't mattered so much when we were younger, but more recently, the differences between us had already started to seem that much bigger and more insurmountable.

And with Thisbe between us, I could feel the distance between us widening.

I looked at the message again and thought of the hanged man card that I'd drawn a couple of days ago. It was all about sacrifice. Giving up your hold on something to gain a bigger view. Maybe I'd have to give up more than I thought. Maybe I'd have to give up Piers.

Upstairs, the light went off.

I clicked off the phone and pushed it into my back pocket. I couldn't let myself think about that. Not yet, at least. It wouldn't do anyone any good to get all upset about things I couldn't change right this minute.

By then, Lucy had been gone for about seven, maybe eight minutes. The house still stood silent, though, the doorway dark and still. I tried again to take a step forward, but again, my effort was met with pain in my chest and my feet feeling like lead.

Another minute passed.

Two.

Any minute now she'd come on out of there and we could go. But that minute passed, and so did a fistful of minutes more, and I started to get a feeling that something wasn't right.

I pulled out my phone to call Mama Legba, cursing myself for letting Lucy talk me into doing something so stupid, but when I went to turn it on, the screen was dead. I shook it a little, like that was going to do anything, but of course it didn't. I'd had plenty of battery a minute before, but no matter how long I held the power button, nothing happened. Not a flicker of energy, not any sign that the phone was anything but dead.

Still, no Lucy.

Maybe she'd left her phone in the car, I thought, knowing even as I hoped that it was a long shot. Still, I had to try.

But I didn't take but three steps back when the wind picked up. It was the kind of wind that rolls as it blows through, up from the ground and then around you like the beginnings of a storm. It was enough to make me stop dead in my tracks.

I thought about the bottles breaking, and the light flickering at Odeana's house, and the wind tearing through Mama Legba's back rooms, and a feeling of dread started inching right down my spine. I had to force myself to calm down.

But even when I got my breathing steady, this wind felt different, and it didn't stop. The trees started to sway in the gusts, the wind whistling and whipping through them with more and more force.

I started for the car, but stopped again when I heard the buzzing—a metallic sound that started off slow and grew and grew, coming up from behind me. Coming from the house, I realized as I glanced over my shoulder. There, just beyond the roofline, the sky was dark, and the darkness was growing.

No, not growing. Coming closer.

I tried to take another step toward the car. I didn't want to be out without anything protecting me, not with that dark cloud coming. Closer and closer. But I couldn't make my feet move.

The cloud grew and billowed—I could barely make out the roofline now, because the cloud had almost swallowed it. And the buzzing was getting louder and louder.

That's when I realized it wasn't a cloud. It was a swarm.

I tried to run again, but the minute I tried to lift up my foot, I found that I couldn't. Magic stronger than my fear or my panic was pinning me there.

The buzzing was heavy in the air and the house almost completely obscured by the dark swarm. My heart beat frantically in my chest, and I managed to take a step, maybe two, but then my feet wouldn't budge. And then they were upon me. All around me thousands of legs and wings and tiny, hard bodies brushed against me, beat against me. I crouched low to the ground, trying to keep them off me, but still they swirled, a hurricane of living things, buzzing and angry and *hungry*.

The swarm was so dense it felt like a solid wall. My arms stung where some of them scraped at me, and my throat burned from my screams.

I am going to die here, I thought. *Eaten alive by an army of bugs*.

But just when the cruelness and rightness of that thought was solid and firm in my chest, everything stopped. Everything—the wind stopped and the day went completely still. The insects froze in mid-flight, dropping from the sky and pelting me like hail.

I stayed crouched down like that, afraid even to move in case something I did started it all up again, but instead of more of the swarm, I heard a new sound—a crackling noise as footsteps crushed the brittle bodies underfoot. Closer and closer. When the shadow fell over me, I finally looked up.

"What are you doing here?" I said, ignoring Odane's outstretched hand.

"You're welcome," he said, still holding out his hand like he was waiting for something.

"You're telling me that you stopped all that?" The ground all around my momma's property was covered with a thick blanket of the shiny, blue-black shells of the beetles.

He nodded, his face tense. "For now. But we need to go."

"I can't," I said, finally taking his offered hand and letting him pull me up. I was afraid to move because I didn't want to hear—or feel—the crunching of the hard little bodies littering the ground. "Lucy's still inside."

"Inside there?" His brows flew almost clear to his hairline. "You'd have to be all kinds of crazy to go in there."

"It's my house," I said, suddenly and unaccountably angry with him for being there, for finding me so helpless and afraid. And most of all, I was angry for him being the one to save me when I wanted to be able to save myself.

"You're telling me you can't feel what's coming from that place?" he asked. "Black magic. Dark as anything I've ever felt." He practically shuddered.

I frowned. "I never did before, but I feel something now. I can't even get as far as the door anymore," I told him. "There's some kind of spell to keep me out."

He shook his head, his eyes still trained on the house. It's like he didn't even see the mess of bugs laying all about—he only had eyes for the building itself. "No, it's more than that. There are spells woven all through this place. They go deep into the land." He looked at me then, suspicious-like. "You're telling me you can't feel any of it?"

"I grew up here," I said, like that was some sort of explanation, and maybe it was, because he didn't ask me anything else.

"Who'd you say is in there?"

"Lucy. The girl who came with Mama Legba and me the other day. Red hair. Carries a camera everywhere?" I added when he didn't seem to understand at first.

He was still staring at the house, like he was trying to decide whether to go in or to leave Lucy to her fate.

"I'm not going anywhere without her," I said before he could suggest it. From the look on his face, it sure did look like he wanted to suggest it. "What are you doing here anyway?" It was my turn to be suspicious.

"My mom saw something. She sent me over."

"Saw something?"

He nodded, still staring at the house like he was getting up his nerve. "Sometimes she sees things, and in this case, she must have seen you."

"We need to get Lucy out of there," I said. "She was supposed to come out a while ago, but I can't go any farther than this." My meaning was clear—he'd need to go in for me.

He let out a long, frustrated sigh. "Fine. You go on and get in your car. If anything else happens, you'll at least have something to protect you."

"Thank you," I said, meaning it as I retreated. The windows of the house were still dark. Lucy either hadn't heard all the commotion outside or something was wrong inside.

Odane looked back once to make sure I was in the car before he made his way toward the house, but he didn't look back again after that. Not when he made it to the top of the steps. Not when he disappeared inside.

I sat, my hands shaking and my skin clammy despite the heat of the closed-up car. Waiting. Watching.

After a few minutes, something shifted in the doorway, and a moment later, Odane stepped through carrying Lucy, unconscious in his arms. Not caring about the crunch of the bugs anymore, I jumped out of the car and ran as far as I could to meet them, my heart hammering in my chest and the guilt and horror of what I was seeing burning my eyes.

Odane carried Lucy easy as if she were a child. Her head flopped back, bobbing a bit as he walked, the wind lifting her hair as it hung listlessly. She was completely limp, except for her arms, which were wrapped around something she was holding—a dark wooden box.

Even unconscious, she was holding onto it like it was the only thing that mattered.

FIFTEEN

By the time we got to Mama Legba's shop, Lucy still wasn't quite coherent. We couldn't take her through the front door like that without people noticing and asking questions we didn't want to answer or calling the police on us, so we shuffled her in through the back.

"Auntie O!" Odane shouted.

Seconds later, Mama Legba appeared in the doorway. "Odane?" Then she saw Lucy, limp and still mostly unconscious in Odane's arms, and her face flashed with confused worry. "What happened?"

Odane looked at me as he set Lucy down onto the low couch and waited, like he was giving me a chance to explain. When Mama Legba realized he wasn't going to talk, she looked at me, too.

"We went to my house," I told her, and before I could say anything more, she tore into me.

"You went to *what* house?"

"The house I grew up in. Lucy had this idea—"

"Lucy did?" Mama Legba interrupted, glancing at Lucy's still figure and then back at me. "Why would Lucy think about doing a thing like that? She heard you talking about the spell that kept you out the other day. She should have known better."

"It wasn't exactly all her idea," I said, backtracking a bit. "I was thinking about maybe going out to Thisbe's cabin again—"

"Thisbe's cabin?" Mama Legba's eyes narrowed even more, if that was possible.

"Are you going to let me finish, or are you going to keep interrupting me?" I snapped, my temper finally starting to melt some of the fear that had paralyzed me most of the drive over.

Mama Legba pursed her lips at my sass and then gave a wave of her hand to indicate that I should continue.

"Like I was saying, I had this idea to go to Thisbe's cabin, and before you say a word, I *know* it was a stupid idea, but we have less than two days before that aloe mixture you made might open up something bad and . . . " I felt the beginnings of a breeze sliding across my neck and my voice caught in my throat.

"And what?" Mama Legba asked.

I took a second and tried to settle myself down. I didn't speak again until I was sure that no other wind was kicking up. I still wasn't sure what had happened out there at the house. I didn't think I'd called up those bugs, but I couldn't be certain.

Taking a final, steadying breath, I went on. "I asked Lucy to go with me to the cabin, but she had this idea that where we really needed to look was my house, because it was the last place my mother had lived."

"Actually, that wasn't such a bad idea," Odane said thoughtfully, like he was impressed we'd come up with it.

I glanced over at him, unsure of how I felt about his comment. I didn't need his approval, but even so, part of me was glad I had it.

"So you went to your house," Mama Legba said. She still didn't sound none too happy. "Did you get yourself through the door this time?"

I shook my head. "No, I still couldn't even go as far as the front porch, but Lucy could. At first everything was fine, but then ... " I took a shuddering breath. Just thinking about it and I could almost feel that unnatural wind and the sharply buzzing wings of the insects that had come down from the sky like a plague.

"Then everything wasn't," Odane finished for me. "I've never seen nothing like it, Auntie. When I got there, the whole place was covered in a swarm of bugs so dark you'd think night had fallen over that one little piece of land. Chloe was standing there like she couldn't go nowhere else, right in the middle of it all."

I'd been doing pretty well holding myself together until that point. All the way back from my house to the Quarter, I'd focused on following Odane's truck and I hadn't let myself think about the bugs. But at his description it all came back—the sound of their demanding wings, the sting of their shiny black bodies pelting my skin like bullets. The way they'd surrounded me, almost swallowed me in their dark mass. I had to close my eyes and take a couple of deep breaths to ward off the nausea that rose up in my stomach.

"And what was you doing there, boy?" Mama Legba asked, her hands on her hips and her attention, finally, not on me.

"Mom sent me," he said simply.

Mama Legba blinked, her expression tense. "Odeana saw it?"

Odane nodded, and Mama Legba sank into her chair.

"What?" I asked, not understanding why the mood had shifted so suddenly, so dangerously, in the room.

Mama Legba glanced up at Odane and then, after he gave a slight nod, she met my eyes. "My sister was born behind the veil. She got the second sight," she said reverently, like that was supposed to mean something to me. "Some babies is born in the caul, and they has the sight—the ability to see what will be. Odeana been having her visions since we was girls, but she only sees certain things. Important things. Usually, when she gets the sight, somebody's gonna die."

"She saw one of us about to die?" I asked Odane.

"I'm not sure exactly what she saw, but she yanked me out of bed and told me I needed to get myself to the address where I found you. I learned a long time ago not to question my mom when she's got a vision."

"Well, I'm glad you didn't question her this time either," I told him, and I meant every word of it and a whole bunch more that I didn't say.

"Me, too," he said softly, and maybe for the first time, his voice didn't hold even a hint of scorn. Then he turned back to Mama Legba. "I found Lucy in the basement. I almost didn't find her, though—she'd crawled through a smaller door that went down into a second cellar. It was so dark in there I couldn't see a foot in front of me. I almost turned back, but I caught sight of the white toe of her shoe right before."

We all looked over to Lucy, who was curled on the couch and still holding the box securely in her arms even though she hadn't quite come to completely. Her eyes were open now, but she was sort of staring off.

Mama Legba went over and kneeled down next to her. Brushing some of the hair back from her pale face, she made some cooing noises to try and wake her. Lucy stirred a little, but only to adjust her hold on the box.

"Try to get her all the way awake while I make her something to help clear up her energy," Mama Legba said as she pushed herself up. "She's got mixed up in something dark and we need to be getting it off her."

While the tea was brewing, Mama Legba lit a smudge stick and wafted the smoke around. Little by little, Lucy's eyes began to look more focused. Little by little she stirred enough that we could get her to sip the tea. Finally, Mama Legba managed to get her to give up the box she was holding and set it aside.

When she was feeling well enough and her eyes had finally taken on their usual sharpness, Mama Legba settled herself down in the chair across from her. "You feeling better, Lucy-girl?"

She nodded and took another sip of tea.

"What happened, child?" Mama Legba asked.

I sat next to Lucy, to help keep her upright, but Odane took to lurking in the corner, a hip propped against one of the countertops, his arms across his chest. He had a look of utter concentration on his face as he listened.

"I went in the house," Lucy told us, her eyes far off, like she was remembering. "I looked upstairs first, but there wasn't anything that seemed important, so I decided to try the basement, like Chloe had suggested."

Mama Legba glanced at me, one dark brow raised.

"I wasn't allowed down there as a kid," I said, sounding more defensive than I meant to.

"At first I didn't see anything interesting in the basement either. Just a lot of old stuff, and I didn't think that Thisbe would leave something important sitting out in the open." Lucy paused long enough for another sip of tea. "But then I noticed the door. I almost missed it, since it was so dark down there and there were a couple boxes stacked in front of it. So I moved them and found this other part of the basement."

"That's where I found her," Odane confirmed.

Lucy's face went a little pink. "Thank you for that," she said.

Odane nodded, but he didn't add anything more.

"Anyway, I had my phone, so I used the light and went in." She hesitated then, and her eyes were far away and serious.

"Take your time, child," Mama Legba said, touching Lucy's knee.

She blinked a few times, then closed her eyes for a long moment, like she was trying to visualize it. "There wasn't any light in there at all," she said. "But when I pointed my flashlight up on the walls, they were covered in symbols. Kind of like the symbols that were on that tomb."

Mama Legba frowned. "You mean Thisbe's tomb?"
Lucy nodded.

"Wait," Odane said. "Back it up. Thisbe has a tomb?"

Mama Legba gave him an impatient look. "Last place they saw the old witch was in one of the cemeteries. She'd been hiding the boy's body—"

"Alex," Lucy interrupted, glancing up at Odane to explain. "She'd kept his body in one of those old above-ground tombs, only it wasn't a normal tomb. It was all carved up with these strange markings, and they must have had some sort of magical properties, because they seemed to glow."

Odane thought about this. "I didn't see any markings in the cellar, but I didn't have a light. I tried to use my phone, same as you, but it was dead."

"Mine went dead, too," I told them. But when I pulled my phone out of my back pocket, sure enough, it was fine. Plenty of battery. Plenty of reception.

Still no other messages from Piers.

"So whatever happened must have done something to interrupt the power," Odane said, checking his own phone and finding it was also just fine.

"That's about all I really remember," Lucy told us. "I went down into the room—it had an even lower ceiling than the regular basement—it was all made of dirt, like someone had dug it out by hand or something. And the walls, like I said, were covered with these weird inscriptions. There was an altar or something there, but it wasn't like yours," she told Mama Legba. "It didn't have anything but red candles that had been burned down to stubs and a tarnished silver bowl. Underneath the bowl, I found the box. I almost didn't notice it, because it looked like a stand or something for the bowl, but the second I picked it up..." She frowned. "I don't know what happened."

"Sounds to me like you tripped some kind of alarm," Mama Legba said.

If Lucy had tripped an alarm, it meant that I probably hadn't been the one to cause those evil bugs. That realization made me feel a little better. Not much, but a little.

Mama Legba looked at Odane, her patience at an end. "Now what about these bugs you was talking about?"

"It's like I was telling you, when I pulled up, the whole place was dark as night, but it wasn't night. You think the cicadas can get bad? They don't have nothing on what I saw out there." Even Odane looked uneasy remembering it. "The whole bed of my truck is *still* filled with them."

Mama Legba perked up at this. "You best show me, then. You girls wait here. We'll be back."

By the time Mama Legba and Odane came back, Lucy had more color to her and almost seemed to be back to her own self.

"Please tell me you didn't bring any of those things in here," I said when I saw that Mama Legba had something cupped in her hands.

"Oh, hush," she told me. She went into the hallway—the one that led out to the front shop—and after a minute returned with a heavy stone bowl. "Let's see what we got here," she said, using a wooden dowel to crush a couple of the black bugs in the bowl.

I shuddered at the sound of the exoskeletons crunching beneath her pestle.

"Scarab beetles," she said, though I'm not sure if she was talking to us or to herself. "But not really." When she was done, her brows went up as she examined the contents.

"Well?" Odane said. He didn't seem half as bothered by what was happening as I was.

"They might look like scarabs, but that's not what they is. See?" She thrust the bowl toward him.

He examined the contents critically and then licked his finger and dabbed the tip of it into the bowl. Then he examined the fine powder coating the tip of his finger before touching it to the tip his tongue.

"Ugh." I couldn't hide my disgust.

"They're not real bugs," he said, as though that excused it.

"They looked real enough to me, and who goes around putting nasty stuff in their mouth like that? Just ... ugh."

Odane kind of chuckled at that, and I felt the sudden urge to throw something at him.

"They're made of dirt," he said, taking the bowl from Mama Legba and bringing it to me. "They looked like bugs and acted like bugs, but look—they crumble into nothing when you press on them at all."

Sure enough, he was right. There wasn't any sign of anything that remotely looked like a bug in the bowl. Certainly, there should have been some kind of wetness from their bodies—the insects hadn't been dead that long. But the bowl only held some dry, dark dirt.

Not that I was going to taste it.

"So what does that mean?" I said, stepping back. Dust or not, I didn't want to be anywhere close to it.

"It means that we was right about Lucy tripping some sort of alarm. These are just a bit of magic. Entering that cellar or touching that there box must have released a kind of energy, enough to animate this bit of earth into something fearsome."

I shuddered. Fearsome wasn't the half of it.

Mama Legba frowned as she walked over and settled herself on the couch to look at the box. "Sure don't seem like much," she said, letting her hands hover above it. "But it must be or she wouldn't have gone to the trouble of protecting it like she did. I wonder what it's hiding."

"There's only one way to find out," Odane said.

"We need to open it," Lucy agreed.

Mama Legba's mouth went tight, but she didn't disagree. "We need a protection charm before we start," she said, placing the box on the low table near the couch. "You want to try, Chloe-girl?"

It was the first time she'd offered to let me try any sort of charm since everything had happened, and I felt a little jolt of excitement as something shifted inside of me. Something that yearned to reach out and take the opportunity she offered.

"No," I told her, slamming that yearning back into its own box. "You can do it."

"I know well enough that I can do it," Mama Legba said, "and I know you can do it, too. The question is if *you* know."

I glanced away, unable to meet her eyes. "I'm not ready for anything like that," I told her. In truth, though, I *wanted* to be ready. I wanted to feel that same spark of excitement that had flickered through me when the candles snuffed themselves out or when Odeana's electricity flickered. But I was worried the part of me that wanted those things was way too much like my momma.

Mama Legba seemed to understand. Her hand rested on top of mine, and finally I looked up at her. "You afraid of the wrong thing, Chloe-girl. Not all magic means you linked to

Thisbe, child. There ain't no reason for you to keep running from what's inside of you. I tried to tell that boy of yours that much, but now I'm telling you as well."

It was too much of a temptation, and far too much of a risk, so I drew my hand away. "I'm not afraid," I lied. "I just don't want to."

Mama Legba considered me a moment or two longer, and then seemed to decide it wasn't worth arguing for now. She lit a stick of incense, and then holding her hands over the box, chanted the protection charm. Taking a deep breath, like she was trying to steady herself, she eased the latch on the box free and gently opened the lid.

We all seemed to be holding our breaths, waiting for something to happen when Mama Legba eased the lid up. When nothing did, the relief in the room was palpable.

"Let's see what we got here," Mama Legba said, gently lifting the topmost object.

Whatever I'd been expecting, the contents of the box were a disappointment. Inside I didn't see anything at all worth protecting. The box didn't hold nothing but a mishmash of useless junk: a faded silk ribbon gone brittle with age, a few buttons, something that might have once been a Gris-Gris. And some scraps of paper, most of which had long ago turned brown.

"What is all that?" I asked as Mama Legba picked through the pieces.

"Seems like a record of some sort. They're all in a sort of order, too—most recent on top," Mama Legba said, sorting through them.

She laid it all out on the table in front of us, piece-by-piece, as she went through them. "There are some more recent ticket stubs for flights, but the older they get, the more interesting they look. This here looks like a receipt for passage on a ship of some sort, right around the turn of the last century." She read over one of the more fragile bits before looking up at me, her eyes dark with some unspoken emotion as they met mine. "I think this might be Thisbe's free papers. Looks like it was dated 1810, when she wasn't more than about eighteen years old." She went to hand the paper to me, but I shook my head, refusing it.

It was hard enough knowing what my momma was without also having to think about what she'd been. I couldn't think about her being no older than I was and owned by another person.

"I wonder what she did to get her freedom," Odane said as he took the outstretched papers from Mama Legba.

"What do you mean by that?" I asked, not liking the note of amusement in his voice.

He glanced up at me with a lazy shrug. "Only that she must have had some sort of leverage to get her owner to let her go. Either that or she earned enough on the side—or someone else did—to purchase her freedom. Whatever the case, these didn't come cheap," he said, setting the papers back down on the table.

"This looks like a record of her life," Lucy said, looking at another bit of paper—one that looked like a ticket. "She wouldn't have been able to stay in one place without people catching on, so she traveled around."

"Not just around," Odane said, tapping the scraps. "Look here, this one is a transatlantic crossing to Liberia in the mid

1800s. Then she travels through Haiti and Jamaica before coming back to America."

Mama Legba made a thoughtful noise. "There's a pattern, sure enough. She could have gone most anywhere, but she didn't. She wasn't off in Paris or Rome, like she could've been. Look here, West Africa, the West Indies—all places on the Middle Passage. And they are places that have their own practices and beliefs when it comes to the spirits," she said. "These are places where Voodoo was born and grew up in different ways."

"So she was learning?" Odane asked. "Maybe collecting different parts of the tradition from different places."

"Maybe so," Mama Legba agreed. "From the looks of it, she certainly got around enough over the last hundred years that she could have learned all sorts of things."

Lucy picked up the last of the pile of scraps. "What are these?"

Mama Legba held out her hand and Lucy gave her the fragile bits of paper. When she gently unfolded one, it nearly broke in two along the crease. "Looks like these are some newspaper clippings that date back..." Her brows went up. "Some date *way* back."

Odane leaned in for a better look. "What are they clippings off?"

"I don't rightly know," she said. "These here seem to be a couple of death notices." She placed the clipped columns of newsprint on the table. "And these are just reports about that plantation out there Lucy's daddy works on."

Lucy leaned in and tapped a finger on one of the scraps before scooping it up. "I remember my dad talking about this. The state was going to reclaim the property because the last owner hadn't kept up with back taxes before he died. The house was abandoned for decades before some private owner bought it for cheap, but he couldn't afford to actually restore it, so he sold it to the university." She glanced up from reading. "That's when they hired my dad."

"A lot of these have to do with the plantation," Odane said, pulling another of the clippings from the pile. "Says here this guy owned Le Ciel back in the 1920s, but he went missing sailing off the coast of Cuba." He held the obituary out to me.

Without really thinking about it, I reached for it and—

It had been years since I'd seen the place, but the mansion looked the same as it always had. Like the years couldn't touch the sanctity of those white walls.

I almost didn't go around back, to the servant's entrance, like I knew I was supposed to. I'd been so many places, learned so many things, and it was easy to forget that in this place, I wasn't anything at all.

The woman who answered the door wiped her hands on her apron as she looked me up and down without so much as a word. Her lined face didn't show any sign of recognition, but all the same I had to hold myself steady while she looked over me. When she decided I'd do, she ushered me into the stuffy warmth of the kitchen and then on past that to the coolness of the hall beyond.

"Mister La Rue will see you in his library," she said.

"Mister?" I asked, surprised. Usually it was left to the woman of the house to interview new servants.

"Missus isn't well today," the woman said, giving me a look that let me know that the missus was often not well, and that

"not well" was a nicer way of saying something that shouldn't be spoken about in mixed company.

When I entered the library, La Rue was sitting behind his desk. His attention was focused on some big ledgers he was looking over, and he waved me to sit on the stiff-backed sofa without so much as looking up.

I did as he bade me to do, keeping my hands tucked in my lap and taking a moment to look around the place. I'd never been inside the big house, and now that I was, I hated Roman Dutilette that much more for building it.

"Name?" La Rue asked, still not bothering to look at me.

"Sarabeth Johnson," I said, supplying the name I'd been using for the last few years.

He scribbled something down on the pad of paper. "Experience?"

"I've been working as a domestic since I was about fifteen years old." I pulled the forged papers out of my purse. "I have referrals from my last three posts."

LaRue glanced up to accept the papers, but as he put his hand out for them, his dark brows beaded together and he studied me for a moment that drew out long and painful and slow. "Well, well, well." Then his mouth curved up into a feral-looking smile. "Sarabeth, indeed," he drawled.

My hands froze on the papers. "Roman?" I whispered, even as I knew it was impossible.

His smile widened. "Thisbe."

As the shock of his words wrapped around me, I lost hold of the papers and—

With a strangled gasp I came back to myself, to Mama

Legba's shop. My brain raced, trying to put together what I'd seen.

"Chloe?" Lucy asked. "Are you okay?"

I shook my head. "It just happened again."

"What happened?" Odane asked.

I explained to him about the visions I'd had when I touched the charm before, and the ones I'd had in her cabin. "I thought it was maybe some kind of magic that was still on the charm or in the places where she worked those spells, but . . ." I looked up at Mama Legba. "When I touched that clipping, I was back there. I was seeing her life again."

Mama Legba was considering me with an uncomfortable intensity. "So it ain't only the charm that causes them." She picked up another scrap of paper that had been taken from the box. "But I can't get no sense of Thisbe on these, so I don't think it's anything she's doing to you, either." Mama Legba frowned. "Though I don't rightly know how that could work."

"People leave bits of their energy behind all the time, Auntie. You know that. Everything in this world we touch becomes a part of who we were, what we are. She's got her mother's blood, so I don't see why she shouldn't have a touch of her power. Maybe that's why she can sense traces of this Thisbe on the things she touches."

Mama Legba shook her head. "It don't feel right."

"Nothing about any of this feels right," Odane said.

"What did you see?" Lucy asked, picking the clipping from where it had fallen to the floor. She frowned a little, like she'd expected to have a vision, too.

"Thisbe came back to Le Ciel. Must have been about the

time of that clipping. The guy it talks about, the one who was lost at sea—La Rue—he was hiring a new maid and she wanted to get into the house, so she applied. But he recognized her."

"What do you mean 'recognized her'?" Mama Legba asked.

"I mean, he seemed to know somehow that she was Thisbe and not the 'Sarabeth Johnson' she'd called herself by."

"How could he have known that?" Lucy asked.

"I don't exactly understand," I told them, "but I got the sense that Thisbe thought he was Roman Dutilette."

Mama Legba made a small sound of disbelief.

"He didn't look anything like Roman," I said, trying to explain. "I mean, he had the same coldness in his eyes, but he was a rich white man looking at a black servant, so maybe that accounted for his expression."

"But Thisbe didn't think so," said Odane.

I shook my head. "No. She didn't. She called him by name, and he didn't deny it."

"How is that even possible?"

Mama Legba took the clipping from Lucy. She closed her eyes for a second, like she was trying to get a reading on it, but then opened them, clearly confused. "I don't rightly know, but you came back, Lucy-girl. You found your way back here to finish what Armantine left to be finished, didn't you?" She set the clipping back on the table, like she didn't want to hold it for too long. "Maybe Roman did as well."

"But it sounds like he recognized her so quickly," Lucy said. "When I first met Alex again, I had a sense that I was being drawn to him, but it took me weeks of dreaming before

I pieced everything together and could really remember who he'd been to me."

"Maybe it wasn't a coincidence that he came back," Odane said. "This Thisbe found a way to live for more than a century beyond her natural life, so what's to say that Roman Dutilette couldn't have done the same?"

"How would he have learned to do a thing like that?" Mama Legba asked doubtfully.

Odane shrugged. "You can get any information you want if you're willing to pay enough for it."

"Let me try again," I told them.

"I don't think—" Mama Legba started, but I cut her off.

"You just said you don't sense any of Thisbe's magic on these. Whatever's causing the visions, it's probably nothing she's doing, right?"

"We can't be sure, Chloe-girl," Mama said, but without much conviction.

"You're all here. If something happens, there are three of you and one of me. I think it's worth the risk if we can learn something more."

Mama Legba frowned, but after a few moments of hesitation, she gave me a small nod. "You right. I don't like it, but it's what we have right now."

"These older articles are written in French," Odane said, already sorting through the pile. "This one looks to be from 1811." He studied it, his brow drawing together as he read it over. "Some sort of attempted slave revolt, it looks like. My French is pretty bad, but maybe you can get something more from it."

He handed it to me, and, ready for anything, I reached

out. The second my fingers touched it, heat shot through me, so powerful and angry that I gasped as Mama Legba's shop fell away and I found myself standing alone on a road, with the scent of death so thick around me that my stomach clenched.

SIXTEEN

Bile rose in my throat, and before I could stop my insides from turning over, I stumbled over to retch onto the side of the road until I felt emptied out, body and soul.

Trying to catch my breath, I wiped the corner of my mouth with the hem of my apron. I wasn't even close yet and the stink was already so thick I could practically taste it. Not that I had any intention of turning back.

I'd known that something was coming. For months now, I could practically smell it in the air. But I hadn't realized how fast it would come, and I hadn't understood how much it would take.

My fault, I thought. Because I hadn't been strong enough to protect him.

I looked down that dusty road, the heat shimmering off the surface of it, and for a moment, I remembered another road. Another time.

The first time I saw him, the cane had already been boiling away in iron pots wide enough and deep enough to cook *a man. I'd been walking down a road just like this one when Jean-Pierre Dutilette came driving around the bend with a wagon filled with a new crop of men to replace the ones his plantation had cut down.*

Except that time, one of the dark heads didn't bow. That time, one figure sat straight and proud as the driver who held the whip.

Without a mother around to protect me, I'd been fighting off unwanted attention ever since I understood a smile wasn't always a welcome. But when I saw the man with the straight back and too-proud eyes, I knew I wanted him.

But not even magic as strong as mine had been enough to keep him.

So I walked on, ignoring the ache in my chest, and I didn't let myself stop again for anything—not for the heat licking at my skin. Not even to retch on the side of the road when the breeze brought with it the smell of death.

Ahead, I saw a row of poles that looked like crows were perching on the tops of them. But I knew that what I was seeing didn't have anything to do with feathers even before I came to the first pike.

As I approached it, the skin on the man's face seemed to be crawling alive, there were so many flies on it. All that was left of his eyes were dark, empty sockets staring sightlessly up at the sky. I don't know whether it was relief that I didn't recognize this face, or the horror that I'd have to keep on walking that made my legs go out from under me and a sob tear free from my chest.

I wanted to take the poor man's head and give it the proper ritual to protect the soul as it went on its way, but I knew I couldn't risk it. Not with everything that had happened. Not with the hate still spinning through the air and suspicion hanging in the breeze.

Still, I took a moment there on the side of the road and, like my mother had taught me, I said the words to call for the spirits to reclaim the man's soul.

Then I moved on to the next pike, and the next man who didn't have Augustine's face. And as I walked, I thought about the other women who walked this same path, mothers and lovers who hoped for the best but found instead the beaten faces of the men they loved. But with each pike that didn't show me Augustine's features, I hoped a little more.

He'd been gone for fifteen days already. Fifteen days when I didn't know what had become of him. Fifteen days since I woke to find him no longer in my bed.

Ten days ago, the River Road had gone crazy with violence and death. Eight days ago, those who could went back to the ordinary dangers of the lives they'd been handed. Five days ago, they'd driven the first pike into the ground and severed the first soul.

Every night since, I'd gone to wait in our place, and every night I hadn't found anything but the empty stars.

Another pike that isn't topped with a crow. Another face that isn't his. And each face I find is a fresh wound in the ragged thing that was once my soul.

Had I been stronger, Augustine never would have left me that night. He never would have been able. Had I been stronger, I wouldn't have to be searching for him here.

I vowed not to make that mistake again.

On and on I walked, until the sun was so hot beating down on me, I thought my own skin would peel like the corpses I met. The hot wind cut across my skin, searing me, forging me into something stronger than I'd ever been before. With each step, the rip in my soul grew a little wider, a little deeper. A little more impossible to ever be mended.

I walked all the way to the Quarter, following that road of death, all the while followed by the sightless eyes of the damned.

SEVENTEEN

I heard somebody calling out, but the voice came from so far away I thought it was the wind itself calling to me. But the wind doesn't tear at your hands with claws. It doesn't tug at you and shake you.

"Let go of that now," another voice said. "Give it here," it commanded.

Suddenly, the sharp bite of something like vinegar burned through the stink in my nostrils, cutting through the vision. My chest ached, but when I took a shaking breath, all I could manage was a keening moan that sounded like it came from something more animal than human. Grief tore me in two and pinned my halves to different corners of the lonely world.

"They killed them," I sobbed. Because even though I knew I was back in the safety of Mama Legba's rooms, the memory of those sightless eyes, like empty holes, was still burned into my vision. My nose was still filled with the sticky smell of flesh rotting in the sun.

"Chloe-girl," Mama Legba said, her voice sharp as her hands held my arms steady. "Come on, child. You need to come on back to us."

Slowly, the room swam back into focus and eventually I had enough hold on myself to realize that everyone was close by, watching me with wary eyes. All around me, the room was in shambles.

"What happened?" I asked, blinking up at them through my tears.

"That's what you need to be telling us," Mama Legba said.

My skin felt feverish as I looked at the crumbled bits of paper that used to be the clipping. They'd destroyed it trying to get it away from me. The rest of the scraps from the box were scattered on the floor around the table.

"You said, 'they killed them,'" Lucy said gently. "Who killed who?"

"I don't know," I told her. And then I explained the heads on pikes that lined the River Road. I told them all about what I'd seen, and I told about the hate that had burned in me during the vision. But I didn't tell them that the hate still warmed some part of me, searing deep down like a fire banked by the memory of what I'd seen.

Mama Legba frowned. "Could be one of the rebellions that flared up 'round these parts way back when."

"There were human heads staked like scarecrows all along the River Road, all the way from the plantations to the Place d'Armes in the Quarter," I said, bile rising in my throat at the memory of the vision. "I don't remember learning anything like that."

Mama Legba's mouth turned down. "That wouldn't

exactly be a welcome tale in schools anywhere, but especially not 'round these parts, now would it?"

"But you didn't get anything else about Thisbe and Roman?" Lucy asked.

"No. But if it was only 1811, maybe that was too early for Thisbe to have known him? Let me try again," I said, reaching for another scrap.

Mama Legba caught my hand before I could grab it. "Wait a minute, child. That wasn't just a vision you had there."

"She's right, Chloe," Lucy said. "The first time, I barely noticed anything had happened to you until it was over, but this time when you touched that clipping..." She hesitated. Finally, looking almost embarrassed, she glanced away. "It was different this time."

"It felt like a storm was blowing through," Odane said, his voice tight and his eyes curious and assessing. "The second you touched that bit of paper, it was like you weren't even in there anymore. Then, a moment later, a wind kicked up that didn't stop until we ripped it out of your hand."

"There's something more than visions happening," Mama Legba said with a frown, "and I don't think we should play with it anymore until we know how much more."

"What about the dreams?" I asked. "If these visions are connected to Thisbe, the dreams I've been having probably are, too."

"You're having dreams, too?" Odane asked, his expression unreadable.

I gave him a tight nod and briefly explained what I'd seen in my dreams, then turned to Mama Legba. "If you help me dreamwalk, like you helped Lucy, maybe I could find out what

Thisbe was doing back then, maybe find out what it has to do with what's going on now?"

Mama Legba studied me for a second, but then her mouth screwed up and she shook her head. "It might could be, child, but that maybe ain't enough for us to take that risk."

"But you did it for Lucy—"

"You saw what happened to Lucy last time, and she knew more about her dreams than you do," she said, stopping my argument. "When she came to me, she'd already been able to control parts of her dreaming. What you told me don't sound like you have no control at all."

"But—"

"No." Her voice was more forceful now. "Lucy was dreaming of her own past. But you're saying you dreaming of Thisbe's past? That still just don't seem likely to me, or at least it don't sound natural." Mama Legba frowned. "Dreams maybe tell us our own lives, but we can't get into someone else's without some sort of violation. *If* these is even dreams about her actual life, to try breaking into them means breaking through into part of Thisbe. Our souls is meant to be our own, and it would take a darker magic than I know to do what you're asking. I don't want no part in that kind of magic," she said.

"But we both know someone who wouldn't mind working that sort of magic," Odane said thoughtfully.

"Don't even start," Mama Legba said, pointing a finger at him threateningly.

He shrugged. "I'm just saying... You and I both know Ikenna could help with this. He knows more about darkness like this than anyone around. He might even be able to help keep her safe if she wants to see what all this is really about."

"There ain't no safe with him," Mama Legba snapped. "And there's no way I'm letting Chloe go messing around with dreaming or these visions, not till we know for sure what's causing them.

"So that's it?" I asked, my stomach twisting. "You're giving up and shutting me out of this, too?"

Mama Legba pursed her lips. "It isn't about shutting you out," she said. "It's about taking our time and making sure we don't misstep. There's too many parts to this to go jumping in feet-first without looking where we jumping. That wind you called up wasn't like nothing I've ever seen before, child. It was stronger than most people can conjure when they trying, and you weren't even trying." She paused, frowning when she met my eyes. "At least let me think on it before we do anything else."

"We don't have time for you to think," I snapped. I knew it was only temper that had me lashing out, but after all that had happened that morning, I couldn't seem to stop myself.

"I'd rather take the time than rush in and lose you to this," Mama Legba told me.

I stood up and turned to Lucy. "You ready to go?"

She studied me with a frown for a moment before she agreed.

"Now don't rush off in a huff," Mama Legba said.

"I'm not in a huff," I lied. "I just need to go. I want to try to call Piers again before it gets too late, and—"

Mama Legba touched my arm. "Wait a minute, child." She stood and made her way back to the front of the shop. When she came back, the deck of tarot cards was in her hand. She drew one card from the top and then set the rest aside before coming over to me. Taking me by the wrist, she turned my hand palm up and slid the card into it.

The hanged man.

"You can't hold so tight, child. Knowledge and power can't be forced. It's only going to come when you let go."

I tried to hand the card back to her, but she wouldn't take it.

"I can do this," I told her, one last plea. "Please. Let me try again."

"Can and should are different things," Mama Legba said.

But that wasn't how it felt to me. Can and should felt exactly the same. "So we're going to ignore what's right in front of us?"

"Chloe," Mama Legba said gently. "That bit of magic you called up wasn't anything good. If Odane hadn't pulled that scrap out of your hand when he did, I don't have any doubt you'd have pulled this whole place down on our heads, and that wouldn't have helped anybody at all. We can try again, but not right now. I need to build up the protections and figure out a way to keep you safe if you gonna be purposely giving yourself over to something like these visions again."

I shook my head, tired of arguing. "Let's go, Luce."

"Chloe-girl," Mama Legba pleaded.

"I get it," I said before turning to Lucy. "You coming?"

She frowned and glanced at Mama Legba, but then she stood to come with me.

"Where are you parked?" Odane asked. "I'll walk you out."

"I don't need you—"

"Never said you did," he said pleasantly, "but I can't let

the chance to be with a couple pretty girls pass me by." He gave me a too-charming smile that could've melted the Ice Queen herself. But it didn't melt me. Not much, anyway.

He walked next to me, his hands deep in his pockets, without saying a word, but there was something expectant about his body language. Like he was waiting for something. Lucy followed silently behind us, like she was still making up her mind about who was right and whose side to take.

Finally, we reached my car, and he kind of hung himself over the door when I slid in. I tucked the card Mama Legba had given me into the overhead visor, because it didn't seem right to throw it away. She'd want it back eventually.

Something about the way Odane looked at me made me feel uncomfortable, like he already knew everything there was to know about me and was still making up his mind about it.

"My aunt is wrong about this," he said, looking down at me. "I know she's trying to protect you, but that's only because she's scared for you and that's clouding her judgment. If this Thisbe is really going to summon Samedi, we don't have time for people to sit around and wait."

I didn't say anything at first. He was voicing everything I felt in my heart, but it seemed too much like a betrayal to speak against Mama Legba.

"I meant what I told Aunt Odette back there," he said. "My father probably could help with all this if you want him to."

"Mama Legba doesn't seem to trust him," I said, remembering the conversation at Odeana's house and thinking of the almost visceral reaction Mama Legba had when Odane said his name.

"She doesn't," Odane agreed.

"And you think I should?"

Odane shrugged. "My aunt has her reasons. See, she basically controls the market on Voodoo in the Quarter. My father—at least in the biological sense—kind of runs things on the other side of the river, over in Algiers." His dark eyes met mine. "He'd do just about anything—and has—to get a foothold on this side, which is why Auntie O doesn't want anything to do with him."

"So, what, it's like some sort of turf war?" Lucy asked, peering across the car at Odane.

He didn't smile. "Something like that."

"No, thanks," I told him, because the way he looked at me told me there was more he wasn't saying. A lot more. I reached for my door, and he was forced to back off.

When I rolled down my window to let out the heat that had built up inside, Odane leaned down and rested his arms in the open space. "I don't know about this Thisbe person y'all are worried about, but I know enough about Baron Samedi to not want him anywhere around my part of the world. If you want it, you've got my help on this. Think about it," he said, his face only a couple of inches from mine.

He smelled nice, I realized, like some sort of woodsy, clean scent with the hint of something darker, like incense.

I mentally shook myself—I didn't have any reason to be smelling some boy, no matter how he might have looked at me like we were at the beginning of something. "Nothing to think about," I said, starting up the car. I gave the engine a little gas, just because I could, and when the Nova roared, I was glad I didn't have one of those eco-friendly cars.

But Odane didn't back up. His mouth lifted a little, like he was amused, but then the smile fell flat. "I'm not asking you to decide right this minute." He looked so damn sincere that I almost thought about it. Almost. "But whenever you decide, I'm willing to help."

"Or maybe you're willing to help your dad," I said, watching him for some sign that he was playing me.

He shook his head. "I'd be doing it for you, not for him." Something about the way his voice went all gravelly made me think he was telling the truth. Still . . .

"I'm not standing against Mama Legba. I wouldn't do that to her."

"Even though she doesn't trust you?"

I didn't have an answer for that, so I gave him the sweetest smile I could and leaned my head closer, like I wanted to tell him a secret. He leaned in, like he wanted me to.

"Unless you want to lose that big, strong arm of yours, I'd suggest you get it off my car."

His mouth did pull up into a grin then, and damn if it wasn't like a kick to my stomach. So I did what any self-respecting girl would do. I pulled away without saying another word.

EIGHTEEN

Odane's words had me so unsettled as I pulled into the traffic of Canal Street, I mis-shifted. The clutch ground out its displeasure, and angry with myself, at Mama Legba for not trusting me, and for my mother for being what she was, I slammed the car into a higher gear and shot off.

I knew Mama Legba had a point. We didn't know anything about these visions, and with the other things that had happened—the icy fingers trying to strangle me, the way something had messed with Lucy when she tried to dreamwalk at Mama Legba's, and the wind that had scattered the contents of Thisbe's box all over the floor—I knew there was a good chance that there was something more to what I was seeing. But we were running out of time.

"I need to look at the other things in that box," I said, my voice tight with impatience.

"Good luck with that," Lucy said. "Mama Legba isn't

going to let you anywhere near that box again." To my surprise, she sounded as frustrated about it as I felt.

"You don't sound like you agree with her," I said carefully, glancing to see her reaction.

Lucy frowned. "It's not that I don't think she and Piers are right to be worried about Thisbe. I probably know better than anyone how dangerous she is. I mean, I have some very vivid memories of her killing Armantine to get what she wanted, and I don't doubt she'd do it again..."

"But?" I asked, prodding her to go on when she stopped.

"But, I think you understand that, too," she told me. "I think you've probably lost more than any of us, and you still have the most to lose in all of this."

I knew just how much she'd lost, so I couldn't quite speak through my surprise at her statement.

"I lost Alex," she continued, "and that about killed me, but I have to believe that I didn't lose him for good. I know that whatever happens in this life, he wants me to be happy and that eventually we'll meet again. But, Chloe, you didn't just lose your mom; you lost who you thought she was."

I tightened my grip on the steering wheel, but I couldn't speak through the tightness in my throat. Because Lucy had nailed it. She understood.

"I can't even begin to understand what you're going through, but I think that you wanting to stop Thisbe makes you stronger than any of us. Mama Legba and Piers are worried about you because they saw firsthand what Thisbe did to you. I saw it too, but I think something has happened to you since then. I watched them cut off your hair, and I don't think I could have been that brave or selfless. Not without a lot of convincing and maybe someone to hold me down.

"And I see the determination in your eyes when we talk about finding Thisbe and stopping her. You aren't the person you were before all this happened, and I'm willing to bet on you being the one that comes out on top."

I let out a long, shaking breath. I'd been frustrated, sure enough, but I don't think I'd *really* realized what it meant to not have Piers believe in me until Lucy handed me her trust like a gift, whole and unsolicited.

"Thank you," I whispered, because it was all I could say.

"Don't thank me," Lucy told me. "Prove me right."

There was a tone in her voice that had me glancing over at her. "What do you mean?"

"I'm saying that I can't have lost Alex for nothing. I need to see Thisbe stopped for his sake as much as my own."

I waited, knowing there was more to what she was getting at, but Lucy seemed to be wrestling with something internally. Finally, she took a determined breath. "I think it's time you saw Thisbe's tomb."

St. Louis Number Two has crypts that date back to the early 1800s. Like most cemeteries in New Orleans, it's usually filled with groups of tourists during the day, but it closes well before dark. After that, it's not really safe to go wandering around, because the dangers it's filled with have nothing to do with the dead.

Even during the day, the city's cemeteries are about my

least favorite place to be. Once you get inside their heavy walls, the tombs rise up on all sides and it feels like they might topple over on you at any moment. The narrow pathways are often uneven, and there's usually a sort of hush that falls over the whole place, like everybody's afraid of waking whatever might sleep there.

Lucy had her arms wrapped around herself as she shuffled through the alleyways, trying to remember which route would lead us to the tomb where Thisbe had kept Alex. But as we rounded a corner, I knew which one it was before she even pointed it out. Where every other tomb in the cemetery was worn from the years of rain and wind and coated with a century's worth of dirt and grime, the tomb at the end of the last row we'd turned down was a brilliant white. It was covered in carved symbols that hadn't been touched by time, and it didn't even have the dark waterline that the others had to mark where Katrina had invaded.

"Is that it?" I said, knowing her answer even before she gave me a silent nod of her head.

The tomb wasn't any bigger than the monuments around it, but its thick columns made it seem fancier than the dull, aged marble of its neighbors. Rather than having the flat roofline of most crypts, this particular tomb was topped with an obelisk.

I took a step toward it, but Lucy made a sort of mewing sound that had me hesitating. "What? I thought you wanted me to do this."

"I did ... I mean, I *do*. We have to figure out what Thisbe's up to, but I saw what happened when you touched that news clipping. I'm just a little nervous about what might happen this time."

"You want to go wait in the car?"

She frowned for a second, like she was considering it, but then she finally shook her head. "No. If you go all glassy-eyed and start calling up a hurricane, somebody's going to have to stop you."

I couldn't stop the huff of laughter that escaped when I pictured skinny Lucy trying to hold back a hurricane. "Okay then," I said, grateful that she was still willing to stand behind me.

Slowly, I approached the tomb with my hand stretched out in front of me. I hesitated only for a moment before pressing my palms to the marble. It was warm from the heat of the day, and the moment my skin brushed against it, the sun went dark.

My skirts brushed against my legs as I pushed the heavy stone from the door and stepped into the coolness of the tomb's interior. The beam from the flashlight in my hand swept across the surface of the walls, revealing the charms that I'd carved bit by bit over the years.

A lifetime before.

I let the flashlight glide over the walls and felt pride and satisfaction heat my blood. I'd built this monument years ago for Augustine, and since then, I'd inscribed it with every bit of magic I'd come across in my travels. Every charm I'd learned and every spell I'd ever collected to summon the one I loved and keep what belonged to me safe were on these walls. At some point, it stopped being just for him and became a testament to my own power, my own life.

I traced one of the markings on the wall near me, a symbol that I'd learned in some tropical jungle years ago meant to ward off energies that mean a body harm. Another right above my head was a rune for resurrection that a powerful sorcerer in Egypt had taught me. He'd spent a whole afternoon showing me the order I was supposed to trace those lines, because he thought it would get me into his bed. And because he didn't believe I could ever use the power.

Men always thought they had the power, but most were all the same. All it took was a slow, inviting smile and they were yours. I never did get into his bed, and he never got out of it— not once I was done with him.

But the rune hadn't been strong enough. Augustine never came.

Finally, I let the beam of the flashlight fall on an altar-like table against the far wall. After all these years, the French boy's body was still there, still barely breathing.

I approached him with a sort of reverence for the sacrifice the boy had made. Not that he had a choice. That girl—what had her name been?

It didn't matter. That girl had sealed this boy's fate the minute she'd walked through my door and handed him over all in the name of love.

Setting the flashlight on his chest, I aimed the beam of light so I could focus on what needed done. Then I took out my knife and unfastened the locket from around my neck. I let my mouth form the words I'd said so many times before as I sliced into the skin near his shoulder, watching the blood well.

The dark liquid seeping slowly from the wound was barely

enough to coat the locket, and when I placed it around my neck, I could hardly feel the warmth of the power it contained.

Ignoring the shiver of worry that passed through me, I dipped two fingers into the blood pooling around the wound and called on the energy within it as I traced over the lines of my face. But the flash of heat I usually felt when the spirit responded was barely a kiss of warmth, and I knew that the connection the boy gave me to the source of all life and power wasn't working as it once had.

Even though I could feel the power in his blood transforming me, taking back the years that had gone by since last I'd visited him, I knew it wouldn't last for long. Not like it once had, when the energy I took from him could push back decades and hold off the years.

I should have seen this coming.

Panic raced through me, and I pressed my hands to the chest beneath the red string. Waiting for the slow rise and fall. Willing him to keep breathing still.

Until I could find another way.

I didn't know how much more time he had left to give me, and I didn't know how much longer I could wait in this skin.

Augustine hadn't come back yet, and I knew that he would have if he could have by now. Something was stopping him, or rather, someone.

Roman. I'd killed him three times already, and still he'd come back. That couldn't be a coincidence, and no single soul could have that much luck. There had to be a connection between him reappearing and Augustine's absence, but in all those lifetimes I still hadn't figured out what it was.

And now I was running out of time.

I'd figure it out, though. I would find a way to live a bit longer, to find Augustine. To make sure Roman was destroyed once and for all.

It was early afternoon by the time we got out of the cemetery and made our way back to Le Ciel. I gripped the steering wheel so Lucy wouldn't see how my hands were still trembling. I hadn't called up a hurricane or anything, but my muscles were achy and sore, like I'd just run for miles. Seeing Thisbe's life through her eyes was unsettling enough, but this time seeing her thoughts and feeling the desperation she felt to survive and the fury she felt when she thought of Roman had left me shaken and unstable. It reminded me too much of that part of myself that stretched and purred anytime I brushed against any sort of power.

"It was definitely more recent than the others—I was holding a flashlight—but I got the sense that what I was seeing still happened a while ago. She was starting to worry that the power she was taking from Alex was getting weaker, and she was scared. She knew she needed another plan, because she was convinced that Roman was connected to Augustine's disappearance somehow."

"So it's not all about Augustine?"

I glanced over at her. "No, it's definitely about Augustine, but I think maybe there's more going on than we first thought."

Lucy was silent for a long moment, like she was thinking

things through. "Does that mean Roman could come back again?"

"Thisbe thought it was possible."

"Could he *already* have come back?" Lucy asked nervously.

"I don't know. It might be why my momma got the job at Le Ciel, though. Maybe she was waiting for him to turn up again?"

I took the off-ramp that led away from the highway and out toward the plantation. Lucy was quiet on the other side of the car.

After a few minutes, Lucy turned to me. "But if Thisbe's trying to get back at Roman, and Roman keeps coming back somehow, why would she need this Baron Samedi guy?"

I frowned, trying to think it through. "Maybe she wants something else from him?'"

"Like what?" Lucy said, letting out an overwhelmed-sounding sigh.

"Maybe she wants him to take Roman and keep him on the other side of the divide for good. Maybe she just wants Samedi to help her get Augustine. It's hard to know why anyone would want to summon him. But we have a lead, right? We can start with this Augustine. If we can find out exactly what happened to him, maybe we'll understand more."

"Right. I guess we can start by looking at those plantation registers."

"Byron is going to hate that," I said, thinking of how pissy he'd been when we talked to him the day before.

Lucy shrugged. "I'll bring him some coffee. He'll get over it."

NINETEEN

We were almost back to Le Ciel when I finally gathered enough courage to say what I'd been thinking about ever since I walked out of Mama Legba's shop. "I don't think I should stay with your folks anymore."

"What?" Lucy asked, turning to me in surprise. "Why not?"

"I'm not stupid enough to ignore what Mama Legba said. There's a good chance that Thisbe has more of a link to me than we thought. I could still be dangerous, Lucy." And there was one other thing I couldn't quite make myself say out loud—if Thisbe had worried about her old skin not being enough, maybe she would be looking for a new skin. She'd already tried mine on for size once, and I wasn't sure anything would stop her from doing it again.

I could feel Lucy staring at me, but I wasn't brave enough to take my eyes off the road and see what she was thinking.

After a long minute, she reached out and touched my

shoulder. Her voice was steady and full of conviction when she finally spoke. "I don't believe that, Chloe. I think if Thisbe wanted to use you to get to me or my family, she would have by now."

"Lucy, you saw what happened in Mama Legba's shop. That's not the first time I've felt like I rustled up some sort of power, and I didn't have any control over whatever was happening. And what about what happened the other day to you, when you tried to dreamwalk?" I pressed. "You're saying that wasn't something to worry about?"

"I don't know," Lucy admitted weakly, and I knew she could see my point. "Where would you even go?"

"I could move back into Piers's place," I told her, shrugging off the unease I felt when I thought about letting myself into his apartment after the way he'd sounded on the phone. I wasn't sure how he'd react to coming home and finding me there.

"You can't stay there alone!" Lucy huffed. "What if that's what Thisbe wants? Maybe these visions are her way of pushing you away from the people who want to protect you and help you?"

"He'll be back in a couple of days," I said.

"No way," Lucy told me, crossing her arms. "If you want to move into his place once he's back, fine, but until then you're staying with someone. If you don't want to stay with me, move in with Mama Legba."

But that was the last thing I wanted to do.

When we finally began to approach the heavy gates that welcomed visitors to Le Ciel, I realized something was wrong. The road, usually empty except for an occasional tour bus or car, was littered with vehicles—police cars with their lights flashing and news vans with their doors open. People buzzed around like carrion birds looking for dinner.

I shifted uncomfortably in my seat as I pulled up slowly to the place where an unmarked car blocked the drive. Like a good responsible driver, I stopped to wait for clearance to pass.

"What do you think's going on?" Lucy asked as she leaned forward, as though getting closer to the windshield would help her see.

"I don't know," I said.

The thickset deputy who was blocking the main gate motioned for me to pull over. Leading with his stomach and taking his good old time about it, the deputy swaggered over to my car. Mirrored lenses covered his eyes when he leaned down and rested his elbow on my open window. My stomach went tight, but I made sure to keep my hands on the steering wheel—right where he could see them.

"Sorry, folks. Grounds are closed today. You're going to have to turn around and head home."

"I live here," Lucy said, leaning over to speak across me.

His caterpillar eyebrows raised above the mirrored lenses. "That so?" He turned to me. "What about you?"

"She's staying with us right now," Lucy said, before I could even answer.

With those mirrored glasses, I couldn't tell what he was looking at—me, the interior of the car, or something else. He didn't seem to be in any hurry to talk. "I'm going to need to you to step out of the car."

"What?" Lucy asked, clearly confused.

"Out of the car, please. Both of you." He stepped back to let me out. "Turn it off, first, and put the keys on the hood."

By now, my hands were shaking, but I did what he asked and got out, slowly and carefully. Lucy met my eyes over the roof of the car, and I could tell she was just as uneasy as I was. Maybe more so. She'd probably never been through a traffic stop like this.

"Stand over there," he drawled without so much as a "please."

Lucy looked like she wanted to argue, but I snagged her arm and pulled her over to the spot where he'd pointed. The last thing I needed was her getting us arrested. We watched in silence as the officer went around the car, opening the doors and using my keys to open the trunk. After tossing my purse out onto the road, he bent down to look under the seats and then wedged himself into the car to examine the cluttered glove compartment. Finally, apparently satisfied that I wasn't hiding anything—or maybe not satisfied at all—he grabbed a clipboard from his car and came over to where I was standing. He didn't give me back my keys.

He looked at me. "Name?"

"Chloe Sabourin."

"Address?"

I gave him the number to my own house and said a silent prayer to any well-meaning spirits who might have been listening that he didn't go check it out. Somehow I didn't think the dead rooster and piles of beetles would go over well.

"Your name?" he asked Lucy, and she gave it to him. "You got some ID on you?" he asked us.

"In my bag," I said while Lucy fished hers out of her pocket.

He sauntered back over, grabbed my bag from where he'd tossed it, and pawed through it with his sausage-like fingers. When a tampon fell out, he didn't bother to pick it up. Finally, he located my ID and came back over to me.

"You say she's staying here?" he asked Lucy. Again with the brows and the scowling.

"Yeah. She's staying with my family while her mom is out of town," Lucy told him, peering over his shoulder like she was trying to see something, anything, in the distance. But the house was still a ways off, and trees blocked our view. "Can you tell me what's going on? My family should be back there."

The officer looked up from what he was writing, and this time he slid his glasses down his nose a bit so I could see his eyes. Ice blue and without a hint of warmth. But he never answered her question.

After a few minutes of writing down my information and calling it in to the station, he handed me back my ID.

"So can we go?" Lucy glanced past him again, to the house.

"I'll get you an escort to your house," the officer said.

Relief washed over her features

"But your friend here's going to have to wait until the unit's done with the scene."

"The scene?" My knees went weak as overcooked noodles.

"What scene?" Lucy asked.

"Not at liberty to say," he told us, motioning for another deputy to come over. "Take this young lady home." Then to me, "You'll need to be behind the yellow line with the rest of them until everything's sorted out."

"Miss? If you're ready?" the second deputy said.

"But—" Lucy started, but when the deputy's brows went up again, it was enough of a warning for me to speak up.

"It's okay, Luce. I'll wait here." She still looked like she wanted to argue, but I shook my head. "Go find out what's happening. I'll be fine," I said, trying not to let her see how upset I was.

"You're going to need to move that," the officer grunted, gesturing toward my Nova. "Can't have you blocking the road."

As Lucy walked up the long drive, looking back like she wasn't sure she should leave me, I did what he asked and moved the car out of the drive and off to the side of the road with the news vans. The second I parked and cut the engine again, one of the plastic-haired reporters came over and leaned down into the window. He was young—not all that much older than me—and he was basically vibrating with eagerness.

"Could I ask you a few questions?"

I looked up at him. I'd never seen anybody with teeth that straight and white in real life. "I don't know any answers," I said, resting my forehead on the steering wheel and trying to remember how to breathe.

Apparently, my abruptness didn't dissuade him. "Did the police give any details about the victim?"

"Victim?" I lifted my head, my heart in my throat. I'd been trying to hope that the scene had something to do with vandalism, maybe.

The news guy looked disappointed. "Did the police mention anything at all?"

"Who's the victim?" I said, ignoring his question.

He frowned. "Maybe he mentioned where the body was found?"

"What body?" I was getting angry now. Or rather, terrified, but it came out like angry.

"The rumor is that a body was found in the mansion. Can you confirm that?"

"I can't even get back there. How could I confirm anything?"

The fake smile fell from the guy's face. "Well, if you hear anything…" He handed me a card that I tossed on the floor of the car the second he walked away.

Another body. Another murder. I had to let Mama Legba know. I reached for my bag and dug around for my phone, but … nothing. I swore I'd grabbed it on the way out the door that morning, but after digging for a few minutes, I came up empty.

I could always drive back to the city to tell her, but it was a good twenty minutes each way. If I left, I might miss my chance to make sure that Lucy and her family were safe.

Pounding my fists against the worn steering wheel, I let out a string of curses. Usually that would've been enough to make me feel better, but this time it didn't. Not when I was stuck on the outside of everything, again. Not when I didn't know if my friend's family was hurt, or worse. Not when the thing blocking my path was a fat-ass policeman who looked at me like I wasn't worth his time.

I was stuck, alone. And all I could do was wait.

TWENTY

The afternoon had grown thick and sultry by the time a silent ambulance made its way out of the gate. The news vans weren't giving up, though. Not with the yellow police tape still up, blocking the entrance to the property, and Officer Eyebrows still standing guard. Eventually, I slid into the backseat, where the sun wasn't hitting. The old, cracked vinyl was stiff and sticky against my skin, but I was too nervous, wiped out, and just plain scared to care.

I closed my eyes and tried to think of something besides the heat beating down on me or the fear that was twisting my insides into knots, but the only thing I could seem to think about was the coolness of that pine grove from my dreams. The empty darkness of the night, the silence of the stars, and the girl with cheekbones that could cut and a mouth that reminded me of my mother's.

And then, the heat of the day was gone. The constant chatter of the reporters in their vans dwindled until it was nothing but a far-off murmur, and then silence. All at once, I was no longer just imagining the grove of trees—I was there.

So was the girl.

She was a little older than the last time I'd seen her, closer now to my own age. She sat alone, her back against the base of a thick tree, her arms wrapped around her knees, like she was protecting herself from the night. Her mouth was moving, but I couldn't hear what she was saying. Maybe she was talking to herself, but from the way she rocked, maybe she was singing.

After a while, the girl looked up, found the moon high in the sky, and frowned. Her eyes tracked the darkness, searching. She looked right through me, like she didn't see me. She must not have seen what she'd been looking for either, because a moment later, she stood, brushing the pine needles from her skirts as she gathered her things, and started walking. She never looked back.

I didn't hesitate to follow her.

On and on we walked, the girl a little ways ahead of me, picking her way between the trees confidently, even though the night was dark and thick, like she knew exactly where she was going. She didn't stumble once, which is more than I could say for myself.

This time wasn't like before, when I had run and run and never got past the same bit of wooded land. This time, the trees eventually grew farther apart, and with each step we took, the pines gave way and moonlight began to find its way to us, lighting up the land so I didn't have to stumble through the darkness as much.

Eventually, we found the end of the grove of pines and stepped out into a clearing lit up by a heavy moon and a canopy of stars so thick I'd never seen the like. There, I could make out the features of the land—the broad expanse of a field thick with cane. The shadow of some low building off in the distance with lights flickering in its open windows. I looked back once, but the grove of pines I'd just escaped looked so much like a dark, empty mouth that I didn't look back again.

The girl walked on, rubbing her arms like she was trying to warm them with her hands now and then, but mostly she walked with the determined gait of someone who had somewhere to be. In the distance ahead, strange shadowy shapes rose from the land, but we were too far away to make out what they were. As we got closer to them, I understood at once what I was seeing—two straight lines of sturdy-looking trees formed an alley of sorts, leading out into darkness. On the other side, I knew, would be the river. On this side, where we were walking, should have been Le Ciel.

But there was no house.

My steps slowed so much as we neared the property that I almost lost track of the girl. She continued walking, on and on, but I came to a stop. Those giant live oaks that dripped with Spanish moss and made tourists trek from the Quarter just for a picture in their shade looked exactly the same. There was no mistaking where we were—there's nowhere else in all of the delta region with trees planted in just that way—purposefully, like someone wanted them to lead up to the river. But the mansion wasn't there yet. So *when* were we?

The girl was far ahead now, and if I hesitated any longer I was going to lose her. I wanted to know where she was going, so I left the comforting—and unsettling—familiarity of the oaks behind and ran to catch up.

On she walked, past the place where the big house would someday stand. Past a row of small shacks dotting the dark horizon—probably slave quarters for the plantation that would someday become Le Ciel Doux. The original slave quarters hadn't made it through the years when it was unfashionable to have any reminders of the less-than-pristine parts of the area's history sitting around. But they were here now, in whatever time this was.

The girl didn't turn toward them, though, and she didn't stop walking. She went past the area that would one day hold a small, picturesque pond, through another line of trees, and to the clearing that held Thisbe's cabin.

Her steps slowed as she approached it, and when I looked beyond her to the shaded porch of the ghostly white structure, I realized it was because someone was waiting for her—a shadowy figure who held a narrow cigar between his teeth. Its tip flickered a deeper orange as he took a long drag on it.

I couldn't feel anything—not the cool of the air or the breeze rustling the trees—but I could feel the frustration and anger radiating off the girl when she saw the man on her porch. She squared her shoulders and took the last few steps toward the cabin, toward *her* cabin. The man sitting on the porch didn't so much as stand to acknowledge her arrival, but as we got closer, I realized he was younger than I'd expected. But there was something familiar about him.

It took me a second to place him, but when his mouth turned down at something the girl said, it clicked into place. *Roman.*

Once I recognized him, there was no way not to see the Roman Dutilette I was familiar with in the man's features. But he was younger here than he was in that daguerreotype Dr. Aimes had showed us. Younger than in any of the portraits that hung on the walls in the big house. His hooded eyes seemed to look right through the girl, like he didn't believe she was worth seeing, and his smile was more a sneer than anything else.

The girl was clearly agitated. I couldn't hear a thing she was saying, but from the way she held her body, she was strung tight. Angry.

Roman listened with disinterest to whatever it was the girl told him, blowing streams of smoke from his thin mouth. When she was finished, her hand pointing toward the land we'd walked through as though to direct him on his way, he threw his head back and laughed. Then he got up from the porch and stepped up to her, his eyes cold, his skin dusky in the moonlight. He was still sneering, his light eyes glinting with expectation as he reached for her, brushed her cheek with his hand.

She jerked her head away, a look of disgust and hate filling her eyes, but he took her by the arm with one hand and, flicking his still-lit cigar aside, roughly grabbed her chin with the other, forcing her to look at him. She struggled but couldn't free herself.

I moved closer, wanting to help her get away from him.

But my hand passed clean through them both, like I was nothing more than a ghost. There was nothing I could do. Not as he pulled her against him. Not as he forced his cruel mouth against hers.

He kissed her long and hard and without any affection

at all, his hands groping her roughly as she struggled against him, and when we was done, he sneered at her again.

Then he looked up at me, a mocking smile wiped across his mouth, and said my name.

TWENTY-ONE

"Chloe?"

Someone was shaking me, and my only thought was panic. I had to run, to get away from Roman's cold eyes and cruel hands, so I lashed out wildly.

"Chloe!" The voice pitched higher. That's when I realized I knew the voice—it wasn't Roman who was saying my name.

"Lucy?" Pulling myself slowly off the sticky vinyl of the seat, I sat up, my head still muddled from the last bits of the dream. Lucy was standing over me, her skinny body silhouetted against the softening sun. It was late—almost evening.

She backed up to allow me to scoot out of the car, and I took my time stretching out my sore neck and back and focusing on breathing, on letting the rest of the dream wisp away in the warmth of the day. That's when I remembered why I'd been waiting in the car.

There was one news van still hanging around on the

road, but the rest had left, apparently. The cop with the too-big gut and mirrored glasses was gone as well.

"I'm sorry it took so long," she said.

My mouth felt like I'd been chewing on a cotton ball. "Did you find out what happened?"

Lucy didn't look so good. Her freckles stood out more than usual against her pale skin. "They're not sure what happened…"

"Some reporter said there was a body."

She closed her eyes, like she was willing herself to be somewhere else, to see something else. "It was Byron."

My mouth fell open. "Someone killed Byron?"

"It's bad, Chloe. They found him at the foot of the stairs in the main hall of the mansion. His neck was broken, and they think he was pushed down them."

"How do they know he didn't just trip?"

Lucy grimaced. "Remember the daguerreotype of Roman and Josephine they found the other day?"

I nodded.

"Those are actually printed on glass. Someone smashed it and used one of the bigger shards to stab Byron. Before he fell. There was blood all the way down the steps."

But Lucy was so pale and her expression so distant that I knew there was more.

"What else?" I asked.

"They arrested him," she whispered. Her eyes were glassy with tears when she looked up at me. "Someone told the police that my dad and Byron had been fighting over Piers taking the charm to Nashville. I guess it was pretty bad, and since my dad was the one to find Byron…" She took a deep breath. "The police took him downtown in handcuffs a few minutes ago. My mom's frantic. She's on the phone with my uncle, who's a lawyer in Chicago, and they're trying to figure stuff out, but..." Her voice broke.

"Oh my god, Lucy." I wrapped her in a hug. She kind of slumped in my arms.

"He didn't do it," she said. "He *couldn't* have done it."

"I know he didn't," I told her, looking over her shoulder to the mansion in the distance. "They'll figure this out and he'll be back here in no time."

She pulled away from me. "It has to be Thisbe," she said. "It has to be related."

I didn't disagree, but I'd seen how Dr. Aimes had lashed out at Byron before and I wasn't so sure *how* it was related.

"He didn't do it," she said again, her voice hollow and breaking. But it sounded like she was doing all she could to convince herself.

That night, Mrs. Aimes left T.J. with us so she could go downtown and try to figure out was happening with Dr. Aimes. I don't think anyone slept much waiting for them to get back. When I did manage to drift off, I'd dream of the shadowy figure on the porch who had been waiting for the girl. Usually, it was Roman's face I saw there, but other times it was Byron's. And once, it was Dr. Aimes who looked back at me with cruel eyes.

TWENTY-TWO

By the time we woke, Dr. Aimes was back at home, looking shaken and unsettled. Not that I could blame him. Finding a body and then being accused of the murder would make anyone look like that. Still, there was something in the way he held himself all closed off and quiet that made me uneasy.

Before breakfast was even over, though, a knock at the door shook everyone up again.

Dr. Aimes answered it, and his voice carried into the kitchen where we were sitting: "I already answered all of the questions I'm going to. You can talk to my lawyer..."

Lucy glanced at me and we both got up to go see what was happening. When we came into the front parlor, Dr. Aimes was still standing at the door, as though barring it from the two police that were standing on the porch.

"We're not here for that, sir," a plain-clothes detective said. "We found some things in an abandoned vehicle that we believe belong to you." The male officer held up a clear bag. "May we come in?"

"I don't understand," Dr. Aimes said, taking the bag.

"The vehicle was found outside of Picayune," the female officer told him.

Dr. Aimes took the items out of the bag—a torn envelope clearly labeled with the university's logo, and a cube of sea-green-colored foam that was also ripped in half—and examined them. "These are . . ." His voice trailed off.

"You recognize them?" the detective asked, his face not giving away any emotion at all.

"I think I do, yes. Please. Come in." Dr. Aimes stepped back to let the two in as he turned the foam over in his hand. He was silent as he traced the indentation inside. "I sent an artifact to be delivered by an intern of mine. I think this is the packaging," he said, his eyes never leaving the empty foam cube. "And there was a book as well," he added, gesturing absently to the torn envelope.

"We didn't find anything in the envelope, sir," the female officer said. "Can you tell us the name of this intern?"

"Piers. Piers Dumont," Dr. Aimes answered, his voice hollow as he handed back the packaging.

"When was the last time you heard from him?" The officer asked pulled out a pad of paper and a pen.

"I sent him to Nashville on Thursday," he told them. "He's a student at Vanderbilt and was delivering some things to a colleague of mine there. He was supposed to help with a few tests and come back next week with the results."

"Why was his car in Picayune?" I interrupted, dread making my stomach feel like lead.

"Who's this?" the detective asked, looking between Dr. Aimes and me and obviously not seeing the connection.

"This is Chloe Sabourin. She's been staying with us. She's Piers Dumont's girlfriend."

"Why would his car be in Picayune?" I asked again, panic clawing at me.

"I'm sorry. We can only divulge information to family."

"His parents are out of the country for the summer. He doesn't have any family in town right now," I told them, dazed.

The officers just frowned.

"Where is he?" I asked. Vaguely, I felt Mrs. Aimes's arm go around my shoulder, and the freely offered comfort had the words dying in my throat. I looked at Lucy, and her eyes were filled with the same worry I felt choking me.

"We're still trying to piece things together," the detective told me.

"So you haven't heard from Mr. Dumont since Thursday?" the female officer asked. She exchanged another silent glance with the detective.

"I spoke to him after that," I said. "On Friday."

"Did he confirm that he'd made it to Nashville?"

"I . . ." *Had he?* I couldn't remember. The conversation had been so short, so gruff, that he didn't tell me much of anything. "I think so."

The officer looked at Dr. Aimes, dismissing my information and me. "What was the value of the artifacts?"

My stomach sank at the implication in her words. "Piers would never have stolen those," I argued.

"Chloe…" Dr. Aimes warned, his voice serious. Then he turned back to the officers. "I'm not exactly sure. With items of historical significance, often it can be hard to put an exact dollar amount on them." His voice grew darker. "But they were valuable to the historical record. To this property."

"We can help you fill out a report," the detective offered.

"What about Piers?"

The detective looked up at me and then pulled a card from his pocket. "If you hear from him, you should contact me immediately."

"You're not going to look for him? He wouldn't have done what you're suggesting. He could be in trouble some-where—hurt."

The female officer frowned. "There wasn't any sign of trouble other than the packaging we found. There's nothing to indicate that Mr. Dumont was in any distress. You're welcome to come downtown and file a missing persons report if you'd like, though."

Anger lashed through me and I felt a breeze brush against my skin, but I forced myself to tamp my anger down and not lash out. "Thank you. I will," I said.

———————

The house on Desire Street looked the same as it did a couple of days before, so I didn't understand why I was so nervous. But the longer I hesitated out on the sidewalk, the more I started to think that the whole plan was a really bad idea. I'd left Lucy behind at Le Ciel to look into the registers, but she thought I was filing a police report, not doing this.

I turned on my heels. "Stupid," I said to myself, starting back toward my parking spot a few blocks over.

"What's stupid?" called a voice from behind me.

I cursed under my breath and turned back to the house to find Odane standing at the top of his porch steps, grinning like someone who knew exactly what effect his smile had on people.

"What brings you to my side of town?" He didn't bother to come down the steps, just kept his place at the top of his porch, the king of his would-be castle.

"I . . ." *Shit.* I didn't have any good excuse for being there except the real reason—the one I'd just decided not to go through with.

His brows drew together and that always-present smile of his disappeared. The look that replaced it was a new one—a sincere one—and damn if that wasn't a thousand times more dangerous.

"What is it?" he asked as he jogged down the three steps and came out to where I was standing. "Did something happen to Aunt Odette?"

"No, Mama Legba—your aunt—she's fine."

He was right up close to me now, so close I could detect the warm, woodsy scent of him. It reminded me of the way a forest smells at night—dark and wild with the bite of pine cutting through—and the memory sent little shivers of awareness through me.

I locked those down. Hard. I didn't need any shivers of anything, especially not coming from him.

"Then what is it?" he asked, still all sincere concern.

"Nothing. I changed my mind."

He cocked one eyebrow and crossed his arms over his broad chest. "And you think I'm gonna let you get away without telling me what you changed your mind about?"

I shook my head and turned to keep walking.

"Hey," he said, his words as gentle as the hand that grabbed my arm to stop me. He turned me to him gently, but his hands were steady on my arms to keep me in place. "Really. Tell me what's up. You didn't come this far out of your way for nothing."

I pulled away, but I didn't go any farther. I'd come this far, hadn't I? He was being so nice, so concerned, that I almost did want to tell him.

"Admit it," he said after a few seconds of undecided silence from me. "You couldn't stop thinking about me. You want me."

My head whipped up before I could stop myself. "You—" But the words died in my throat when I saw the laughter in his eyes. "You're kidding." Which was about the dumbest, most obvious thing I could've picked to say.

"Maybe." His mouth turned up at the corners. "Maybe not." He gave me a wink, and when I rolled my eyes at him, his expression went serious again, changing the whole layout of his face. With his eyes focused on me, his mouth in a grim line, and his whole attention turned toward sincerity, he almost looked like a different person. "I already volunteered to help you. Why don't you come on in and tell me what's what?"

I glanced back up at the house—the steady droning rattle of the window air conditioner, the crooked shutter, the warmth the whole place seemed to be surrounded by.

I didn't belong there.

"Come on," he said. Not giving me time to refuse, he took me by the hand and led the way up the steps.

TWENTY-THREE

Across the Mississippi from the Quarter is a neighborhood called Algiers. It's been around as long as New Orleans has been a town and has seen as much as any other bit of land around these parts. It's the first land slaves saw after being kidnapped from their native countries and the place they were kept until they were sold. It's where the Acadians were held after they fled from Canada when the British conquered it three hundred years ago. It's a land that's soaked up all sorts of blood and pain and suffering over time, and at the very tip is a place that was once called Slaughterhouse Point, which was where we were heading.

By boat, it would have only taken a few minutes to get over there, but by car, it took closer to half an hour from Bywater, where Odane's family lived. I, for one, was happy to have the time to think. Everything had happened so fast—once he had me settled with a sweet tea, I'd started talking, and once I started talking, I couldn't make myself stop. So we were going to see his father—Ikenna Gaillard—a man I wasn't none too sure about meeting.

"When we get there," Odane was saying, "you let me do the talking."

"Excuse me?"

He glanced over at me as he drove. "It's not that I don't think you can handle yourself, but I know how his mind works."

"Why are we doing this again?"

"Because he's the only person I know who can help you break into your dreams if Aunt Odette won't." Odane's jaw ticked as he focused on navigating the truck through the last bit of traffic in the Quarter and headed for the Crescent City Connection Bridge.

"You don't like this any more than I do, do you?"

"Not overly," he admitted, "but Auntie O can be stubborn—sometimes too stubborn. Just look at the whole mess between her and my mom."

"Yeah, about that. They obviously care about each other, but it doesn't look like they can stand being in the same room for more than five minutes."

Odane gave a soft grunt of agreement. "That's putting it mildly."

"So, what's the story there?"

"It's family stuff…"

"I told you my family stuff," I said, a challenge in my voice. "Seems like it's only fair that you do the same."

He hesitated for the length of a few blocks, but then finally gave in. "It goes back a long ways, but the bottom line is that Aunt Odette was always the oldest and because of my mom's leg, she was always looking out for her baby sister. When her baby sister didn't want to be looked out for anymore, they had words."

I studied his profile. "There's more to it than that, though."

"A little bit. See, they were supposed to be going into business with each other. Aunt Odette's shop used to be my grandfather's, and he was supposed to pass it on to both of his girls. His name was Luke Turner—he claimed to be a nephew of Marie Laveau. Although, I have to say, half the Hoodoo doctors in a fifty-mile radius say the same, so I don't know if it's true or not.

"Anyway, my grandfather willed the two girls his shop, because they both seemed to have the touch when it came to the spirits. Everything was all set, from what I understand, and then my father came strutting in and messed everything up."

"Messed it up how?" I asked.

"First he tried courting Auntie O, but when she realized he was more interested in the shop than in her, she turned him down flat. Then he turned his sights on my mom. Auntie O tried to warn her off, but my mom wouldn't hear any of it. She was convinced that her sister was just jealous that my father chose her instead.

"She let Ikenna sweep her off her feet, and before she knew it, she had me on the way and no ring on her finger. When she pressed my father to get married, he wanted to have his name added to the lease of the shop—as a gift for the wedding, or so he said. When Auntie O refused, it caused a big fight. The sisters haven't been the same since then. My mom asked Aunt Odette to buy out her half of the shop, since she didn't want anything to do with her sister or the shop anymore. Aunt O refused, saying half the business was still and always would be hers. My mom refused to have anything to do with it, and now they don't talk much anymore."

"Did he end up marrying your mom?"

Odane shook his head. "Nope. Once Ikenna found out that Aunt Odette wasn't going to budge, he cut my mom off almost completely. He must have heard through the grapevine that my mom had a son, because when I was thirteen, maybe fourteen years old, he started coming around trying to make nice with me—offering to buy me smokes or liquor or take me out on the town. Make a man of me, he used to say."

"Charming," I drawled.

"Yeah." His voice went dark, dangerous, like there was barely leashed anger skimming across the surface of it.

"And you still think going to see him is a good idea?"

"Honestly, I wouldn't call it a good idea, but it's the one I've got. If Aunt Odette is dead set against helping you figure out these dreams you've been having, and if you're dead set on knowing what they're trying to tell you, he'll be able to help. For a price."

"That's what I'm worried about," I told him, shifting uneasily on my side of the truck. "This price of his—how much will it be?"

"No way to tell until he names it," Odane said as he steered us onto the bridge. To the right and left of us, the Mississippi's dull waters glinted in the sun. "We don't have to accept what he offers, though. If we don't like his bargain, we'll walk away—no harm, no foul. If it seems doable, we maybe can learn something."

Odane navigated through a residential area before finally

pulling up to a small neighborhood bar. It was painted white with decorative wrought-iron bars over the dark windows. The sign read *Crossroads* in scarlet over a design that looked like a compass rose without the points.

"This is it," Odane said, shutting off his truck and peering out through the windshield. His arms resting on the steering wheel, he looked at the entrance to the bar with apprehension on his face.

"We don't have to do this," I told him. "I can find another way." Now that we'd arrived, part of me wished that he would take the out I was offering him.

"Maybe," he said as he opened his door. "But we're here, and he probably already knows it. Might as well go in and see what's what. Otherwise, he'll think we're running scared."

———————

The interior of the bar was dark except for the glow of amber-colored bulbs hanging from the ceiling, and it took my eyes a minute to adjust. The bar was the definition of a dive. Dark, scarred wood lined the walls. Most of the booths had rips in their red vinyl seats, some of which had been repaired with silver duct tape. The windows were darkened, and the barroom was empty except for a couple of older men huddled over their drinks. The baseball game playing on the big, old-fashioned TV kept fuzzing in and out as they ignored it.

"Can I help you?" an older woman with a sagging bosom and a missing eyetooth asked as she leaned against the bar and dried a hazy glass.

"We're here to see Ikenna," Odane said.

"Are you now?" She looked us up and down, but then something like recognition lit in her yellowed eyes. "Go on back, then. You know the way?"

Odane gave a tense nod and grabbed my hand. "Come on," he whispered, pulling me along gently.

We made our way through the narrow place, which seemed to only get darker the farther back we went. At the very back of the main barroom was a hallway, and at the end of that hallway was a room with only a beaded curtain for a door. We weren't even halfway there when a tall, wiry man stepped through the beads.

Odane's dad didn't look as old as I'd expected him to be. He looked more my momma's age—or what I'd thought her age was—than Mama Legba's. Tall and lean, he wore his hair plaited in braids close to his head, and he was dressed—head to toe—in black. A gold ring flashed on his right pinkie and a diamond stud winked in each ear.

When he saw who it was, he smiled, a flash-of-teeth kind of grin that exposed a crooked front tooth.

All at once, he was someone else—deep-set, empty eyes, hair like snakes, bones for fingers, and a crooked-toothed grin that said I was about to meet my fate. But then the vision from my dream faded as quickly as it had come, and he was just a man. Just Odane's father.

"My boy!" He opened his arms, as if in welcome, and Odane moved in front of me.

"Hello, Ikenna." There wasn't any greeting in his voice.

The man's smile never faltered, but his eyes found me. "And who's this?"

"A friend," Odane said. "Can we talk?"

The man laughed, a deep, hollow-sounding laugh that was all cold amusement. "That's how it's gonna be? I like it. All business. I like it a lot." He pulled back the dark wooden beads and gestured us in. "Come on back then, and let's get to this."

I followed Odane, his hand still securely wrapped around mine, into the room behind the curtain. Ikenna didn't so much as move to give us more room to pass, and I had the feeling he was taking my measure as I brushed by him.

There was something oily about him. Something that reminded me of a snake creeping or an eel sliding away. I couldn't look right at him—not without him looking right back and seeing more than I wanted him to. So I kept my eyes busy taking in the room.

The walls were washed in a deep burnt ochre, and there weren't any windows at all. On one end of the room, incense burned on a small altar lined with the kind of glass-jarred candles you'd find in a church. It made the air hazy with its too-rich, too-spicy scent.

The bench-like altar was piled with trinkets and roughly carved statues. It reminded me a little of the one Mama Legba had in her shop, but these small effigies looked twisted and bent compared to hers.

On the other side of the room, a desk that looked like it belonged in an old-fashioned detective show was piled haphazardly with papers and folders. Behind the desk was a wall of shelves holding different pictures, more of the strange, gnarled statues, and a leathery-looking alligator head, its mouth open to expose its sharp, yellowed teeth.

Ikenna settled himself in a large leather chair on one

side of a round table that stood in the center of the room and gestured for the two of us to take the other seats.

"Y'all want something to drink?" he asked, leaning back in his chair.

"No," Odane answered. "This isn't a social call."

"I can see that plain enough," Ikenna said with a grin that seemed more like a leer. "Your mama okay?" He didn't really sound like he cared.

"Mama's fine," Odane ground out. "She's not why I'm here and she's not up for discussion."

Ikenna's mouth went tight, and his eyes flicked to me for a second and then back to Odane. "What about this one? Can we discuss her?"

I bristled at the tone in his voice, but as I opened my mouth to say I wasn't up for anything with him, Odane squeezed my hand tightly and beat me to it.

"She's a friend, and she's not for you. That's all you need to know for now."

Appreciation gleamed in Ikenna's eyes. "She's more than a friend, or you wouldn't be so jittery right now."

Odane tensed, but he didn't respond.

"And she's more than that, too, isn't she?" Ikenna's eyes focused on me, and my breath went tight. In the dim light of the hallway, I'd thought his eyes were dark, but that wasn't the case. His eyes were actually more the color of honey, and they fairly glowed in the dim light. One of his pupils was almost completely dilated, so the iris was nothing but a ring of gold around the dark, empty center, giving his gaze an unbalanced intensity.

Ikenna took a deep breath, his unnatural-looking eyes

closing like he was savoring the moment. "Mm-hmm," he murmured without opening his eyes. "It's like she bathed in power and then sprinkled on some more, like powder." His eyes flashed open, hungry. "Where'd you find her, son? And how much for her?"

I started to get up, because no way was I sitting here being talked about like I was something to be bought or sold, but Odane's hand tightened almost painfully around mine.

"She's not part of this negotiation," he said, calm and easy.

"Everything's part of the negotiation," Ikenna said with a sharp-toothed kind of grin that reminded me of an alligator just sitting in the bayou, waiting for its prey. "But you finally got to your point, so we'll set the girl aside for now. Why don't you tell me what you came here for—and how much you're willing to give up for it?"

Odane released my hand then and leaned his elbows against the table, like a poker player waiting for the deal. "I'm not giving up anything until I know what you can do for me."

Ikenna laughed at that. "If I was worried your mama was raising you soft, I ain't no more. Nice." Still looking more amused than anything else, he also leaned forward. "Start at the beginning, and we'll see if we can't come to terms."

I didn't like any of this discussion, not one little bit. Not the intensity that seemed to hum between father and son, and definitely not the fact that Ikenna wasn't looking at me at all, but still seemed to be focused on me.

"I don't think we should do this," I whispered to Odane. "We can find another way."

"Ain't no way but my way, sweetheart," Ikenna said.

I looked up and forced myself to meet those eerie eyes without flinching.

"Good. She got a backbone. She's gonna need it."

"Why's that?" Odane asked.

"You really can't see it?" Ikenna said, and for the first time since we'd arrived, he looked confused. Maybe even a little disappointed.

"See what?" I asked.

Ikenna scratched his chin as he considered me, and I noticed that he had a ghostly tattoo in white ink covering the dark skin of his hand. It replicated the bones that lay beneath his skin, giving the impression that he was a living skeleton. "You don't know either, do you?"

"Why don't you stop talking in circles, old man, and tell us what you're playing at?" Odane's voice was tight. Dangerous.

Ikenna wasn't pleased—not in the least—but his curiosity apparently won out over his irritation. He turned his full attention onto me—those creepy eyes bore right into my own. "Not all the power she's dripping with is her own."

TWENTY-FOUR

"What do you mean it's not all hers?" Odane demanded.

"I mean that she got an energy about her that don't belong to her. It's covering over what she might have underneath."

"But Mama Legba never saw anything like that," I said, confused.

"Odette might be good at some things, but there's a lot she don't know. She don't know how to dance with the darkness. Not like I do," Ikenna said with a slow, knowing smile. He wasn't bragging on himself, I realized. He was simply stating his truth.

"Can you tell whose energy it is?" Odane asked, trying to get back the control he'd had moments ago.

Ikenna frowned, his eyes finally coming back to me, studying me. Looking at me and through me right at the same time. "It's female in nature. Feels powerful, old. But connected to you somehow."

"That can't be," I whispered, reaching for the dreads that no longer covered my head. "We got rid of her control."

Ikenna shook his head. "I'm not sure what you think you did, but your power sure enough ain't alone. In fact, whatever you have is buried so down deep beneath this other that it's no wonder Odette didn't see it, 'specially if she wasn't looking for it. She probably thinks this other power is yours." His eyes narrowed at me, appreciative and cunning all at once. "Whose power you carrying, girl?"

"Don't answer that," Odane told me as I shifted uneasily under his father's too-perceptive stare.

Ikenna waved his hand to silence him. "Enough of this. What did y'all really come here for?"

"We have some questions about Baron Samedi," Odane told him, taking a different approach than I'd expected. Still unsettled, I sat as still and calm as I could and waited for their hands to play out.

"Baron Samedi?" This seemed to intrigue Ikenna. "I didn't think you were interested in that . . . what did you call it once upon a time? Oh, yeah—*stupid dark shit* I believe were the exact words you used. What's got you so interested now?"

Odane hesitated, but then he spoke. "Someone might be trying to summon him."

Ikenna couldn't mask his surprise, or his apprehension. "Someone *who*? Better not be someone *you*."

"A witch named Thisbe," Odane said.

"Never heard of her," Ikenna said, like he was dismissing the information. But his shoulders were still tight and his expression couldn't hide his interest. "She from around here?"

"You could say that. She's been from around here for more than a hundred years."

"That ain't possible." Ikenna looked more impatient than ever.

"It shouldn't be, no. But it is."

"You say. Have you seen her with your own two eyes?"

"No," Odane said slowly.

"Then you chasing fairy tales, son."

"He's telling the truth," I interjected, ignoring the look Odane shot me. "She's my mother."

"Your mother?" Ikenna's eyes narrowed. "Your mother is over a hundred years old?"

"That's what they tell me," I said tightly.

"Who's they?" Ikenna asked, still suspicious.

"Mama Legba. Others who saw what she can do."

Ikenna's expression was filled with doubt. "You say Odette saw this?" His attention was all on me, and I suddenly understood why Odane had wanted me to let him do the talking. When Ikenna focused on you, I mean *really* focused on you, it felt like being caught in a hunter's sight.

"She did," Odane said, drawing his father's attention back to himself.

"Well, then," Ikenna said thoughtfully. "That *is* something, all right."

"Your turn," Odane said. "We need to know what summoning Baron Samedi would entail."

Ikenna's brow furrowed. "Why would you think I'd know a thing like that?"

"You're the most powerful bokor 'round these parts— anyone who knows anything knows that. You telling me you don't serve Samedi and his Loa? You trying to tell me you don't know the process of calling him?" Odane asked with more than a little disdain.

A bokor? Odane hadn't mentioned that his father was a bokor. In Voodoo, most priests were called houngans and priestesses were mambos. They served the light Loa—the spirits that dealt with life. I'd only heard tales of bokors, sorcerers who served with both hands—the light *and* the dark. Damballah and Samedi. If the stories were true, they couldn't ever be trusted, but here we were, negotiating with one.

"I know enough," Ikenna said slyly. "I may serve, but I've never been stupid enough to mess with summoning him."

"But you know how someone *might* go about it?"

Ikenna pursed his lips, but eventually he nodded. "You need an ointment—"

"Aloe in black cat oil," Odane said, to Ikenna's surprise.

He nodded with a concerned frown creasing his face. "Mixed with a few other things," he said slowly.

"What other things?"

Ikenna looked distinctly uncomfortable, but he leaned back in his chair, pretending to be at ease.

"If we don't know what Thisbe's collecting, there's no way to stop her, now is there?" Odane said. "Unless, of course, you want Samedi showing up looking for you once he's been called to this side of the divide?"

Ikenna's eyes narrowed, like he knew Odane was out-maneuvering him and didn't know how to stop it. "You need the blood from a living body and graveyard dust. It takes a sacrifice, too. Samedi is the one who escorts the souls, so you need a freshly departed soul for him to come harvest. The rest involves trapping him for long enough to make the deal you want to make."

"What kind of sacrifice?" I asked, my throat tight at the thought of Piers gone missing.

Ikenna narrowed his eyes at his son, but then he turned to me. "Depends on what you want from the Baron. If you only want to talk to him, any old thing will do—even an animal. If you want to do more, you have to give more." Ikenna drummed a fingertip on the tabletop. "If you want to make a trade, to bring back your dearly departed, you'd need to trade in kind. A youth for a soul who departed young. A man for a male who left this world, and a girl for a female soul you want to bring back."

"That's it?" Odane asked.

"Ain't that enough? You're talking at least two deaths to summon him, more depending on what he asks of you. Knowing Samedi, he probably would want more." He pinned Odane with his golden eyes. "My turn now. What does this Thisbe want to summon the Baron for?"

"We don't know," Odane said.

"That's a lie," Ikenna said flatly.

"*You* say—"

"I more than say. I *know*. And you'd know you can't lie to me if you'd come around more than once or twice in your lifetime."

"You never gave me a reason to."

"I offered to teach you . . ."

"You offered to *use* me," Odane snarled. "That ain't a reason."

The two of them squared off after that in silence.

"What'd you really come here for, son?" Ikenna said. "I

know it wasn't just to ask about Samedi. Most the people who practice 'round these parts could have given you those answers."

Odane looked at me, as though asking for permission.

If what Ikenna was saying was true—that I was carrying someone else's power with me—that power might be my mother's. It might mean that I'd been right—cutting off my hair might not have done anything at all but make me feel like a newly shorn sheep. But there was something worse— Piers was missing and Thisbe needed a sacrifice, a young soul for a young soul. I would pay any price I needed to if it meant finding a way to make sure Piers didn't end up in Baron Samedi's hands.

I gave Odane a small nod, conveying my consent to go on.

"You're right. We didn't come here just to ask about Samedi, though we thank you for the information. We came because we need help breaking into her dreams."

"Breaking into dreams is easy enough. Child's play, really. Dreams ain't nothing more than the soul at play."

"She's been dreaming about Thisbe, and we want to know why."

Ikenna pinned me with his uneven gaze. "If you want to see someone else's life, that isn't breaking into dreams. That's channeling a soul, and with the other power you're wrapped up in, y'all might want to think twice about doing anything stupid as that. There's no telling what might happen."

A shiver went down my spine, but I forced myself to shrug it off. "I'm willing to risk it."

Ikenna smiled then, and this time the smile didn't hold a hint of derision. "I bet you are." The curve of his mouth faltered. "But I also bet you don't have any idea what you might be stepping in to."

"I'm already into it," I said, feeling the truth of those words more than ever.

"You might think you are ... " Ikenna said, but he seemed almost unsure.

"Can you do it or not?" Odane asked, before his father could back away from the negotiation.

"'Course I could ... for a price. You did say you came to talk business." He gave his son a slippery smile as his gaze glided over to me.

Odane's jaw muscles ticked. "We did, but it depends on what it is you want."

Ikenna shrugged, easy like. "What don't I want? Power. Money. The key to the city. You got any of those?"

Odane stayed silent.

"No. You don't got nothing to give," Ikenna said, the smile dropping from his face like a bad habit. "So maybe I don't got nothing to tell."

"I got myself," Odane said, and damn if Ikenna's crazy eyes didn't light with something that looked like eagerness.

"Who says I'd want it?" he drawled.

"You do." Odane's voice never wavered. "You've wanted a piece of me ever since you realized I could be your ticket to the Quarter. Must have chapped your ass some when I turned you down a couple of years ago."

Ikenna's eyes narrowed.

Odane shrugged and kept on talking. "Aunt Odette's been hounding me to develop my gifts lately. She seems to think she's the one who should help me."

226

"That so?" Ikenna asked. His expression had gone thunderous. Deadly, even.

"That's what *she* thinks. I'm not so sure she's right about that." He kept his eyes steady on his father.

No way was I going to sit there and let him talk about Mama Legba. She wasn't supposed to be part of what we were doing, but Odane grabbed my hand tight and sure, and when he squeezed it, I felt a little jolt of warmth and peace that couldn't have been natural.

I looked up at him, trying to figure out what he'd done, but he was focused on Ikenna.

"I'm sure she's dead wrong," Ikenna said, emphasizing the word *dead* like it was a wish.

"You leave her out of this, and maybe we can work ourselves something out on the business side of things," Odane said.

"Why would I leave her out?" Ikenna asked, his brows flying up. "She's the whole point."

"You leave her out because I won't have my family involved. You do anything against her, and you won't *ever* get what you want."

"And what do you think that is?"

"Her shop. Her part of the city." Odane leaned forward. "The Quarter is all you ever wanted. I was just the path you thought you'd take to get it." The bitterness in his voice practically choked the air out of the room.

Ikenna considered this. "That's true enough, but how am I gonna get what I want if I leave that old bat out of this?"

"Because you don't need her to get it."

"No?" Ikenna seemed confused by this idea.

"Not if you have me."

Ikenna frowned like he wasn't getting it. I wasn't either.

"Who do you think is gonna take over once Aunt Odette is gone?"

Now I did yank my hand away from Odane. "You can't—"

But all at once, the voice went out of me. It felt like my vocal chords seized up.

Odane glanced my way, his eyes flashing in warning. "You wanted my help, so maybe you should settle down and take it."

My eyes widened and I opened my mouth to tell that double-crossing ass exactly what he could do with his deal, but I felt like I couldn't move a muscle. Odane glanced at me with a lazy sort of confidence that let me know he was the one responsible. My anger spiked, but there wasn't a thing I could do but seethe inside and hope he understood how dead I was going to make him when this was all over.

He either didn't understand what the look I was giving him meant or he didn't care. Dismissing me, he drew his attention back to Ikenna, who was watching the exchange with amusement and appreciation.

"Why would you think I want to wait around until she's gone?" Ikenna asked. "I'd be an old man myself by then. I want my portion *now*."

"My mom doesn't want her half of the shop. I could have her sign it over to me," Odane suggested.

Inwardly, I was screaming, but I couldn't get my mouth to make a sound or any part of me to work. It was like something or someone was holding me down so I couldn't speak or move.

The holding was gentle enough, but it was impossible to break just the same.

Ikenna scratched at his chin again, the skeletal tattoo mirroring the motion of his hand. "What are you saying, son?"

"I'm saying that if I had my half, I might be inclined to welcome my *father* into the family business."

"And you'd double-cross your aunt like that?"

"She double-crossed my mother." Odane shrugged.

I let out a huff of breath, the only sound I could seem to make, but I was so angry, so unbelievably furious that he'd play us like this. On the desk, the stacks of papers rustled like they were being stirred by some invisible breeze.

Ikenna's uneven eyes looked my direction and then at the papers on his desk that were starting to flap more violently now. The candles near his altar flickered in the unnatural wind.

Odane squeezed at my hand and shot me a look. *Give me a minute here*, that look seemed to say. *Trust me.*

But I wasn't about to sit there knowing he was betraying Mama Legba. The more my temper spiked, the more I seethed, the more the wind rustled.

Ikenna's mouth curved up as his eyes lit in anticipation.

"Chloe," Odane snapped, and something in his tone made me go still. The wind went silent, too.

"Well, well," Ikenna said. "So she has a name."

Next to me, Odane flinched. "Don't you—"

"You don't have to worry none," Ikenna interrupted. "As long as you follow through on the terms we set, I'll never have any reason to use her name." He smiled at me, and my stomach turned.

Odane glared at his father. "So you'll help us?"

Ikenna stared at him like he was making up his mind. "You get your mama's half of Odette's shop," he said finally, "and I'll help you with whatever you and *Chloe* need helping with."

I repressed a shiver at the sound of my name on his lips.

"That's it?" Odane asked, wary.

Ikenna laughed. "That ain't enough?"

"It might take some time to get the papers in order," Odane said.

"Well, you come on back when you do, and we'll talk more then," Ikenna said, standing as though to show us out.

"We don't have that kind of time. Someone stole some aloe from Aunt Odette, and by our figuring it has a little less than a day left to cure."

"I see," Ikenna said, looking more disturbed than I would have expected him to show.

"So unless you want someone to summon the Baron here, to your city..." Odane leaned forward. "Without the understanding in her dreams, we don't know how to stop the witch from summoning your boss. You see our dilemma."

"I do indeed." Ikenna scratched at his chin again, clearly unhappy to be pushed. "It'll take some doing to round up all I need for the ritual, but I could do it later tonight."

"Where?"

"We need to be somewhere that has some link to the person we're trying to summon in her dreams."

"There's a cabin that used to belong to the witch," Odane said, giving him the location. "There's a tomb, too."

Ikenna considered the options. "If someone's about to

summon Samedi, I ain't in no hurry to be lurking around a graveyard. The cabin should do fine."

"What time?"

"Right around sundown," Ikenna said. "I'll ask for your marker on the payment."

Odane gave a terse nod and unclasped his necklace. He gave it a long look, rubbing one of the beads between his fingers, and then tossed it across the table to his father, who took it up and tucked it away without even looking at it.

"Thank you," Odane told him, holding out his hand.

"Don't be thanking me yet," Ikenna said, ignoring the outstretched offering. He remained seated, as if on a throne. "I'll expect those papers soon."

"You'll have them," Odane said through gritted teeth.

"Y'all can see yourselves out?" Ikenna smiled at me, his uneven eyes aglow. "It was very nice to make your acquaintance, Miss Chloe."

————

Odane didn't say anything else until we were in his truck and already pulling away from the bar. I *couldn't* say anything, so I sat and seethed, wishing I could punch him.

He drove a ways and then pulled over. "Dammit!" he shouted, pounding on the already worn steering wheel. He threw out a few more curses, and then rested his head on the wheel.

"What the hell was that?" I asked, my voice finally working as I slugged him in the arm.

Odane's head snapped up, his eyes wide at my sudden burst of violence. "Chloe, I'm so sorry—"

"You didn't seem so sorry in there while you were stopping my mouth and holding me back. And *yes*, I knew that was you," I said, poking a finger in his direction before he could make any sorry excuses. "You ever lift a finger against me again and I'll—"

"I had to do it," he said, taking another blow without flinching.

"I just bet you did," I said, trying to slap at him again.

He leaned away from my fists but didn't try to stop me. "Don't you see? He had to believe that I was selling out Aunt Odette. If I'd have warned you what I was going to do, there was a good chance he would have seen right through our act. But you fought me, and that made him think I was really willing to betray her."

I frowned. "So you're not?"

Odane rubbed the back of his neck and looked at me, his dark eyes giving away the worry I felt. "I wasn't planning on it, no. We got information we needed, didn't we? And he's agreed to help you break into those dreams you've been having. With both those things, maybe we can stop Thisbe."

"And then what? You'll hand over Mama Legba's shop?"

"That was never the plan. And it still isn't." He sighed and slumped down in the driver's seat.

"You think you can get out of the agreement?"

"Deals are made to be broken," Odane said with a playful grin. When I didn't respond, the smile slid from his face, and he scratched the back of his neck, as though he was uncomfortable. "I'll figure something out."

I just sat there, my arms crossed and my expression murderous.

"We still have the threat of Samedi," Odane offered. "See, Samedi usually operates on the other side of the divide. He don't usually come on our side, but when he does, he has a bad habit of seeking out those who serve him and making them, well, serve. And if we have the key to stopping him from being summoned … We can renegotiate."

"Oh … " I said, feeling a little better.

"Yeah. It's one thing to play at prayers and spells. It's another thing to come face-to-face with the demon who happens to be your boss, and who you've pledged your obedience to. Ikenna doesn't want Samedi to be summoned any more than we do. He might have helped us no matter what, just to stop it from happening, but then you started up with all the energy and the wind, and I slipped up."

"Because you told him my name," I said, understanding.

Odane nodded. "The marker I gave him would have only affected me, but then there was that wind, and I knew he was getting excited." He hit the steering wheel again. "I was just trying to stop you before you let him know how powerful you really are."

The memory of how Ikenna's eyes lit up when Odane said my name sent a shiver of unease through me. I'd heard tales of people being called out of their name—usually scare-me stories told around bonfires late at night. But I'd learned enough in the last few weeks to not dismiss something because I thought it was a story.

"I'm so sorry, Chloe."

"What could he do?" I asked, studying Odane for some

sign that he'd set this all up on purpose. But he seemed sincere enough.

"I don't know for sure, but he has more leverage now to get me to come through on my end of the deal than he did before he knew your name."

"He could force you to betray Mama Legba?"

"He could try." Odane's jaw went tight. "But I'll never let him, Chloe." He hesitated for a second, then offered, "We could still call it off. I'll figure out a way to get my marker back, and—"

"No," I said, cutting him off. "I need to go through with this." And then I told him about Piers and how he'd gone missing.

"You're thinking he's the sacrifice Thisbe needs," Odane said when I was done.

I nodded, unable to say those words out loud and hear their terrible truth. "Let Ikenna try to do whatever with my name. There's more riding on this than just me now."

"So we'll stick with the plan," Odane said. "We'll meet Ikenna tonight. And we'll deal with whatever problems he brings as they come."

TWENTY-FIVE

By the time I got myself back to Le Ciel, my nerves were jangling, but I tried to put the thoughts of Ikenna out of my head and went to find out what Lucy discovered in the registers. She was in the main office building at the plantation, a small, plain-looking structure on the outskirts of the property.

I found her in her dad's office, sitting behind his cluttered desk. "Hey," she said, studying a large ledger when I came in. "So how'd it go?"

"It didn't."

"What?" She looked up at me.

"I didn't go to the police station," I told her, and then before she could ask why, I explained. "There's no point. The police aren't gonna be interested in a missing black man, not when they already think that Piers is the one who stole that stuff."

Her face pinched, like she wanted to argue, but she didn't.

Because she knew I was right. As long as he was a suspect, there was no way the police were going to care if he was in trouble.

"But you've been gone for hours," Lucy asked, a question in her voice.

"I was with Odane."

"With Odane?" She didn't bother to hide her surprise.

"That's what I just said."

"Why, exactly, were you with Odane?" Lucy asked, her brows drawn together in confusion.

I sighed. "He offered to help the other day, and I thought it was time to talk to him about it."

She didn't say anything right away. I could tell she was waiting for me to explain, but she wasn't going to wait forever before she started pressing. But I wasn't sure how much I should tell her.

"Well?" She was staring at me expectantly. "Did he help?"

"We went to see his father."

Her eyes widened a little, and I knew that she didn't like what I'd said. "You mean the father that Mama Legba doesn't trust?"

"The very same. Turns out he's a houngan over across the river in Algiers," I told her. It wasn't a complete lie. A bokor usually is a houngan first. "A Voodoo priest of sorts," I had to explain, when it was clear she didn't understand. "Like Mama Legba, but a man."

"Does Mama Legba know about this?"

"No. And we're not going to tell her. She and Odane's dad have some sort of argument from way back—something involving her sister and the shop—and she doesn't like him. You saw how she reacted to Odane's suggestion—she wouldn't want me to talking to him, much less having him help us."

"Then maybe you shouldn't," Lucy suggested. "I know you're scared. We're all scared for Piers, but—"

"But what? We wait for the police to solve the murders and find Thisbe?" I gave a dry, hollow laugh. "The police aren't looking for Thisbe. They don't even understand *what* to look for when it comes to her."

"Chloe…" Lucy warned.

I sank into the chair on the other side of the desk. "Ikenna had a lot to say about summoning Samedi. Thisbe needs a sacrifice, and the sacrifice needs to be an equal for the person you're trying to get back." I looked up at her to make sure that she was paying attention so she understood. "Augustine was about Piers's age, Lucy."

"Oh…" she said, like that information was too much for her to process right away.

"Did you find anything?" I asked, trying to distract her from trying to talk me out of the path I'd already chosen. I nodded toward the ledger.

I watched a couple different emotions flash across Lucy's face, but it was clear she'd found something and her desire to tell me what it was outweighed her desire to argue about Odane and Ikenna.

"Actually, I think I did." She flipped back through the oversized pages and, using a finger to track down a column, found what she was looking for. "There was an Augustine at Le Ciel. It looks like Roman's father, Jean-Pierre, bought him when he was about sixteen, back in 1806."

Relief shuttled through me. "So my visions—they're true."

"Maybe," she said, but she was frowning down at the book.

"What is it?"

"I could be wrong about this, because it's really hard to understand what I'm seeing here, but from what I can tell, this Augustine was busy. Not long after Jean-Pierre purchased him, there are a whole series of entries to show where he'd received permission to hire himself out to other plantations." Lucy pointed to some notations, then flipped to other pages and did the same. "I guess that was common enough. Sometimes masters would let their slaves earn some money to buy things for their cabins or extra food. But then, right around 1811—about the same time as that news clipping that affected you—the entries stop." She glanced up at me. "That's the weird part—there isn't any other entry for him after that."

"Why's that so weird? Didn't slaves die or run away all the time?" I asked, trying to figure out what she was seeing.

"They did, but Jean-Pierre kept records of *everything*. Every time he bought or sold something—or someone—he wrote it down, so every time a slave died or was sold off, it's noted in here. See?" She showed me a couple of the records so I could understand what she was saying.

"But there's no death or sale note for Augustine?"

"Nothing. I've looked through about a decade's worth of ledgers for some sign of him after 1811, but there's no other mentions or notes about what happened to him. It doesn't say that he died. There's no record of him being sold, and there's nothing noting him as a runaway, either." She looked up at me. "It's like he disappeared."

"People don't just disappear," I told her.

"I know, but he seemed to." Lucy frowned and closed the ledger. "On paper, at least."

"So it's a dead end?"

"This is. But we know he was real now," Lucy said with no little satisfaction.

I sank into one of the chairs. "But we don't know what happened to him."

She frowned. "No. We can probably assume that whatever happened, it wasn't good. But it's still a mystery."

"We have to solve it," I told her. "Tomorrow that ointment is going to be ready. And if we're right that Thisbe has Piers..." But I couldn't make myself finish that sentence.

Looking up at the note of desperation in my voice, she frowned at me. "There's still a little time left. You don't have to go to this hangman—"

"Houngan," I corrected.

"Right. Sorry. *Houngan*. If Mama Legba doesn't trust him, I don't think we should either."

I shook my head. "It's already been arranged."

"Well, unarrange it," she told me. "We can go to Mama Legba and let her know what we found out. She's got to be willing to help you once she hears what we found here."

"It's not that simple," I told her, and then I explained what happened—and how Ikenna had my name. "I don't think backing out is even possible now."

Lucy frowned. "I don't think you should trust him, Chloe."

I nodded. Lucy was right—I couldn't trust Ikenna. I *didn't* trust him, but I also didn't know how else to get the information we needed. There was knowledge buried in the dreams I'd been having, I could feel it. The question was what I was willing to sacrifice for it.

Sacrifice. I thought of the card I'd drawn just days ago—the man hanging from the tree. He'd put himself through that pain to gain the knowledge and the freedom he wanted, Mama Legba said. How much was I willing to sacrifice to put an end to this once and for all?

TWENTY-SIX

When I came through the line of trees and looked across the clearing toward the cabin, it felt like the whole world was hushed and waiting. Like every plant and insect around knew something was about to happen and they were all still deciding if that something was going to be good. I checked my phone and saw that I was already running late.

Two people were already waiting in front of the cabin. Odane and Ikenna. Side by side, they looked nearly identical. I hadn't noticed before how Odane had his father's build. His shoulders sloped the same way, but Odane was an inch or two taller. And his eyes had Odeana's intelligence and wit shimmering in them.

Odane had a large rucksack over his shoulder, and Ikenna was looking over the cabin like he already owned it. When Odane saw me coming across the clearing toward them, he waved.

"You got yourself quite a place here," Ikenna said, finally

shattering the uneasy quiet. His eerie eyes took in the whole cabin—its rusted roof, the worn shutters, and the rickety steps that had been stained by the rust-colored dust someone had once used to keep intruders out.

"It's not mine, so you best come on in before someone sees us out here." I opened the door and motioned them both into the cabin.

Odane came first, his jaw tight with caution and his dark eyes taking in everything all at once. "This is Thisbe's place?" I couldn't tell what he thought of it from the look on his face.

Ikenna stepped in behind him, looking distinctly uneasy. "There sure is magic rubbed off on every inch of this place. Dark magic, too."

"Supposedly, this is the cabin her father—the man who owned her—gave her after he freed her," I told them. "The university owns it now, and technically we're not supposed to be here. Dr. Aimes has been more on edge than usual the last few days, so we need to do this quick and get out before someone from the staff sees us."

Ikenna kept looking around, like he didn't hear a word I'd said.

"Will this place work or not?" I asked, impatient to get started and nervous all at once.

Ikenna nodded. "It should do fine. The energy up in here can only make things easier, especially if it's her energy."

"I don't know who else's it would be. No one's ever lived here but her," I told him.

Odane was still staring at me, but finally he spoke. "You sure you still want to do this?"

"What's done is done," Ikenna said, taking the rucksack his son was carrying.

"It ain't done until it's over, old man," Odane countered, his voice low and dangerous. "If Chloe wants to back out, she can."

"Maybe she can, and maybe she can't. But you're all in now," his father said, meeting his son's gaze with a cold resolve.

"I'm not backing out," I said, stepping forward to break up the father-son pissing contest. "How's this gonna work?"

The two stared at each other for a couple more tense moments, but then Ikenna smiled. "She's got nerve. You should keep this one."

"I'm not his," I said, glancing over at Odane. I was surprised to see hurt flash across his expression, and for a second, I felt an answering twinge of guilt. "I'm not anybody's but my own," I added, trying to ease the offense.

"Well then," Ikenna said, and he let out a husky laugh. "Go on and strip down."

"Ikenna!" Odane practically growled the word.

"It's okay," I said, trying not to show how nervous I felt. "Strip down how far?"

"I need some skin for the spell to work," Ikenna said.

I slipped my T-shirt over my head, until I was standing in my bra and shorts. I was still wearing more than I'd usually wear to swim in, but I felt exposed nonetheless. "Good enough?" I didn't look at Odane, but I could feel the heat of his gaze on my skin. I wasn't sure what to do with that, or with the heat that I could feel rising in my cheeks, so I did my best to ignore both.

Ikenna glanced at me and gave a short nod. "You'll do."

He was already opening the rucksack and starting to take out a weird assortment of items. After he made a partial circle of salt on the floor of the cabin, he picked up a narrow brush and a jar of something dark that smelled sour and spicy when he opened it.

"In the circle," he said, motioning that I should stand in the center. Then without any other explanation, he began to paint.

I couldn't understand what he was saying as he worked, because I'd never heard anything like those words before. Slowly and methodically, he painted a jagged line all the way down across my back. The cool wet of the paint gliding across my skin made goose flesh rise along my arms, then up along my neck, but Ikenna was methodical and he took his time about it, chanting all the while. When he was done, he closed the circle and set the salt aside.

"The candles, Odane," Ikenna said gruffly, like Odane should have already known what to do. He set six of the black candles around the perimeter of the circle and then positioned the six white candles between them. "Three and three and three twice more," he murmured as he lit the candles with a smoldering stick of something that made my eyes burn. It certainly wasn't sage. "A good number to summon a soul."

I took a step toward the salt line, but something pushed against me, holding me back. "I didn't agree to summon anything," I said, panic spiking in me. "You said channeling, not summoning."

"Settle down, girl." Ikenna came over and stood across from me, the diamond stud in his ear catching the candlelight in the quickly dimming room. "You want to see into your dreams, you're talking about seeking the life of the soul. Since the dreams aren't yours, you need the soul they belong to. You can't see nothing if you don't summon it."

"But Thisbe isn't dead," I said.

Ikenna gave me a slow smile. "That's what's gonna make this interesting."

Odane stepped forward. "You sure about this, Chloe?" he asked, his voice tense, worried.

I nodded, not sure at all that it was the truth. I tried to settle myself back down. *I had to do this.* If the cards I'd drawn were right, I was destined to do this. Whatever happened, the sacrifice I was making was needed to gain the knowledge I wanted.

"Go on and stand in the center, still as you can," Ikenna said. "Close your eyes and think of the place your dreams take you to."

I glanced one more time at Odane, but his eyes were on his father, like he was watching to make sure Ikenna didn't try anything. Satisfied that I was about as safe as a body could be using a bokor to break into dreams that might belong to someone else, I closed my eyes and blocked out the world.

Immediately, I became more aware of everything around me—the musty, close air. The faint tinge of sulfur hanging in the air from the lit matches. The rough, cool boards of the floor under my feet. The warmth from the candles that surrounded me.

All at once, the darkness behind my eyes grew thicker. Then the fizzling strike of another match and the smell of something heavy and sweet filled the air, along with the rasping chants of Ikenna. They pulsed in an unsteady rhythm and increased in volume, rolling through the air, carrying me deeper and deeper into the darkness.

Deeper and deeper into the night.

My skin grew cold, and all at once light burst behind my eyes, and I opened them. The cabin had disappeared and we were there—all of us—in the pines. Outside the circle the ground had turned to dirt and moss, but inside the circle the worn floorboards remained.

I looked at Odane, and he looked back, his eyes wide with the wonder and the fear that I felt.

"What happened?" I whispered, afraid to disturb the silence.

Odane opened his mouth to speak but didn't seem to know what to say. Ikenna laughed. "What happened?" he said with a leering smile. "What do you think happened? It worked. Just like I knew it would."

"Why are you both here? How can this be my dream?"

"This ain't no dream. I told you, this is a summoning," Ikenna said, like he was disappointed I didn't understand what was happening. "You summoned a soul, and she brought her whole past with her." He gestured to the left, and there was the girl, her toes up to the line of salt, her hands pressed to the air in front of her, as though to some invisible wall she couldn't penetrate. Her eyes were focused on me, and a smile played on her lips. Hope lit her face.

I knew that this time, she saw me. This time, her smile was for me.

With her hand held out the way it was, I knew she was trying to get to me, but I didn't know if I should let her. She beckoned me, offering her hand, but I didn't know what she was offering.

This, after all, was Thisbe, the person who had destroyed so many lives. But now she was also only a girl, still young, with an unlined and almost kind face.

"Go on," Ikenna urged. "This is what you wanted, ain't it?"

I took a step toward the edge of the salt, but I hesitated.

"She won't stay forever," Ikenna said, excitement lighting his words. "Take what she offers or let her go in peace."

I looked to Odane, but the closer I'd stepped to the girl, the more I felt like I was wholly in her orbit. Odane seemed very far away suddenly, his form fuzzy and indistinct, as though I was seeing him through water.

He was saying something, but I couldn't hear him anymore. The only thing left in the world for me was the girl.

She was still waiting, her hand still pressed to that invisible wall, a small smile soft on her face. She didn't look dangerous. Nothing about the moment felt dangerous, either.

I reached out my hand, slowly, because I still wasn't sure, and when our palms pressed against one another, the world slid away.

TWENTY-SEVEN

The pines rose up around me, stretching themselves to the night above like they were trying to catch the stars in their branches. I was alone, but the night wasn't silent as it had been in my other dreams. I could hear the wind stroking the upper boughs of the trees. Unseen insects rustled around me, and I could feel the balmy warmth of a spring night.

I was alone, but I wasn't myself. I had the same feeling as when I'd had the visions of Thisbe—of being in her skin and experiencing her life. But I felt young—*so* young. The trees seemed so much taller. The night, so much darker.

A woven basket was looped over my arm, and the swishing of the rough material of my skirts rustled as I walked through the grove, toward the place where the rows of trunks began to thin. On and on I walked, with a feeling of such purpose and determination that I didn't doubt the pines would end and I would reach my destination. On and on, with a straightness in my spine that I knew didn't match my years.

A straightness I had practiced and learned from surviving so long on my own.

When I broke through the last of the pines, I found myself in the wide-open country, with cane fields on each side of me and the expanse of the cloudless sky dwarfing me beneath its glittering canopy. There was more than enough moonlight to guide my steps as I followed the dirt path that cut between the fields. When I came to the row of shack-like cabins that stood sleeping in the stillness of the night, I took the path that led me well away from them and their slumbering occupants.

Ignoring the way the stalks of cane rustled in the night air, I turned and went toward the great alley of oaks. I approached them solemnly but without fear, and as I walked beneath their broad arms, I felt myself more at home than anywhere else in my world. Because the trees didn't look at me with spiteful jealousy burning in their eyes. They didn't whisper behind closed doors about the motherless girl who the master paid too much attention to. They didn't ask what could be so wrong with a child that a mother would walk away and leave her behind.

The trees didn't pass any judgment at all. They'd seen too much and they would see more still. The oaks would still be standing long after bodies no longer fell in the fields. And when the blood that was spilled on that land had soaked so deep down into the earth that people believed it had been washed away, the oaks would remain still. Steadfast witnesses that blood don't wash. Blood has to be burnt.

My mother had taught me that, just as she had brought me to those oaks on so many nights when I was only a small thing. She was the one who had shown me how to carve cords out of the knotty trunks of those trees and to gather the moss that hung from their branches. *There's a power to this place*, she'd told me, guiding my hand as I wrapped the moss around the bit of wood. *There's a power inside of you*, she'd said as she showed me how to pin my intentions securely by driving an iron needle through the center of the charm.

Lots of people were desperate enough to walk into the swamp, but everyone knew most didn't walk out. My mother was different, though. They all said that if anyone could walk out the other side to freedom, it would have been her. Maybe they were right.

But then again, maybe not.

They called her a witch and they called her the master's whore. They looked at me like I'd been the one who made my mother's choices and, since I was the one left, they hated me for those choices and made me pay for them every day.

But they needed me, too. They knew I had the same spark of power inside me, just like she did. They knew I could weave a charm or heal a wound or save a wife when the babe wouldn't come. Or curse an enemy.

They hated me double for that.

But I pushed those thoughts away. Protection charms needed strength and truth to work, and those charms were what I traded for the extra food to fill my belly and the extra blankets to keep me through the winter. So I took a small knife from beneath some scraps in my basket and I settled my soul before I made the first cut.

The hands holding the knife—the hands that felt like they could have been my own—were so small. They were the hands of a child rather than a woman, but that didn't make them any less skillful. I worked quickly and efficiently, cutting bits of the moss that hung from the trees until my basket was nearly full.

"What are you doing?" a small voice said from behind me, and I turned, startled to find that I wasn't alone.

Standing in the moonlight was a boy who couldn't have been more than ten or twelve. His pale skin looked sallow, and he was pointing a small knife at me. His young face was stern and cold, and I knew immediately who it was. The oldest son of Jean-Pierre Dutilette was a prince in my world—one who came and did as he pleased, and what he pleased was more often cruel than not.

"I'm just getting some moss from these here trees," I said, tucking my own knife into the basket so he wouldn't see it. If he saw it, I'd have to explain how I came to have such a well-made piece, and I didn't think that the truth—that my mother had left it with me—would have been worth the breath it took to speak it.

Panic inched along my skin, but the branches above me rustled quietly, calming me with their very presence.

"What do you need it for?" he asked, his cold, dark eyes looking at me, judging me like I was no better than dung on the road. Not much more than a decade of days on this earth, and Roman Dutilette had already become what he was going to be.

I showed him the contents of the basket. "I'm gathering it for Gris-Gris," I told him.

The boy's face creased in a sour expression. "What's a greegree?" he asked, suspicious.

So I pulled a small pouch out of the pocket of my

apron to show him. "They're for good luck," I said, and then quickly added, "and for protection."

The boy didn't relax, but I saw interest light in his eyes. "What kind of protection?"

"Oh, they help keep the bad spirits away," I explained, watching the interest grow in his expression. "These trees have been here so long, there's bound to be some power in the moss that grows from them. I could make you one, if you'd like."

Ignoring my offer, he raised his knife like I was some kind of threat.

He's scared, I thought. *Something's made him understand that even he can be touched.* I tried not to smile as I wondered what it was that had revealed his mortality to him.

"Who taught you to make them?"

"My mother did," I said simply.

"Who's your mother?"

I glanced away. Most that knew her called her by one name without ever knowing her true name, but I wasn't about to speak either to him. "It doesn't matter. She's gone."

Slowly he lowered the knife. "My mother's gone, too. My baby sister killed her."

I glanced up from beneath my lashes, watching him for some sign of what he would do next. "I'm sorry," I told him.

The boy scowled, but it was clear he didn't want pity from anyone like me. "Are you sure you're not out here plotting to kill us?"

I raised my head, surprised at the meaning of—and the venom in—his words. "Why would I do that?" I asked carefully.

Roman scowled and took a step toward me. "That's what

the maroons did on Saint-Domingue. Père says that Grandpère should have known better than to stay. He said we must be vigilant," the boy said, raising his small knife toward me again.

"I'm not plotting anything," I told him, keeping my eyes down even though hate rose inside of me, hot and sweet and sharp as the blade in my basket.

Show them what they expect you to be, my mother had taught me. *And they'll never see what you truly are.*

The boy seemed satisfied enough. "You better leave all that here. You're not one of ours, and even if you were, you didn't ask to take any of it. These trees belong to me and my father."

This time, I raised my eyes to meet his and let him see the hate simmering there. Because I knew the truth. These trees didn't belong to anyone but themselves, and they never would.

But he either didn't understand or he didn't care. "Go on," he said, stepping even closer with his knife.

I thought about running with the basket. He was younger then me, after all, smaller and most likely not used to wandering at night. I might even be able to get away. But if he caught me . . . Even though I didn't belong to him or his family, it would be bad.

Without much choice, I left the basket—knife and all—on the ground.

"And that other thing you showed me, too," he demanded.

"Why do you want this old thing?" I asked, clutching the small silken pouch of the Gris-Gris in my apron pocket. "I said I'd make you one of your own. A newer one would have more power," I lied.

"I want that one," he said, as though that solved the matter.

And didn't it? He wanted it, so he'd taken it. Because what was I doing but trespassing and stealing from my betters?

Clenching my teeth to keep myself from speaking, I pulled the Gris-Gris from my apron pocket again. Before I handed it over, I took a moment to run my thumb across the lumpy stitches my mother had made long before I'd been born. Then I tossed it into the basket.

"Now git," he said. "Go on now, or I'll have to tell your master what you were out here doing."

I didn't say anything else, but it took everything I had to keep the anger from spilling out of me. I felt the wind pick up as it rustled through the trees, echoing my fury at being treated so badly by this boy. He was no better than I was, and definitely not more powerful, but he had the world at his command. The trees rustled, their branches swaying as my fury at my own impotence wrapped around me like a noose.

Someday, I thought, keeping my back straight and my steps slow and deliberate as I walked away. *Someday* my heart beat in return.

On I walked, away from the oaks and through another strand of woods, and as I walked, I felt myself changing. The plaits in my hair grew thicker, and my body softer even as my own bone-deep knowledge about who and what I was grew unyielding as iron with each step.

It felt as though my journey across the field was a journey of years, and by the time I mounted the steps to Thisbe's cabin, I knew I was a different girl in a different time.

This time, there was no shadowy figure waiting on the

porch, but when I went inside, I stepped into a new piece of Thisbe's life. The world tilted, and Augustine was sitting across from me, our dinner half uneaten on the table before us.

His face was older than I remembered it looking in my other dreams. Already, it was beginning to show the wear of years of labor. It was a handsome face, though. Still blessed with a wide, soft mouth, with intensely dark eyes.

He was looking at me with such devotion...

No. He wasn't really looking at me, I reminded myself. He was looking at *her*, but we were one in the same. I was the girl.

I was Thisbe.

And I was angry. My anger spiraled up from deep within, and even though I could sense how it sprang mostly from fear and from love, I couldn't manage to stop it from burning brighter and brighter. Her—our—veins thrummed with the heat of it.

"You don't have to be the one to lead them," I said.

My anger swirled through the room like electricity. I felt it brush against my skin like a housecat waiting to be stroked.

Augustine either ignored the anger or didn't sense it. He smiled at me, all charm and confidence. "They can't catch me. I have means to tell a man's intentions."

"You have means," Thisbe mocked. "Your spells and Gris-Gris can't keep you safe from a bullet."

The intensity that had lit his face dimmed. "It won't come to that."

He stepped toward me, and I knew what would happen next. He would take me in his arms, and I would melt like beeswax in July.

So I stepped back, refusing to let this routine play out once again, and his face went dark. But I wasn't afraid of him. I'd never been afraid of him, not even when he'd taken the gap-toothed brother of the overseer and beat him bloody when the man had tried to have his way with me. Not even then.

"It's a fool's mission, Augustine. You can't stop all of them."

"I can try," he said, and then his face went serious. "You're free, Thisbe. You can walk away from here. Start over."

"Only if you walk away with me," I said, refusing to turn away from him.

He shook his head, like what I was asking was impossible.

"You think I would leave without you?" I asked, my voice rising in pitch and volume. "You think I would move on and leave you behind after you bought my freedom with your sweat?"

"You know as well as I do that you were the one who convinced your master to let you go. My sweat might have provided the coin to buy your papers, but your powers got you your freedom and all of this," he said, gesturing to the room we were sitting in.

I couldn't seem to hold back the small smile that curved at her mouth. "Because I learned a long time ago how to persuade..." But the smile faltered. "Everyone but you, it seems."

"You know I'll come back when it's over."

"When will that be? When you've burned down every plantation? They'll build another. When they burn you?" I asked, my voice—her voice—breaking.

"I'm asking you to trust me in this."

"And I'm asking you to stop. To come away with me now

before this goes any further. Before it's too late for us to have a life in this world."

He stared at me for a long, long moment, not blinking, his face unreadable. Taking my measure, slow and steady.

I knew what his answer would be before he said it:

"I'm leaving in the morning, before daybreak," he said, placing his fork next to his plate. "That doesn't give us much time."

I flinched as I received the words, but still, I wouldn't let myself go to him.

"I'll always come back to you, Thisbe. Always. You believe me in that at least?"

I nodded, but in that moment, I hated him for it. And I hated myself for letting him wrap me up in his life only to leave me behind.

His voice was soft and low when he spoke again. It was the voice he'd used to tempt, the voice he used when he wanted agreement without a fight. "Thisbe—"

I stood abruptly from the table. "More wine?"

He frowned. "Yes, please," he said finally, as though he understood the wine to be some sort of peace offering.

My thoughts raced as I went to fetch the pitcher. If he went, he would die. It was as simple as that. All those stories of the revolution in Saint-Domingue were nothing but tales. There, the maroons had outnumbered the whites on a small island. The plantation owners hadn't believed defeat was possible, and so they'd not realized the danger until it was too late. But the men in *this* place, the men who owned this land, would have learned from those mistakes.

Yet still Augustine was blind to the risk. He insisted on

plotting and planning. On putting himself into more danger than this life already held. Because he thought no one would suspect him. Because he had been loaned out for work on neighboring plantations for years, and because he had loaned himself out for just as long, he thought he could trust those he spoke to.

Because he wanted to walk through this life like a man, and how could I blame him for that?

But people will turn on anyone if they're scared or desperate enough. Even a cat only had so many lives. A man had far fewer, even a man such as he.

I could let him go. I knew well enough that what was between us wasn't bound to the bodies we wore in this life.

But I *wanted* those bodies. Even as worn and tired as mine often felt, it was the only one I knew, the only one that Augustine had ever known me in. And the wanting I felt, the urgent need for us to be together in *these* bodies, to be with him in *this* life was so powerful, I could barely breathe past it.

Resolved to save him, I slid a small vial out of my apron.

Resolved to save them all from their folly, I put some of the powder into his cup before pouring the wine over it.

The valerian and poppy worked quickly. Not more than a few minutes later, his eyes grew soft, his speech slurred.

"Why don't you come lay yourself down for a spell," I crooned, leading him to the bed. Then I set about preparing the things that would be needed—the knife and the red candle, and the small star-shaped man I'd cut from the great oaks.

With a strange sense of déjà vu, I went through the motions I'd seen in that first vision—the bits of hair and wax, the blood and thread. Until the charm was complete and Augustine would have no choice but to stay by my side. Where he'd be safe. Where we could be together. Where he couldn't lead anyone else on a fool's mission.

When I was done, I pressed a kiss to his lips, satisfied that they were bound by the charm for as long as I lived.

I stayed with him for a while, watching him sleep, but when a rough knock came at the door, I scurried to the front of her home in time to see Roman come through the door.

The girl's fear clawed at me. Roman couldn't find Augustine here, not helpless as he was under the power of the draught I'd given him. "Get out of my house," I demanded.

Roman simply smiled. "Now, now. Is that any way to treat a guest?"

"A guest is someone you've invited," I spat. "This isn't your property, and neither am I. Get out."

"But it's my property that I'm looking for," he said, making himself at home. "Where's Augustine?"

"I'm not his keeper," I said stiffly, keeping myself positioned in the doorway between Roman and the sleeping form of Augustine.

"No, of course not." Roman gave a smirk. "That would be me." Then his expression went tight, serious. "I need to speak to him."

"I don't know where he is," I lied again.

Roman cocked his head, as though he was amused. "Oh, I'm sure he'll be back soon enough." He took another step toward Thisbe.

"Get out," I said again. "You don't have any rights here." I knew it was a feeble statement in the face of my reality, but I held myself as still and straight and fearless as I could.

He took me roughly by the arm and gave me a sharp jerk as he spoke. "I'd like to see you try and prove that," he said, taking up the challenge. He leaned in until I could smell the reek of onions and stale beer on his breath. Then a slow smile crept across his thin lips and he leaned in and pressed his mouth to mine.

Anger flashed through me, hot and wild, and all at once, Roman surged back. He released my arm to reach for his own throat, his eyes wide with panic and fear.

"You'd best be leaving, Monsieur Roman," I said pleasantly enough. Inside of me, the anger pulsed dark and satisfying, even as I felt the panic of what I'd done. Of what I was revealing to him.

Roman's eyes were furious, but his lips were already starting to go blue around the edges.

"Be angry as you'd like, but until you cross back over that threshold, you won't have a breath of air to call your own," I told him, forcing myself to exude a practiced calm.

He struggled for a few moments longer before he shot me a look of such hate, even I flinched somewhere deep inside her skin. Then he backed through the door, one staggering step at a time, until he'd crossed completely over the threshold of the house and was standing on the porch. Only then did he take a long, gasping breath.

"You think because you have some papers, you're safe? You think a parlor trick like that will save you?" he seethed. "I'll kill you."

"I'd like to see you try," I said. I folded my arms across my bosom as much to steady myself from the overwhelming feeling of the power that surged through me as to show my defiance. "You can't touch me."

Still gasping for air, Roman smiled, a horrible twist of his mouth. "You have no idea what I could do to you."

Despite his words, I saw fear in his eyes, and something about the uncertainty lurking in those cold, blue irises eased something in me. I laughed then, because the power that I'd let loose was still curling around me as comforting as a warm blanket, secure and heavy and *mine*. And I knew he could never touch me.

"Tell Augustine I'm looking for him when you see him," Roman said, and there was something in his voice that made me go still. Something in the look he gave me made all that confidence I'd had just a second before drain away, leaving me cold.

"If you touch him—" I warned.

But Roman was already walking away.

I watched to make sure he was gone for good before I shut the door against the world outside and pressed my back against it. Just moments before I'd felt so secure, so calm in the power I'd taken to hand, but now, that knowledge left me cold and unsettled.

In the back room, Augustine slept on, still and peaceful, and I curled up next to him, resting my head against his strong shoulder and pulling the covers over us both.

In the morning, when the sun woke me, I turned over to find him gone. And the knowledge of that loss came crashing down on me, pressing me into myself until I couldn't hardly breathe.

TWENTY-EIGHT

My eyes flew open, and all at once I was back in the empty cabin, but I'd collapsed on the floor and the girl was standing over me. She was inside the circle with me now, and her face flickered from the young girl who gathered moss to my mother to a wrinkled old version of my mother back to the girl my age. Over and over, the surface of her face cycled through the versions of Thisbe as the girl's mouth made the shape of angry words I couldn't hear.

She wasn't touching me, but I couldn't breathe. I couldn't move.

I was stuck there in that circle, somewhere between consciousness and sleep, between living and dying. And that feeling of being so stuck, so trapped and immovable, was about the most excruciating thing I'd ever felt. I couldn't breathe. I couldn't die. I couldn't even feel myself be.

For a moment, I thought about letting go. I thought about giving up and surrendering myself back to the soul

I'd summoned. Something about the girl's expression told me she wanted me to let go, to let her back into myself. Maybe because she had more she wanted to show me.

Maybe because she just wanted more.

But in the distance, I heard someone calling my name, calling me back to myself. That distant voice was enough to pin me to this world until Ikenna could break the circle.

As soon as the salt line was broken, the candles snuffed themselves out and the girl disappeared. I finally pulled air into my burning lungs, but even then, it took me a while to come back to myself. Even then, I couldn't help but feel that something had changed within me from what I'd just experienced. Something still felt like it was gathering deep inside me, something that had maybe always been there. But it had grown stronger when I'd accepted the girl and let her in.

I wasn't sure what to do with that feeling, but it scared me. Ikenna had seen another power layered over my own, and part of me worried that the experience of walking in Thisbe's skin had helped to give that other power more strength than it otherwise would have had. I wondered if I'd ever be able to shake free of it.

Still, I was too weak to do much more about that fear than lie on the floor curled up into myself until Odane knelt beside me and made me look him in the eye. Little by little I calmed myself until I could breathe almost normally. Then, in halting breaths, I told them what had happened, what I'd seen.

"What do you mean, he was gone?" Odane asked.

"I don't know," I told them. "Maybe he realized what she'd done or maybe the spell went wrong. But when she woke in the morning, he was gone, and she was devastated by it. It felt like she was breaking in two when she found out he'd left her anyway, and it was the pain of that, I think, that brought me back."

"Sure didn't seem like you were coming back," Ikenna said, still pacing the boards. "I ain't never seen nothing like that. You lit up like a glow worm when you touched that there girl's soul … " His voice trailed off. "Power filled up this room like the fourth of Ju-ly, and we could hardly get close to the circle. For a minute there, neither one of us thought we'd be able to stop her."

"You couldn't get to me?" I asked.

Odane shook his head. "For a while there, it felt like the whole place would go up in flames at any moment."

For a minute or two, I hadn't been sure I'd get back either, but I didn't tell them that. "She must have realized I was slipping away," I told them, "and tried to grab on again. She almost got me, too. She didn't want to let me go," I realized, shuddering.

"Seemed like she got stronger the longer you were with her," Ikenna said. "Strong enough that she managed to cross through the circle."

"How long was I out?"

"More than an hour," Odane told me.

"An hour?" It had felt more like a couple of minutes.

Ikenna was shifting nervously, gathering up his supplies, spreading the salt so no trace of a circle remained. "We best be going, son."

Odane looked at him, the frown he'd been wearing turning to confusion. "Best be going where?"

"Anywhere that's not here," Ikenna said, packing the last

of his stuff into the rucksack and hoisting it over his shoulder as he moved toward the door.

"I don't think Chloe's ready to go anywhere yet."

"She'll be fine," Ikenna said, his eyes darting nervously toward the open door. "But I'm not going to be around here if someone comes looking."

"Comes looking for what?" I asked.

"You think what happened here was a small thing?" he said, shaking his head. "Whatever that was, whatever connection you have with this Thisbe person, it's going to leave a trace. Energy as bright as that don't disappear, and I don't want to be anywhere near here if this Thisbe you all keep talking about comes around to find out what went down." He pinned me with his eerie, uneven eye. "If she don't already know, that is."

Odane looked like he was about to punch something. Or someone. "So that's it? You're going to up and leave her here? Helpless?"

"I did what I said I would—"

"I don't know why I'm surprised you're running off. Seems like I should be used to it by now."

Ikenna frowned. "Our bargain was to help her access her dreams, not to get me tied up with something as big and bad as this Thisbe seems to be. I've upheld my end of the bargain. I'll expect you to do the same."

"Don't worry," Odane ground out. "I will."

"You coming?" Ikenna asked, taking a couple steps toward the door.

"Naw. I'm going to get Chloe home safe," Odane told his

father, and the disdain in his voice made me realize that as easy as Odane seemed to be, he wasn't someone to cross.

"Suit yourself," Ikenna said with a shrug. "I'll be looking for that paperwork soon, son. Good luck with this mess you got yourself into."

Then he was gone—out the door and across the field and back to the relative safety of the life he had before I came along.

"You feeling any better yet?" Odane said softly.

I nodded, though I didn't really. "I think I can get up now, if you'd help me?"

He threaded an arm around my middle, the heat from his skin brushing against me like a flame. I flinched away and slid back to the ground with a thump.

"Maybe just grab my clothes?" I asked. I was feeling way too unsettled to be that undressed, especially around him. What I'd just gone through had left me feeling exposed in more ways than one.

Odane helped me turn my shirt right-side-out so I could slide it over my head. Once I was more covered, he tried to help me up again, and this time I managed to stay upright on my wobbly legs.

"You think you can walk?" he asked, his warm breath near my ear.

"I don't know," I told him honestly. I brushed off the gentle concern in his voice. "I maybe need to go lay down, I think."

"Which way's home?" Odane asked, so I pointed the way back as he helped me—across the field, back around the pond, and up to the warm little cottage with its lights all aglow.

"Thanks," I said, feeling more like myself by the time we

mounted the steps to the porch. "I couldn't have made it back without you."

Odane grinned. "Yeah?" He turned me in his arms so we were chest to chest. His eyes were intent on me. They were dark as night, but that close I could see they were ringed in the same gold as his father's.

My skin felt warm all at once, but then guilt rocketed through me so strong and absolute that I jerked back.

"So that's how it is?" he asked, his voice gentle as the hands that still rested on my waist.

"I'm sorry—" I started.

"Don't be," he said, cutting me off. "Nothing at all to be sorry for." He gave me a soft, sad smile.

I couldn't help but smile back, but then I thought about Piers and the smile slid from my face. "We'd better tell Lucy what I found out—and that I'm still alive."

Odane raised an eyebrow in my direction. He was pretending that my rejection hadn't bothered him, but it was awkward between us now in a way it hadn't been before.

"She didn't exactly approve of me making any deals with your dad. No offense."

"None taken," he said easily, and I knew he meant it. He meant most of what he said, I realized then. Maybe everything he said. It was a singular quality—a rare quality—to be that sure and true to yourself, I thought.

"You want to come in for a minute? I can give you a lift back to your car after I talk with Lucy, if you want."

Inside, we found Dr. Aimes sitting in the front parlor, deep in concentration over a pile of papers. He looked up when we stepped in.

"Oh, hey, Chloe," Dr. Aimes said absently, his focus turning back to the stack of paper in front of him.

"Hey," I said. "This is Odane, a friend of mine."

The two men did that thing men do when they meet— shake hands, eye each other as they size the other up. Didn't matter that there was nothing to compete over.

"Have you heard anything more about Piers?" I asked him.

Dr. Aimes frowned and shook his head. "The police assured me they're doing all they can ... " But from the way his voice trailed off, I wondered if he believed that any more than I did.

Or maybe there was something else Dr. Aimes was thinking about. He was studying those papers in front of him again, a deep frown drawn across his face.

"What's wrong?" I asked.

"What?" he said, looking up like he'd already forgotten I was standing there. "Oh, sorry." He took off his glasses and rubbed at his eyes. "I was reading over this, and ... well, it's not what I expected."

"What is it?" I asked, stepping closer to look over the papers laid out before him on the low coffee table.

"You remember that book we found? The one that's gone missing."

"The one you sent with Piers, you mean," I said, trying to keep the irritation out of my voice.

Dr. Aimes nodded.

"What book?" Odane asked.

"It was a journal that belonged to the mansion's original owner," Dr. Aimes explained.

"Roman," I whispered, a shudder running through me at

the memory of the younger Roman's cold eyes and stale breath. And of his promise.

Dr. Aimes gestured to the papers on the table. "I kept a copy, and one of my graduate students was working on translating the French and the symbols in it when we heard the news about Piers and the car." He let out a ragged sigh.

"Couldn't they translate it?" I asked, sensing his frustration.

"Oh, they could," he said, shuffling through the pages with a frown.

"You don't seem overly excited..." Which was weird, because Dr. Aimes was *always* excited when it came to old things.

Dr. Aimes looked up at me then, his gentle eyes—eyes that were so much like Lucy's—uncertain. Gone was the professor whose eyes lit up at the mention of anything historical. This man was a different person, a more somber and serious one.

"It's skin," he said finally.

"What?" I didn't follow right away.

"The covering on the book wasn't leather. It was skin. Human skin."

My body registered the shock of those words—my stomach flipped, my skin went cold, my mouth went all dry and rancid at once as I remembered the vision of human heads piked along the River Road. "But how do you know that? I thought the book was gone."

"It is, unless the police find it," Dr. Aimes said as he sorted through a couple of the loose papers. "But it's all in the translation—the way the journal was made, the reasons for it..." His voice trailed off and we sat in an uneasy silence, with nothing but the sound of the whirring air conditioner to fill the space between us. "Roman Dutilette had secrets no one discovered. He made the book made from the skin of one of his slaves because he thought it would give the book power."

You have no idea what I could do to you.

Roman's voice echoed in my memory, as clear and stark as it had been while I was in Thisbe's skin. I knew it could have been any of the Dutilettes' many slaves, but something told me it wasn't. Roman might not have been able to hurt Thisbe, but he could hurt Augustine, and that amounted to the same thing.

I stepped back from the photocopied pages, my stomach turning at the thought of what might have happened to Augustine. Maybe he'd woken in the middle of the night and realized what Thisbe'd done. Maybe he'd woken and hadn't known he couldn't leave her. He would have tried to go back to his own plantation, but he wouldn't have been able to go far—not with that binding charm she'd put on him. He would have been an easy target, and Roman had already been looking for a way to hurt Thisbe, to get back at her.

That journal hadn't been the book of a rich man, I thought. It had been the book of a monster.

Odane shifted uneasily next to me. I glanced at him, and the unspoken look we shared told me he was probably thinking something along the same lines.

Dr. Aimes let out a hollow sigh. "There's more, but I don't know that I have the stomach for it tonight," he said, shaking his head.

Another uneasy moment of silence passed between the three of us, and then Dr. Aimes scooped up the papers and put them into an envelope. "I guess I should take this back to the office. I don't even want the copies sitting around here anymore."

"Is Lucy around?" I asked, realizing suddenly that it seemed like the house was empty.

"She went into town—wanted to tell Ms. Legba about Piers in person, she said." Dr. Aimes frowned. "I thought you'd gone with her."

"No," I told him, but when he looked confused I explained that I'd gone for a walk to clear my head. "I was supposed to meet her in town later," I lied.

No doubt Lucy had run off to tell Mama Legba what I was up to. I needed to catch up with them both and tell them what I'd learned.

"I could take those back to the office for you, if you want. It's on my way out," I offered.

Dr. Aimes didn't look all that certain at first, but his disgust for what the copies contained must have won out, because he handed them over without much fuss.

"Just put them on my desk. I'll figure out what to do with them tomorrow." He glanced up at me. "And if you hear anything from Piers..."

My throat went tight. "I'll let you know."

TWENTY-NINE

"You drive," I said, tossing Odane the keys.

"Me?" He seemed confused. "I thought you were taking me back to get my car."

"Change in plans. We need to get these to Mama Legba's before anyone realizes I didn't drop them off like I was supposed to, so you drive and I'll read."

He frowned but didn't argue.

As he tore down back roads to get to the highway, I tried to make some sense of the journal. The copy was hard to read in some places, but that didn't much matter since it was written in French, which I couldn't make out, and a series of strange symbols, which I *really* couldn't make out. But whoever had done the translating had written the English words in a strong, clear hand right below the originals.

I started reading.

By the time we reached the highway into town, I was starting to get a picture of Roman Dutilette that was different than anything I thought I knew. None of the materials from my training to give tours of Le Ciel had prepared me for the man I met in the pages of his journal.

It turned out that the journal wasn't just a record of his life. There were all sorts of things mixed in—spells from different lands, charms and superstitions from different traditions. Most were darker than anything I'd ever heard of. The spells in those pages required all sorts of death and darkness—black cats buried alive, frizzled cocks burnt as an offering, and blood. So many of the spells required blood and sacrifice.

The more I read, the more I saw a strange sort of logic weaving itself together.

"He was afraid," I told Odane as the lights of New Orleans came into view down the road ahead of us.

Odane glanced over at me, his expression grim. "What did he have to be afraid of?"

"The Dutilettes came from Haiti," I explained. "Jean-Pierre bought the property the mansion is on and moved his family here to make his own fortune right before the slaves staged a massive uprising on that island. Roman's father happened to get himself and his wife out in time, but most of Roman's extended family died at the hands of their slaves. You can see his anxiety all through here that it might happen again." I picked up another sheet. "He picked slaves specifically from countries that had a tradition of Voodoo. He was afraid of it, because he'd heard that the Haitian uprising started with a Voodoo ceremony. It looks like he thought he could fight fire with fire. Everything he did seems to be to keep another massacre like the one in Haiti from happening again."

On one of the pages, Roman had drawn the alley of trees

and the pillars of the house in a rough sketch. I remembered what the young Thisbe had told a young Roman about the trees.

"It's why he built the house where he did—he thought the trees had some power to protect his family," I said. I pulled out another page and studied it. "I think Roman was collecting all sorts of magic—especially dark magic. He wrote the spells and charms in code, so no one would have been able to tell what he was doing." I looked up at Odane. "How did no one ever find out? There had to have been rumors."

"It's secluded out there now," Odane said. "It would have been more so back then. Besides, it's not exactly the sort of thing he'd want to get around, so he would have been careful."

"Which explains the code," I agreed.

"People were scared of what they didn't understand back then, same as they are now. Plus, his standing in the area would have shielded him from suspicion as well."

I sank back in the seat. "So he wanted to protect his family and he collected these spells...They go over most of his adult lifetime," I said, flipping back through the book. "It's going to take a while to sort through all this."

Odane's phone vibrated in the front pocket of his shirt. With a frown he looked at the number on the screen and then answered.

"What's up?" he asked. "Right now? I'm kind of in the middle of...Got it...Of course I'll be careful. Love you, too."

He clicked off the phone. "Change of plans," he said. "I have to make a stop."

"Can't you drop me at Mama Legba's before you do?"

Shaking his head, he shifted and shot off across three lanes to catch an exit we'd almost passed. "That was my mom," he said. "She saw something, and I think you'll want to be there."

"Me?"

He glanced over at me. "She said it was someone connected to you."

"Wait ... You mean she *saw* something," I said, understanding. Then a sort of leaden dread settled in the pit of my stomach. "Do you think it could be Piers?"

"She didn't say, but if we don't hurry, someone's gonna die."

THIRTY

Odane turned off the main highway and took a dark access road that led back into the brush. A little ways down that road, we came upon a broken-down sign that used to welcome visitors to Adventureland, an abandoned theme park just outside the city.

"Your mom saw something here?" I asked, peering through the darkness of the night in front of us and trying to see the park out in front of us.

Most people at school had taken the drive down the lonely stretch of highway that winds around the banks of Lake Pontchartrain, out to the abandoned ruin of the park. It had become almost a rite of passage for the privileged and bored to go out to the sticks and play with some danger.

Back before Katrina, the whole city had been excited about the park opening. People talked about jobs and tourists and money flowing into the area. Then the hurricane came and washed everything out, and the company decided it wasn't worth the money to fix it. They left the park exactly as Katrina left a lot of things, rotted and empty and covered in a layer of whatever the floodwaters left behind.

Even I went out there once with a handful of other girls. We weren't brave enough—or stupid enough—to go at night like a lot of people did, but we spent the better part of one winter afternoon looking around, scaring each other silly, all while the empty ribs of a forgotten coaster lurked above. It had been bad enough in the daylight, and I wasn't in any hurry to see what it was like at night.

Odane cut the headlights so only the running lights of the Nova lit up the way in front of us. A few yards in, we came to an unguarded police barricade.

"Give me a second," he said, getting out of the car. In the dim yellow glow of the car's light, he moved the wooden barricade out of the way and then got back behind the wheel.

The abandoned parking lot was filled with crater-sized potholes and broken glass that glinted in the dim beams of the running lights, but Odane navigated it all with the same easy confidence he always used until we were at the gates of the park. "We'll have to walk from here," he said. "Do you have a flashlight in here or anything?"

I opened the glove box and pulled out a flashlight and handed it to him.

"Ready?" he said, looking at me.

I nodded and eased open my door, careful not to make a sound.

Before us, the abandoned park loomed like a broken city. Here and there, a few floodlights—probably for security—spotlighted areas in a murky yellow. A few shot upward, illuminating the skeletal remains of rides that had never been opened and casting long shadows that fell across them like bars.

We made our way carefully through the broken-down turnstiles that should have welcomed visitors and found a moldering map of the grounds hanging listlessly from its busted-up frame. Odane shone the flashlight's beam on it.

"What are we looking for?" I asked.

"I don't know," he told me, studying the map. "My mom's visions aren't always specific."

"The path to the right is shorter. Maybe we should start there?"

"Sounds like a plan," Odane said, his voice still as hushed as mine, like someone might be listening nearby.

We left the map and followed the debris-strewn pathway to the right, passing a limp, horseless carousel as we went. When we came to the entrance of Mardi Gras World, we had to pass under a half-collapsed archway. Huge, clown-like masks watched with empty eyes as we made our way beneath them, and once we were on the other side, everywhere we looked, more gruesome masks, their surfaces darkened with age and mold, leered at us from every surface.

"This was a mistake," I said, wishing I had picked the other direction. "It's like they know we're here."

Odane took my hand. "Come on," he said, leading me farther into the madhouse world that we'd entered. "We need to hurry."

Onward we walked, steadily, carefully. Past the crumpled frame of a whirling ride, past countless trash bins topped with open-mouthed clowns that looked like they might come alive at any moment and jump up to devour us.

"What's that?" Odane said, training the beam on something that glinted in the dark.

We inched closer to it. "Oh, no," I said, my voice shaking as I stooped down near the camera. Gingerly, I picked up the broken body, but bits of the shattered lens fell to the ground as a feeling of triumph flowed through me.

Bodies pressed around me, but I didn't pay them any mind. Through the eyes of the mask I watched, following her from a distance through the crowd of the Quarter.

I gasped. The vision wasn't as vivid as the others, but I understood what it meant.

"What?" Odane crouched down near me, catching me as I wobbled free of the vision. "Did you see something?"

"It's Lucy," I said, sure. "Thisbe has her."

Odane took the camera from my shaking hands and slung the strap over his shoulder. "Where?"

"I don't know," I said. "The vision didn't go that far."

"Maybe you could try again?" When I hesitated, he gave my hand a squeeze. "I've got you, Chloe."

His eyes were so calm and sure as he urged me to take the camera again. Like he trusted me to do this. Like he knew I could.

"I'm not getting anything else," I said when I took the camera. "It happened fast. Thisbe was hiding in the crowd somewhere in the Quarter, and she took Lucy before Lucy could even fight her." I looked around, the buildings lurking over me, threatening to box me in. To keep me there. "Where would Thisbe have taken her?"

"Not anywhere out in the open," Odane said finally. "She'd find a place to hide out. There—" He pointed to a large, square building with the silhouette of a jester lurking over it like a jack-in-the-box gone wrong. "Let's try in there."

I wasn't sure, but I followed as he led me to the entrance with its broken-down door, and then into the bowels of the building.

THIRTY-ONE

Inside, the air was close, and it choked us with the heavy scent of rot and mold. And something else—something dark and sticky smelling. It was a scent that reminded me of that first day I'd visited Thisbe's cabin.

"I think this is it," I said, coughing on the thickness and dust in the air.

Odane peeled off his top shirt and tore a strip from it, leaving only his white tank covering his chest. "Here," he said, wrapping the fabric around my face. "Don't breathe it in." Handing me the flashlight for a second, he tore another strip from the shirt and tied himself a mask as well. "Come on."

Slowly, we crept into the deep darkness of the building. It had been a funhouse once, so we had to watch our step or trip over the tracks sunk into the floor that should have carried riders through the darkened rooms.

"Do you see that?" Odane said, pointing to a glow ahead of us.

"I think so," I whispered.

"I'm not imagining it?"

"Not unless I am, too."

He looked at me, the whites of his eyes glinting in the light thrown by the flashlight. With a tight nod, he led me forward, carefully stepping along the tracks. When we got to the source of the light—a set of swinging double doors—he put his finger up to where his mouth was under the mask, like he was motioning for me to be quiet. Then he waved us forward, pushing on the door slowly in case it creaked and gave us away, and then suddenly more quickly, and stepped through.

I followed him and stopped dead in my tracks.

The room was empty except for a pile of rags someone had been using for a bed and a rickety metal table, probably used by a mechanic or security guard at one time. But on the floor, laid out like an offering, there was a body wrapped in red string.

"Lucy!" I rushed over to her, but she didn't stir.

She was burning up with fever beneath the string and trembled at my touch, but she didn't wake.

The red string—it didn't seem like nearly enough to hold anyone. I touched a place where it had already rubbed Lucy's skin raw, and as my hands brushed against the thread, I was in Thisbe's mind again...

She'd taken the boy from me, so it was only fitting for her to take his place.

I took out the carved figure, the one I'd made for this occasion. The girl was still unconscious when I sliced into her hand and rolled the little doll in her blood. Carefully, I wrapped the wet figure with the red string until the blood was sealed beneath it, and then, happy with my work, I tucked the bind-ing charm into my pocket.

Energy fairly crackled around her, like her body was trying to call back the part of her soul I'd removed. Yes, the girl was exactly what I'd need. Once I found Augustine, we'd be able to live out our lifetimes together with the power her body gave us.

Satisfied, I began wrapping the sleeping girl in the power of the string.

When her body—and all it had to give—was bound up tight, I went over and crouched in front of the man slouched in the corner, until I was eye-level with him. My knees protested as I balanced on the balls of my feet, but I wanted to be close when I said what needed saying. I wanted to see the under-standing when it finally lit in the eyes that had been following my every movement for the last few days.

But how to begin?

"When I was a girl," I started, "the water ran sweet most of the year, as though the roots of the cane had grown deep down into the soil, down to the cool springs under the earth and sea-soned them. But come late summer, the water would go rancid and taste of iron and rust, like the land had soaked up all the blood spilled during the harvest. Like the land had judged the sacrifice and found it wanting.

"Those were the hardest months—when the heat flayed you. But in those months, your parched throat wouldn't accept the water you tried to give it, because during those months, the water tasted of death. Those were the months we buried our dead in a hurry, without the proper rituals or any time at all to mourn. After, when the cane was boiling away and when the fields lay

massacred by our blades, that's when we waited for the new crop of men to arrive and replace the ones who had fallen.

"There was always a new crop—of cane, of men, and even of hope. We hoped that this would be the last season, and still we hoped we would see the next. Most of all, we each hoped that something else might happen."

I hesitated. Even so many years later, the pain still felt as clear and distilled as the water that used to run from those sweet, sweet springs. But I'd lived with that pain for lifetimes, now. I'd live with it a bit longer.

Lifting the boy's chin between the sharp nails of my thumb and forefinger, I forced him to look at me. To see me. "When I learned what my mother was, that was the beginning of my something else, and when I saw his face for the first time, that was the end of it," I said, waiting for that glimmer of understanding in the prisoner's tired, bloodshot eyes.

The man shifted but never once tried to pull away. "Why are you telling me this?"

"Because you ought to know. Because I'm giving you a gift."

"How is any of this a gift?" The words pulsed with anger.

Good. Anger meant strength. Strength meant life. Life was what I needed from him.

I smiled then, not because I felt pleasure at his discomfort, but because I admired the strength I saw before me. "What I'm about to tell you is a gift, because most people don't have any idea why they have to die."

I surfaced from the vision, gasping for air and shaking with the intensity of what I'd just seen.

"I was right," I whispered, as my own anger warred with the memory of her satisfaction. "She has him."

284

"Who?" Odane asked.

I looked up at him and forced myself to say the rest. "She has Piers. He was here, too, a little earlier. But she took him somewhere. We were right—she's going to trade him to Samedi for Augustine."

THIRTY-TWO

"We need to get her out of here," Odane said as he listened to the shallow breaths Lucy was taking. "She's alive, but barely."

"But Piers—" I started.

"We'll find him," he promised, his jaw tight as he spoke. "But Lucy might know something about where Thisbe went, and she won't be able to tell us anything until we get her some help." He pulled a knife out of his boot, ready to cut the threads away.

"Don't," I said, grabbing his wrist.

He gave me a puzzled look.

"Thisbe did something else before she wrapped up Lucy's body. I think she might have trapped her soul with a binding spell." I tried to think back to everything I'd seen in the vision.

"And a body can't live without a soul," Odane said, understanding. "So we'll leave the thread be for now, and we'll get her back to Aunt Odette."

Getting to Mama Legba's place was a challenge. That late, the Quarter was packed with people—none of them all that sober. As we drove, I watched the crowd, wondering if Thisbe was out there somewhere, hiding in plain sight, waiting to find another victim. Or if we were already too late.

Eventually, we made our way to the shop by the cathedral. Odane pulled into the alleyway behind it and parked illegally, so we could get Lucy into Mama Legba's without anyone seeing us carrying around a tied-up white girl through the streets.

Before we were even out of the car, the door opened and Mama Legba and Odeana came out.

Odane brushed past his aunt and ignored his mother's concerned expression as he carried Lucy in and laid her on the low couch. Mama Legba went over to Lucy and knelt next to her. Carefully, she touched her forehead, her cheeks.

Mama Legba' mouth was drawn tight and when her eyes met mine, I saw a fear in them I'd never seen there before.

"What?" I said. "You can help her, can't you?"

"She ain't in there, Chloe-girl," Mama Legba murmured, and then glanced up at me. "But you knew that, didn't you."

I nodded silently.

"What did Thisbe do to her?" Mama Legba asked.

"I think she bound her soul," I whispered. My hands were shaking as I looked at Lucy's quiet body. "Thisbe used another one of those little carved dolls, but she took the charm with her."

"Can we get these strings off the girl?" Odeana asked, pressing her hand to feel the heat coming off Lucy's body.

"As long as she got that charm, she got Lucy," Mama Legba told me. "We take off the strings, we take away the only thing holding her to this world."

"She has Piers, too," I said, and I told Mama Legba and Odeana everything I'd seen when I touched Lucy and everything Ikenna had told us about what it took to summon Baron Samedi.

"But why not just summon him right then and there?" Odeana asked, ignoring her sister's disapproving murmurs about Ikenna.

"It hasn't been five whole days yet," I told her. "Sunset on day one to sunup on day five. That's tomorrow."

"She could have just as well stayed where she was, though," Odane admitted. "It would have been easier than moving a grown man somewhere else."

"It's because she finally figured out what happened to Augustine," I said slowly, thinking of the book covered in human skin.

"Where you going?" Mama Legba called as I ran out the door and back to the Nova. I returned with the envelope filled with the copied journal.

"There's got to be something in here I missed," I said, pulling out the pages and handing everyone a few. "In the past that Ikenna helped me see, Roman said something to Thisbe right before Augustine disappeared—he basically threatened to get to her through him. When she took Piers, he had this book with him. Not the copy, but the real book—the one with the cover of human skin."

"Which might actually be Augustine's skin," Odane said.

"Yeah, and Thisbe's had this book for days," I continued.

"She has the charm she bound Augustine to her with. There has to be something else that we're missing—something that would make her risk taking Piers somewhere else instead of just performing the ritual to summon Samedi right there at the park."

"This here is nothing but marks and lines," Odeana said, examining one of the pages. "How would this Thisbe make heads or tails of it?"

"It's not random scribbles," I told her. "It's a language from Nigeria." I looked up at Mama Legba.

"You meaning that Thisbe could have read this?" Mama Legba didn't sound convinced.

"I don't know for sure, but you saw all of those tickets and things in that box we found. Thisbe traveled a lot—and she traveled to Liberia at some point. It's close enough that it's possible she traveled other places as well—maybe even Nigeria. It's possible that she could have understood what this all says without these translations. I know, it's a leap, but—"

"Here," Odeana said, holding out a page to her son. "Take a look at this."

Odane took the offered sheet of paper and frowned. "Well, that answers the question of what happened to Augustine."

When he handed the paper to me, I found myself looking at a sketch of Le Ciel Doux. Most of it was notated in French. A few of the strange symbols hadn't been translated yet, but most of them had.

"It does at that," I said, unease turning my blood to ice. "She was already a loose cannon, but if she has this information, who knows what she might do. And she still has Piers…"

"We have to get to the big house," Odane said.

"Right now?" Mama Legba asked, still looking over the papers in her hand.

"What do you expect them to wait for?" Odeana asked. "They either go now, or they'll be going to a funeral."

"Odeana's right," I said. "It's today." I repeated Mama Legba's words back to her: "*Sundown to sunup on the fifth day.* We don't have time to wait."

"It's not morning yet," Odeana told us, but then she pinned her son with the kind of look that only a mother could give. "But don't you even think of coming back unless you all in one piece."

"Wouldn't come back any other way." Odane gave his mom a peck on the cheek, and we started out the door.

"Wait!" Mama Legba yelled from the doorway. When we turned to see what she wanted, her eyes were determined. "Don't forget about the other charm," she told us. "We got to burn it before it does any more damage to Lucy."

"Got it," Odane said as he started to slide into the Nova.

But I stopped him. "I'm driving this time," I told him, taking the keys.

His mouth quirked up as he raised his hand in surrender and backed away without argument. I started the engine with a roar, and then we raced back to Le Ciel and the nightmare that waited somewhere in the darkness. The nightmare I'd once called Momma.

THIRTY-THREE

The grounds of the plantation were bathed in shadow as I pulled through the heavy gates and steered the car down the fork in the drive that would take us to the big house. The Nova's headlights cut through the darkness and lit up the white columns of the mansion, causing them to throw dark shadows against the house.

I cut the engine and the lights, but the mansion still seemed to glow in the darkness, rising up in front of us like an enormous tomb.

Not *like* a tomb, I corrected. The whole place *was* a tomb because of what Roman Dutilette had done to build it.

How many times had I stood in those rooms and told gawking tourists about how the whole plantation system along the River Road was built on the blood and sweat of people who were forced to labor in captivity? I'd never known how much more devastating that truth was in the case of Le Ciel Doux.

Odane sidled up closer to me. "We don't know for sure they're in there," he said in an attempt to build up my courage and his own. "We might be wrong."

"They're in there," I told him, pulling the tarot card from the visor and tucking it into my pocket. Then I got out of the car before I could change my mind.

If my mother—if Thisbe—had any idea that her lover had been captured by Roman Dutilette, if she had read, as we had, how Roman had sacrificed Augustine, she wouldn't be anywhere else.

It was all in the journal. How Roman had learned young that there was more power available in this world than money could buy. How he'd searched for ways to make that power his.

He'd detailed every sacrifice he'd made over the years, every spell or curse he ever tried, but he'd killed Augustine specifically to hurt Thisbe. Because Thisbe had embarrassed him and he couldn't touch her. Because that scared him, and fear made him angry and desperate. He'd written about how he'd collected Augustine's blood to ward the grounds of his father's house and about the intricate process of preserving his skin to bind the book. But he'd never buried Augustine. He'd never done any of the rituals to send the soul on its way back to the beginning.

Because he wanted more than Augustine's death. He wanted his life as well.

By the time Roman inherited the land from his father and was ready to build his mansion, there hadn't been much left of Augustine but some bone, but he'd ground them up with all the rest of the bodies and souls he'd collected over the years and he used them to create the concrete of those pillars that ringed Le Ciel. Because he believed that the power his sacrifices demonstrated would protect him and his descendants from any sort of attack or magic.

Roman had used the man's skin to protect his words, and he'd used his body and soul to protect his house. And somehow, Roman had figured out a way to keep coming back, again and again.

Which is why Augustine had never come back, and why Thisbe was still waiting. Or she had been, until she'd gotten her hands on Piers and, in turn, on Roman's journal.

As Odane and I made our way up to the front of the house, light was just beginning to break at the edge of the eastern horizon. *Sunup on the fifth day.*

"Come on," I said, picking up the pace.

"Were do you think she'll be?"

I thought for a moment. My mother had started working at Le Ciel when I was a baby. She'd started as a tour guide, just like me, and then worked her way up until she helped manage the place. She would have known every nook and cranny of that old house, but there was only one place I thought she would make a stand—the inner sanctum of Roman Dutilette's world.

"She'll be in Roman's library. Whatever she has planned, she'd do it there, because that was his favorite room. It's where he ran his entire empire. It's where she would want to bring him down."

The front door was open when we reached it, and we slipped into the cool darkness of the house. "This way," I whispered, nodding in the direction of the library. From high on the walls, portraits of Roman and Josephine watched us pass, their eyes cold and disapproving of our presence in their domain.

As we made our way down the hall, I heard a voice at the same time that I detected an odor in the air that didn't belong there.

"Smells like gasoline," Odane whispered as I wrinkled my nose. "I think she's already doused the place in it."

My eyes widened. I'd known it would be bad—that she'd want to destroy anything left of what Roman had built—but I hadn't expected to walk into a powder keg.

"We can go back if you want," Odane whispered. "Get some backup before we get in there."

I shook my head. I was more sure now than ever that my mother—that *Thisbe*—was in here, and that Piers would be, too. And I was pretty sure we were out of time.

I nodded toward the library and started again, moving down the hall toward the voice. Outside the library's doors I hesitated. The voice was chanting, a resonant song of sorrow and pain in words I'd never heard, but in a voice that sounded like my momma humming to me as she stroked her fingers down my neck. I couldn't seem to stop myself from closing my eyes, just for a moment, and remembering the mother I'd once known.

"Chloe?"

I blinked my eyes open and found Odane watching me warily.

"Are you sure you're ready to do this?" he whispered. He was looking at me as though he was trying to decide something. "If you can't, go now, and I'll manage. But if you go in there, you have to be ready. Focused. You can't go soft on me. You can't think of her as your mother—not in there."

I took a deep breath to steady myself but gagged on the sharpness of the fuel that soaked the wood paneling and carpets all around us. It was enough to remind me of what I was doing—of who the woman in that next room was to me now. "I'll be fine," I told him, and I hoped I was telling the truth.

Odane nodded, and we both eased ourselves into the library.

Even though it was August and not even a little bit cold, a fire was burning in the library's hearth. Its unnaturally red flames threw shadows across the floor, and its heat made the whole room feel like an oven. In the strange glow of the flickering fire, Thisbe had her back to us and was bent over a low, wide couch where Piers lay, unconscious. I almost gasped at the sight of him, but Odane's hand covered my mouth in time, and his arm kept me still.

Thisbe didn't notice our entrance at first. She was busy with her deep, discordant chanting, and her focus was on the white symbols she was drawing on Piers's half-naked body.

A moment later, though, she went stiff and raised her head to sniff the air like a wolf scenting her prey. A smile crept across her face as she turned to face us.

She looked older than she'd ever looked before—the smooth-as-satin skin I'd hoped to inherit was now creased with lines that should have taken more than a handful of weeks to form. Her hair, which she'd always worn tucked back, was wild about her head and shot through with gray like some kind of Frankenstein's bride.

Her eyes narrowed when she saw me, like she didn't recognize me right away, and then all at once her face lit with recognition and the chanting stopped.

"Chloe?" Her voice sounded like it always did when she was crooning a song or telling a secret just for me, and I had a sudden, overwhelming urge to go to her. To bury myself in her arms like I'd done a thousand times before as a girl. *Do you really believe I would ever hurt you?* a voice whispered.

Before I could take a step toward her, Odane's hand on my arm steadied me and brought me back to myself. The look on his face when I met his eyes—a warning, a question—reminded me what we were there to do. I gave him a small nod, to let him know that I understood and that it wouldn't happen again.

"Thisbe," I said, because I couldn't call her Momma and do what needed to be done, but the sound of that name released something in her. Her face transformed itself into something horrible then, and all trace of my momma was gone.

She smiled at me, a creeping-up-your-spine kind of smile that made me regret ever entering that room, and I had the sudden realization that I'd been wrong. I wasn't strong enough to face her like this. I wasn't strong enough to face what it meant to be her daughter.

I heard a low chuckle rumble through my mind, amused. Like it knew what I'd been thinking and wasn't surprised in the least.

You're mine, the voice whispered. *You've always been mine. Made for me and me alone, baby girl. Come to me now. Come to your momma.*

Odane was there beside me, though, and when he took my hand in his, it gave me strength and anchored me to what was real. When he gave my hand a reassuring squeeze, it helped to mute the droning voice in my head.

"You came," the witch said, her eyes lighting on me. "Just as I knew you would. Just as I intended for you to."

I couldn't speak, but Odane's hand tightened around mine again. "The only thing we came for is Piers," I said. "We're not leaving without him."

Thisbe laughed, a dry-throated cackle that reminded me of nails on a chalkboard. "Then you came for nothing, because this one"—she ran her finger across Piers's throat—"he's mine now."

Odane and I exchanged an uneasy look. We had to get Thisbe away from Piers.

Distract her, Odane's eyes told me.

"I thought *I* was yours," I said, my voice breaking. "Isn't that what you always told me? I thought I was your girl, blood and bone, heart and soul?" I shivered as I said the words she'd crooned to me throughout my childhood, hearing for the first time something more sinister in the words I'd always thought meant love.

"Yes, you are that, baby girl," Thisbe said, her mouth turned down. "But you didn't come to me like you were supposed to. You chose them instead." Her face went thunderous. "You weren't supposed to have a choice."

"Why wasn't I?" I asked, taking another step to the side, but she didn't move from her place near Piers. "Because of those charms you wove into my hair? Is that why you could control me?"

She sneered. "Those? You think those bits of hoodoo were powerful enough to let me control you? No. Those weren't anything more than shielding charms, so you never learned what you really are. I could *still* control you if I wanted to," she said with a wicked smile. "Right now. Tomorrow. Anytime I wanted. *Forever* if I want."

I flinched, my eyes darting to Odane, but he shook his head, letting me know he had my back. Letting me know he trusted me.

I only hoped his trust in me wasn't misplaced, because now that I was away from the protection of his hand, that voice was back, calling me. *Come to me, baby girl*, it crooned. *Leave all this and come be with me.*

"What am I, Thisbe?" I asked, forcing myself to take another step away from Odane, forcing myself to ignore that seductive voice.

"You're nothing at all," she said. A smile as pleasant as it was terrible turned up her lips.

"I'm flesh and bone," I said. "I'm real. Human, unlike you."

She laughed again then. "You think so?" she asked, shaking

her head. "You're flesh and bone, all right, but human? How can you be human without a soul?"

I froze. "I have a soul."

"You say," she scoffed.

"Everyone has a soul," I said. Because didn't a body need a soul? I shook my head. I wouldn't let her mind games get me all tangled up.

You're already tangled up, baby girl. You're already part of this.

"Stop stalling and let him go," I said, ignoring that voice even as I wanted to sink into it. "You can't win. The police are already on their way."

"That's a lie," Thisbe said. "Always did know when you were lying, didn't I?"

She stepped away from Piers then, not far, but just enough that her motion unnerved me. "You ever wonder why I was so good at picking out your falsehoods?"

I didn't answer. She was right, though. I'd learned a long time ago that there wasn't any way to lie to my mother. Not tell her things, maybe, but any lie I spoke and she knew the truth of the matter before the words had finished coming out of my mouth.

"You never could lie because I know you better than you know yourself. I *made* you." She sneered. "I've been deep down inside you since the day I brought you into this world. You can't escape me."

Something deep within me shifted, like it was answering the challenge in her voice. Like it knew she was right.

"That doesn't matter anymore. You won't walk away this time," I told her, feeling the truth of it. With the hanged man card warming my back pocket and the smell of gasoline heavy in the air, I knew I would do what I had to. I'd make any sacrifice I needed to make so that she didn't leave this room a free woman. To make sure she couldn't hurt anyone else. This would end with me, even if it ended me.

"I don't plan to walk away from this, baby girl. Not in this old body, at least." She huffed her delight when I didn't respond right away. "Confused? I thought by now you'd have worked it all out."

"Worked what out?" I asked, stepping aside and hoping to lure her again.

"What you are. What you've always been."

I wouldn't let myself play into her games. I stood silent, waiting for her to show her hand.

"What I made you to be, baby girl. And I did a good job of it, too, didn't I?" She took another step. "Beauty and brains and as empty inside as a vessel. *My* vessel."

I stiffened.

"You've felt it sometimes, haven't you?" she said, her voice so low it was practically a purr. "True, you're flesh and blood, but only because *I* deemed that you should be. *I* picked your father so your body would be strong, powerful—traveled the world wide to find someone worthy for the job. On the day you were born, *I* pulled you from my own body and stopped your first breath before your soul could breathe deep and fill you up. I gave you my breath instead. I put part of who I was inside of you."

"No—" I said, not wanting to believe it.

"Yes," she said. "That's how it's always been. True enough, you had some free will. I had to give you the charms in your hair so you wouldn't suspect the hold I had on you, the connection we shared. After all, you needed to have a life if I was going to take it."

I stepped back, horrified by what she was telling me. "That's impossible," I said, swallowing hard. But I wasn't so sure she was lying. I'd tapped into her past so easily. And without the charms in my hair anymore, the connection between us was undeniable.

"Is it now?" She smiled.

"But why? You had Alex already. Why did you need me?"

"Every soul needs a body, baby girl, but about thirty years back that Frenchman's energy started to wane. He was a powerful one, an old soul, but nothing lasts forever." She laughed. "Nothing but me, I suppose. When I started going back to him more often to refresh my youth, I decided my soul needed *two* bodies. So I created you. Just in case."

"In case of what?" I was shaking, but had to focus. I had to ignore the devastating truth in her words, ignore the voice I could still hear calling me in my mind, and draw her away from Piers. I had to keep her focused on me, but the more focused on me she became, the more her voice called to me, and the more I wanted to answer it.

"For when *he* came back to me," she said, her voice soft and fluttery like a girl's.

"But Augustine never came back to you, did he?" I asked, ignoring the pull toward my mother as well as I could.

Thisbe grimaced but didn't respond.

"You waited and waited. You were faithful, weren't you?" I asked, sliding a little farther away from her, praying she followed.

"I *was* faithful," she hissed, stepping toward me like I hoped she would. "I've always been faithful," she said, like she had something to prove.

"Not always," I told her, poking at her weaknesses, trying to figure out how much she knew. Trying to distract her. "You had me, didn't you? Unless you conjured me out of the air, you were with a man."

Her face twisted into a snarl. "I was *faithful*," she growled. "I did everything for *him*, to be with him. Only him."

I shook my head. "You did all of that—you gave up your very soul and all your possible futures—for a man who didn't come back."

"He couldn't!" she shrieked, and then slumped over with a sob like she'd been punched in the stomach.

I glanced at Odane. *She knows.*

Not good, his eyes seemed to say.

I didn't disagree. She'd be more unstable because she knew. More desperate. Less predictable.

Be ready, I tried to tell him.

He nodded, just slightly, to let me know he understood.

"He couldn't come back because of what you did to him," I said, stepping toward her. "You didn't want him to go."

Her head snapped up.

"Yes, Thisbe, I know all about that."

Thisbe's eyes shifted, like she was nervous suddenly. "You don't know anything at all."

"I know you drugged Augustine—"

Her eyes narrowed, but she didn't deny it.

"You tried to keep him," I said, more confident now in my words, "and that's how Roman killed him. But you didn't know that, did you? Not until recently, at least."

She glared at me, her eyes aglow with something not quite human. "I didn't, no. Not until that boy of yours brought me that evil book."

I froze. "What do you mean?"

Thisbe smiled. "I needed the charm that Aimes took from my cabin. I went to Le Ciel that day to kill him for it, but when I saw Aimes give Piers the package, I decided to change my plans. It was easy enough to get the boy's attention. He was so eager to put an end to me, so eager to be your shining knight. As though a bit of brute strength could overpower me. He did everything I needed—retrieved the aloe from the old hag's shop, helped me kill Byron—"

I couldn't stop my mouth from dropping open. "Piers wouldn't," I denied, thinking of his gentle, scholar's hands.

"Amazing what a little magic will do, isn't it? Easy as playing with a marionette on a string," Thisbe said, her mouth pulling up into a wicked curve. "True, he fought me the whole time, but you didn't seem to notice how much he was fighting when you talked to him on the phone."

My stomach turned. She'd had Piers then, and I hadn't even known he was gone. I hadn't trusted him—or us—enough to know he wouldn't have treated me so short, no matter how mad at me he was.

"But why?" I cried as my guilt clawed at me.

"Because I could. It was easier to use the boy than to take the chance of anyone seeing me."

"What did Byron ever do to you?"

"Nothing at all until he opened himself up to Roman," Thisbe snarled.

"What?" I glanced over at Odane, but he shook his head to warn me against calling attention to him. So I forced myself to focus on Thisbe.

Thisbe chuckled, a dark, hissing sort of laugh. "You didn't read all of Roman's book, did you?" she said, stepping toward me.

I swallowed down my fear and held my ground. But she was right. We hadn't read everything—there was still plenty that hadn't even been translated.

"Roman thought he could control this world, but he wasn't even enough of a man to make himself a son." Thisbe sneered. "You think he was willing to let go of his precious land just because his life was at an end? No," she snapped. "Roman found a way to leave a part of himself behind so he could come back, again and again, to watch over his precious house. He had a portrait done of him and his bride, a daguerreotype."

"He used the picture?" I asked, remembering Roman's cold-eyed stare looking up from beneath the glass of the picture Byron had brought that day.

Thisbe smiled. "People used to be afraid of photographs stealing their souls. It gave Roman an idea, and he found a way to leave some of himself behind in a bit of glass, so when another body found it, he could walk in this world again. Thanks to your boy bringing me the book, I finally knew what to look for. I didn't just kill Roman this time. I destroyed his way of recreating himself. I made sure he'll *never* come back again."

I remembered what Lucy had told me about the strange way Byron had died—with the glass of the daguerreotype shattered and used to stab him.

"I trapped his soul—with Piers's help, of course. Roman is through forever, and now that he's dead, I can free Augustine from the evil he did to him."

"The police will pin Byron's death on Piers," I said, horrified. They already thought he'd stolen the university's artifacts.

"I was careful," she said. "There isn't any evidence they could link to him. If there were, then all this would be for nothing. Aren't they already looking at that professor?" She smiled at me. "By the time they realize there isn't a case, we'll both be far, far away from here, anyway."

"Piers would never go anywhere with you."

"Of course he will. You think I didn't have a plan all along?" She took a step toward me, and I found I couldn't move. Not because I was scared—which I was—but because my muscles weren't under my control any longer.

"I've been watching you your whole life, baby girl. Watching you and then watching him. I always thought he might have something more to him, but after that night where that girl nearly destroyed me, I knew for certain. When I realized your Piers could see that French boy's soul, I knew I'd been right about him all along. About his worthiness." She smiled, a sickening sneer.

"You can't kill him," I said, desperate.

"Kill him?" She looked genuinely surprised. "Why would I kill such a fine, fine specimen? No, I'll use him once I free Augustine. No one will be the wiser—me in your strong little body, Augustine in his. You two have always been so head over heels, it's the perfect cover. Who would suspect?"

I glanced at Odane out of the corner of my eye, but it was enough to remind Thisbe of his presence.

"Oh, don't you worry. You're not going to last long enough to tell anyone," she said to Odane, reaching out her hand and drawing it into a fist.

Odane collapsed to his knees, his hands around his neck like he was trying to pull something away from it.

"Leave him alone," I said, trying to lunge toward her but unable to move. "You can do whatever you want with me, but leave him go."

She scoffed. "I can do whatever I want with you anyway, baby girl."

At a flick of her wrist, I stiffened. Something came over me and bubbled up from inside of me all at once. Suddenly, I couldn't make myself do anything. It was like being trapped inside of my body, paralyzed, but my limbs kept on moving without my say-so. I spun on my heels, my arms and legs all akimbo like a marionette. Then all at once it stopped.

"See?" Thisbe drawled. "You feel it, don't you? Like something deep inside you finally got set free. That something is *me*. It always has been."

It was powerful, the thing she was talking about—that something deep inside me that felt like it could fly. Part of me wanted to let it have all the freedom it craved, but I struggled against it. I fought against Thisbe's power with every bit of energy I had left.

Thisbe's mouth curved into a cold smile. "Go ahead and struggle all you want," she said. "It'll only make the whole process faster. To think, my Augustine has never been gone. He's always been here, just as I suspected, and I'm going to free him now. I'm going to free us both."

I felt weak, so weak. Not in my body, no—it was as strong and young as always, but deep inside myself, I felt different. Suddenly, I felt so far away from the skin I'd always lived in, like the power I was drowning in would overtake me at any moment.

But that other part of me pushed it away again with my last bit of strength. "Won't. Work," I choked out, remembering Lucy and all she'd been through. If Thisbe freed Augustine's soul from the house, she would lose him, just as Lucy had lost Alex.

She me pinned with those devilish eyes of hers, and I couldn't make my voice work. "I won't lose him if I have a body for him to live in," she said, smiling like she knew she'd won. "I have Piers all ready to receive him. There's just the small matter of calling on the one spirit who can finish this once and for all."

Thisbe looked me over, and then she dismissed me and went to stand near where Piers was lying on the velvet settee. On the side table was a bulbous glass bottle. Thisbe picked it up and unstoppered it. Then, chanting the same weird syllables in the voice that sounded so much like my mother, she poured the contents in a circle around them both.

In the corner, Odane was still struggling against the invisible hands that were strangling him, but his movements were getting slower and less forceful. I couldn't move at all, but I knew something was going to happen—something bad.

In my mind, I screamed for her to stop.

Thisbe glanced up at me, surprise in her eyes.

Had she heard me? I tried again: *I know what you're about to do. It's a bad idea, Momma,* I thought, pushing the words in her direction, willing her to understand.

Something flickered in the depths of her eyes when she heard me call her that, and the hand holding the bottle faltered.

You can't trust Baron Samedi, I thought, pushing the words toward her again.

But it was the wrong thing to tell her. As quickly as she'd hesitated, Thisbe was back.

"You think I haven't learned everything there is to learn by now?" she asked as she finished pouring out the circle and then anointed herself—her head, her heart, her lips. "I'm not afraid of a spirit."

"You should be," Ikenna said from the doorway. He looked at me and then saw his son struggling for breath. "Odeana called me and sent me over here," he said, stepping into the room. He placed his hands on his son's head, and Odane collapsed to his knees, his breath coming in huge, heaving gasps.

Ikenna looked straight at me again and asked, "This the witch?"

I couldn't answer. I couldn't move at all.

Thisbe, clearly surprised by this turn of events, growled.

"You're too late, whoever you are," she said, touching her finger to the circle of wetness around her feet. In a flash, blue flames sprang up around her, their eerie glow throwing grotesque shadows across her face.

We have to get out of here, I wanted so badly to scream. The whole place was soaked with gas. It would go up like a bomb the second those flames hit it. But my lips were frozen, my voice stoppered tight.

But when the blue flames started to lick at my legs, I realized they weren't hot. They weren't real flames, or rather, they weren't burning. They traveled across the floor until the entire room was ablaze in their icy glow—the entire room except the circle in which Thisbe stood.

Her voice rang out in strange, foreign syllables as she sliced her palm with a knife and dripped three drops of blood into the flames. When the blood hit the blue flames, they rose up in a blinding flash that I couldn't turn away from or shut my eyes against.

All at once, darkness settled over the room, and the only light came from the blue glow of the circle around Thisbe and the strange bluish glow from Piers's still body.

A man stepped out of the darkness between those spots of light. Drawing himself up to his full height in the center of that darkness, I recognized him as the skeletal man from my dreams. Baron Samedi.

He was dressed in all black, and his purple top hat was tipped rakishly over one of his empty eyes. Although he had the face of a man, his fingers clacked as he moved the bones that made up his hand. The overpowering smell of cigars and unwashed bodies, of the sweetness of rum and the rot of the grave, swept over the room. And all at once, I felt a sense of such desperate desolation that I would have done anything to make it stop.

"Ikenna Gaillard? My faithful servant," Baron Samedi said, in a voice filled with the emptiness of a forgotten grave and the wetness of rattling phlegm. "You dare call me?"

Ikenna cowered in the corner, his body thrown over his son's.

"I called you," Thisbe screeched, obviously displeased that Baron Samedi didn't realize who had summoned him.

He turned to her, his gaunt face scowling, and examined her. As he looked her over, a millipede crawled out his empty eye and down into his black-as-night shirt. "And what are you to summon me?"

"I am Thisbe Bookman."

Baron Samedi cocked his head, breathed her in. "But *what* are you? And why have you brought me here?"

Thisbe, visibly shaken, pulled herself upright. "I want to make a bargain."

"With me?" Baron Samedi took a long draw off his cigar and blew a ring of smoke right into my mother's face. "You don't have leave to make deals with me."

"I brought you a sacrifice," she said, pointing at Piers. "A life for a life. I know how this works. You'll take my offering. You'll bring back my Augustine."

Baron Samedi laughed. His voice was like metal dragging against cement as he laughed and laughed. "You know? *You* know?" He laughed again. Then, with a motion so fast and unexpected that all of us gasped, he flung out his arm and backhanded Thisbe. She tumbled out of her blue circle and hit her head against the marble end table as she tumbled to the floor.

"Momma?" I cried, suddenly free from whatever control she'd had over me. I ran over to her unconscious body and shook her. With her face slack, she looked more like an older version of the mother I knew. Her breath was shallow, though, barely there.

"Ikenna," Baron Samedi said in his rattling voice. "I am not pleased you let this happen."

"No," Ikenna said, visibly shaking as he tried to block Samedi from Odane. "I didn't know."

"A lie," Samedi drawled, puffing again on his noxious cigar.

"I tried to stop it," Ikenna pleaded.

"But you didn't," Samedi growled. "And now I'm here. And I am hungry."

Ikenna trembled, refusing to look at the skeletal man.

"You know my price, Ikenna. You call me to the living, you give me a life."

"Take hers," Ikenna said, pointing at Thisbe. "She called you. Take her with you when you go."

"That?" Samedi puffed on his cigar again. "That is so far past a life that even I won't dig its grave. No, I need a real life. Young and fresh and full of power."

"Then take her," Ikenna said, pointing to me.

"No," Odane rasped, but he couldn't do much more than try to stagger to his feet before his father stopped him by raising a single hand. Frozen in place, he looked up at me, his eyes wide with shock and anger.

"She's young and strong and drips with power. She'd make a welcome addition to your collection of souls."

Samedi turned to me, his head cocked like he was trying to decide. "It doesn't look to me like she wants to be taken," Samedi said. "A sacrifice has to be willing."

Ikenna smiled. "I can help you with that . . . Chloe," he whispered, and I felt an energy wrap around me as his dark voice filled the room. "Chloe," he said again. "Don't you want to go with the good Baron?" he crooned.

No, I wanted to say, but I found that I couldn't. Without me wanting it to, my right leg took a step forward.

"Chloe," he crooned, calling to me again. His golden eyes practically glowed as he watched my other leg step forward.

Everything I was felt pulled toward Ikenna, toward Baron Samedi and his boney hands. I couldn't seem to stop myself from feeling the pull of his words, from following the command in his voice.

Sacrifice, I thought. *Yes. To give myself as a sacrifice.*

It made a sudden, sick sort of sense in that moment. Perhaps this is what I was called to do all along. To give myself to stop a demon. To give myself over to save the ones I loved.

My leg took another step toward Samedi.

No, another voice called, rocketing through my head and drowning out the call of Ikenna saying my name. *Chloe Sabourin, you are mine. Body and soul, baby girl, and no one else's.*

My feet went still and I felt pulled in two directions at once.

You weren't meant for that side of the grave, the voice said. And then it called to me, until my own name sounded like a chant. Over and over, the syllables of my name rolled through my head, Ikenna's voice warring with my mother's. Over and over, until the soft chords of her voice began to drown out his.

I took a gasping breath and fell to my knees, Ikenna's hold broken.

Samedi's skeletal fingers scratched at the skin drawn taut against his sharp chin. "It don't seem like the girl is willing, Ikenna," he growled, turning on Odane's father. "Are you so weak that you can't bring me what I require?"

"But I've been your faithful servant all these years," Ikenna pleaded from his knees.

"You have, at that, haven't you?" Samedi said, examining Ikenna. "Maybe it's time you see another realm then," he said, smiling around his cigar.

Ikenna's eyes widened. "No—" he started to say, but in a blinding flash of fire, they both were gone.

The blue flames died out completely then, leaving the room lit only by the light of the candles Thisbe had used while summoning Samedi.

"Odane," I said, leaving my mother to go to him. "Are you okay?"

He sat up, dazed. "I think so. Ikenna—?"

"He's gone."

"The Baron?" he asked, still looking more than a little dazed.

I nodded. "We have to get out of here," I said, choking out the words. "Help Piers, and I'll get my mother."

"Leave her. The police can deal with her later." Odane pulled himself up, still rubbing at his throat, and then he walked over and struggled to get Piers upright. Straining, he managed to get Piers's arm looped over his own shoulders. Piers moaned like he was trying to come to, but his legs were unsteady.

Cursing, Odane tried again, this time struggling to sling Piers over his shoulder. Piers isn't a small guy, but Odane's days on the rig must have helped, because eventually he was staggering under Piers's weight. "Ready?" he asked, turning toward the door.

But when he turned, he knocked over one of Thisbe's candles, and flames licked at the carpet. I lunged for the flame, but it was too late. Before I could smother it, the fire flared up, crawling across the carpeting my mother was laying on, making a quick meal of the ancient fibers as it consumed them with its hungry glow.

"We have to go. Now!" Odane shouted, stumbling a bit under Piers.

I looked back at my mother. "I can't leave her here."

"Now, Chloe!"

"Get Piers out," I said, stepping back. "I've got to get my mom."

"After all she's done?" Odane's eyes were wild.

"She stopped Ikenna," I tried to explain. "And if I leave her here, I won't be any better than she was. I can't be like her, Odane."

"You're *not* like her," he shouted, stepping back from the heat of the growing blaze.

But I felt something stir inside of me, and I didn't know if I believed him.

Flames began to lick their way up the far wall. I knelt next to Thisbe and tried to slap at her face to wake her.

"Chloe!" Odane still hadn't left.

"Go! Get him out of here," I told him as smoke started to fill the room. It was only a matter of time before the flames hit the gas-soaked hallway.

"I'll be back for you," he said, straining under the weight of Piers's body.

And then it was just me and Thisbe.

I shook the still-unconscious body of the woman who was my mother. "Come on, Momma. We have to go." I could already feel the heat from the flames as they engulfed the room. "I have to get you out of here," I said, mostly to myself.

"Baby girl?" my momma mumbled, her eyes glassy and unclear as she blinked at me. "Chloe?"

It wasn't just the smoke stinging my eyes as I gasped and hugged her. "I knew you were in there somewhere."

"What happened?" she asked, still looking like an older version of my momma.

"You summoned Baron Samedi."

"Did it work? Where's Augustine?" she asked, struggling away from me.

"He's not here, Momma." I tried to pull her upright. "Come on. We have to get out of here."

Her eyes went flat. "Leave me."

"What?" I tugged at her. "No. You have to come with me. I can't leave you here." *Not after the way you saved me.* But I couldn't make those words come out.

She pulled away, and then met my eyes. Hers were dull, dead, like a woman who had given up. "There's no reason to go out there. It's all over. Everything's over. I'll be with him now."

"No!" I tugged at her again. "You'll be with *me*. What am I supposed to do all alone?"

She stared at me with those dead eyes. "You've always been alone, baby girl," she said, pulling away from me. "I've only ever been living for him."

I saw the truth of her words, then—the stark truth of what had always been my life.

"Go on," she said. "Get out of here."

I hesitated still, feeling the way the heat licked at my skin. In a moment, it would be too much to bear. In a moment, the halls would go up in flames and the smoke already hanging heavy in the air would be too much to breathe through. I couldn't leave her, not to that kind of death. Even with all she'd done, nobody deserved that.

Outside the room, the hall crackled with flames as the gas-soaked carpets began to ignite.

"Go!" she growled. "I don't want you here."

I pulled away. She didn't want me. Maybe she never had. And I wouldn't die here for her.

Grabbing one of the side tables, I heaved it through the window, and then, my shirt covering my nose and mouth, I worked as quickly as I could to clear the rest of the glass away so I could climb out. Carefully, I hoisted myself over the low windowpane and eased myself outside, but a piece of glass sliced open my calf. Hissing at the pain, I looked back into the library in time to see the walls go up in flames completely, but the heat was so great that I had to turn away.

I staggered off the veranda and across the lawn to where a crowd of people had gathered. Odane was there, laying on his side and coughing up the smoke he'd inhaled. When he looked up and saw me, his eyes were full of the terrible relief that comes from having outsmarted death.

Dr. Aimes was kneeling over Piers, who was beginning to stir, and Mrs. Aimes had T.J. caught inside the circle of her arms, but her eyes were wild as she searched the crowd for Lucy. I staggered over to her and let her know that Lucy was safe at Mama Legba's. She sobbed her relieved thanks before she took T.J. off to the side and pulled out her phone, leaving me alone to watch in a daze as the mansion that had defined my childhood was engulfed in flames. As my mother burned right along with it.

I didn't realize I was sobbing until a voice said "*shhhh, shhhh,*" low and gentle near my ear. "It's okay, baby," the voice murmured as strong arms wrapped around me.

"Piers?" I said, finally realizing who had me. I turned into the safety of his broad chest and I clung to him with all I had, with my very life.

By the time we heard the sirens sounding far out in the distance, it was too late. The orange flames had devoured the mansion, and black, sooty smoke was already pouring forth from every window.

I didn't leave when the screaming ambulance took Piers off to the hospital. We'd have time enough to figure out what was left between us now that he was safe, so instead I stayed where I was to make sure it was truly done. I watched the fire engulf Le Ciel Doux until the flames licked high up into the morning sky. Rooms collapsed and columns fell. As I watched the mansion burn, I thought I saw something move in those flames. Two figures reaching for each other in the bright heat of the cleansing fire.

EPILOGUE

Long after the fire had burned itself out, I sat on the gnarled roots of one of the massive live oaks and watched the smoke rise from the smoldering ash of what once had been the grandest house on River Road. Le Ciel Doux had burned for almost twenty-four hours before the flames were finally controlled.

Everyone was safe. Lucy had snapped to as soon as the charm Thisbe had bound her soul to had caught fire in the house, and Odane didn't even need to be treated for the smoke he'd inhaled. Piers was still in the hospital for observation, but he was stable and he'd recover. I knew I needed to go see him. I knew staying away was probably cowardly. I knew that nothing that had happened between us had been his fault, not the call or the distance, but still, I felt different. I felt changed somehow, and I wasn't sure what that meant for us. We had things to say, but I wasn't ready to open all that up. Not quite yet.

A shadow fell over me, blocking the morning sun. "You gonna sit here all day?" Mama Legba asked.

I glanced up at her, but I didn't answer.

"You know, if she didn't love you somewhere down deep inside, she wouldn't never have let you go," she said, taking a seat next to me. "She'd have made you stay and watched you burn right along with her, just for the spite of it."

I wanted to believe those words, but I wasn't sure. I'd been thinking about this very thing for the past day. Maybe she'd let me go because I still carried a part of her with me. Maybe I *should* have burned up with her.

Mama Legba put her hand on my arm. "You ain't your mother, Chloe-girl. Whatever she told you, you ain't her at all. You never was. You was never gonna be."

I didn't believe that either, because I could still feel something deep down inside of me. Something that reminded me of the young Thisbe, the hopeful girl who waited in the coolness of pines and whose eyes lit up when Augustine had come for her.

"She wasn't all bad, you know," I said, finally squinting over at Mama Legba. "She did what she because she loved him."

Mama Legba shook her head. "What Thisbe did those many years ago didn't have nothing to do with love, Chloe-girl." She tilted my chin up gently so I was forced to look her in the eye. "What that girl did way back when, what she kept on doing, only had to do with fear."

I pulled away from her, swallowing hard.

"I don't even know who I am," I said softly. "It's like my whole life's been nothing but a lie."

Mama Legba patted me on the knee. "It don't matter what has been as much as what's gonna be, Chloe-girl. You gonna let your fear rule your future or is you gonna let go of that worry and live? Choice is yours, and you get to do with it what you will."

She stood then and gave my shorn head an affectionate pat before she sauntered off, leaving me to my thoughts.

Odane found me not too long after. "You okay?" he asked, settling down next to me on the root.

"No," I told him honestly, and he wrapped an arm around me. I didn't pull away this time. Because in the circle of his arms, I knew at least that someone understood everything I'd just been through—without explanation or excuse.

"You will be, though," he said. "You beat a demon and destroyed a witch. You're strong enough for anything, Chloe. You'll get through this, and you'll be okay."

"Yeah," I said, starting to feel the truth of Mama Legba's words. "Maybe one of these days."

"Not one of these days," he told me. "You need to start now."

I pulled away from him. "How am I supposed to do that? People died because of her." My voice got softer. "You could have died because of her, and I feel like there's still a part of her inside of me."

"Maybe there is," Odane said.

I looked up, surprised.

He smiled. "You have her blood in you. You're never going to be able to erase that." He shrugged. "Maybe she was telling the truth and you have something more of hers in you, too. Maybe not. It doesn't matter."

I shook my head, wanting to disagree. Because *of course* it mattered.

"It *doesn't*," he insisted. "I got my father's blood in me, but you don't condemn me for it, do you?"

I shook my head, because he was right. I didn't blame him for being Ikenna's son. "How can you be so sure about me?" I asked, resting my head in my hands.

His mouth kicked up into a grin. "I'm not usually wrong about things." Then his expression was soft, thoughtful. "Stop being afraid, Chloe. Aunt Odette can help you figure out what you are. You've been running for a while now. It's time to stop and claim whatever you might have inside of you as your own."

"I don't know if I can."

"You can," he said, and he walked over to the edge of the charred remains and cupped his hands around some of the ash. He brought it to me, and I held out my hands to receive it. "Start with love and send her spirit on its way, Chloe."

"I can't—" I started to say, moving to give him back the ash he'd given me. I didn't want any power.

But he wouldn't take it. "You can. Come on."

He helped me up, and we walked together to the riverbank. Up over the levee until we could see the muddy breadth of the Mississippi glinting in the morning light.

A breeze rustled through the trees, like the land itself was waiting.

"Go on," Odane said, urging me forward.

I walked, alone, to the shore, and then I walked a bit further, until the mud and muck of the river pulled at my shoes. Silently I called to Damballah, to all the spirits of the light, but I didn't feel anything.

I looked back at Odane, but his expression was calm, confident. He gave me a small nod, as though urging me to try again.

Closing my eyes, I drew on that part of me, that deep down part of me that I knew wanted to be set free. The part I'd been feeling ever since they'd cut my hair. I'd been too afraid to look at it before, but I looked at it now. I pulled it up from the depths of who I was and let it uncurl and stretch itself out. It warmed in response and practically purred its satisfaction, but to my surprise, it didn't feel anything like my mother. I staggered back at the unexpected welcome of it.

I couldn't stop the smile from curving at my mouth as I took a deep breath and raised my ash-filled hands to the sun, the stars, and the world wide. When my voice rang out, it chanted words I never realized I knew. Words that had always been deep, deep inside of me.

This time, the spirit answered.

The End

Acknowledgments

Writing a book is such a solitary process. It's hours and hours staring at a small, glowing screen, buried in a world that only you can see. And yet it's a process that depends on so many people that readers rarely notice. So as I wrap up the final book in this series, I need to take a moment and thank those people who made this possible: first, Brian Farrey-Latz, who took a chance on the world in these books and allowed me to finish the story of Le Ciel Doux, and the entire team at Flux for helping to make these books a reality.

Kathleen Rushall deserves my unending thanks. It's having an ally like her in my corner that makes this whole publishing thing work, and I count myself fortunate every day that I get to work with her.

So many people read versions of this book and gave me invaluable feedback along the way: Hope Cook, Lisa Robinson, Kathryn Rose, Emma Kress, Kristen Lippert-Martin, and Marci Curtis. This book wouldn't have happened without their astute eyes and willingness to be open and honest.

When I wrote *Sweet Unrest*, I'd always planned on Thisbe being more than just the big bad. Much of her story, especially the gory details of the German Coast uprising, comes straight from the history books. Daniel Rasmussen's book *American Uprising* is essential reading for anyone who wants to know more about the brave men and women who made a stand for their freedom in 1811 and the horrible cost they paid. But while I've tried to make the history in this book accurate, I've taken quite a few liberties with the magic. For more about what Voodoo really looks like in the

Delta region, I'd suggest the incomparable Zora Neale Hurston's *Mules and Men* and *Tell My Horse*.

Finally, I have to thank my family—I'm grateful for my boys, who didn't mutiny while Mama was staring at her computer. And, of course, to Jason, who never ceases to amaze me with his willingness to support my writing and me, even when I'm at my worst. None of this would mean anything without my guys.

© Cameron Whitman Photography, LLC

About the Author

Growing up in Northeastern Ohio, Lisa Maxwell liked reading so much that she gave up her rather sensible idea of becoming a lawyer and decided instead to get a not-so-sensible degree in English. And then she got another…and another. It seems to have worked out. When she's not writing books, she teaches English at a local college. She lives near DC with her very patient husband and two not-so-patient boys. You can visit her online at www.lisa-maxwell.com or find her most days on Twitter @LisaMaxwellYA.